THE EPIC STORY OF AMERICA
1777-1779
TRIALS, TURNING POINTS, AND TRIUMPHS

JENNY L. COTE   LIBBY CARTY MCNAMEE   CHASE ADAM
MIKAYLA BADENHORST   CHLOE FROST
PAYTON GRACE   CAMERON GRAHAM   NAOMI HAYES
PERI JORDAN   PIPER JORDAN   ELLIOTT LAY
EDAN MACNAUGHTON   ROXANNE MESSIER
CARMENE MILLER   ZOE MILLER   KIT PACENTRILLI
ELLA QUILL   ALEX ROBERSON   ANNA ROBERSON
HANNAH SCHNEIDER   THORSTEN SCHOEN
JOY ELIZABETH TARDY   EMMA URRUTIA
JACOB WALTER   CHRISTOPHER J. WATT   BELLA WAUGH
MADELEINE ROSE WENZEL

EPIC PATRIOT PRESS

Copyright © 2023 by Jenny L. Cote and Libby Carty McNamee

Published by Epic Patriot Press

All rights reserved.

No part of this book may be reproduced in any form or by any electronic or mechanical means, including information storage and retrieval systems, without written permission from the author, except for the use of brief quotations in a book review.

The Epic Story of America 1777-1779: Trials, Turning Points, and Triumphs

Print Edition ISBN: 9781732220218

ePUB Edition ISBN: 9781732220263

Printed in the USA.

—For the Children of Epic Patriot Camp 2023

HUZZAH!

"Studying history is one of the great pursuits in life, because all of the answers to the future can be found in the past."
—Mark Schneider
Colonial Williamsburg's Marquis de Lafayette

"Three loud HUZZAHS for 'The Epic Story of America: 1777-79!' For young Americans, it is vital they know their roots. This book inspires our youngest generations to explore and research the founding of the United States of America."
—Author Bruce E. Mowday
Lafayette at Brandywine: The Making of an American Hero
Lafayette: America's Young Hero & Guest
September 11, 1777: Washington's Defeat at Brandywine Dooms Philadelphia

CONTENTS

Virtual Epic Patriot Camp	vii
The Original Epic Patriot Camp	x
I. AMERICAN PATRIOTS	xiv
1. General Benedict Arnold: The Unappreciated Turncoat	1
2. George Blakey: The Untold Story of a Rifleman	11
3. Benjamin Franklin: Spies, Strings Attached, And Stained Secretaries	20
4. General Horatio Gates: The Spies of Saratoga	31
5. General Nathanael Greene: Integrity Forged by Fire	42
6. Alexander Hamilton: The Life, The Story, and the Legend	56
7. Governor Patrick Henry: Surprises at Every Turn	66
8. General Henry Knox	77
9. General Charles Lee: Paper, Bullets, and Impulsivity	87
10. Benjamin Tallmadge	94
11. General George Washington	104
12. Martha Washington: Revolutionary Winters	111
13. General Anthony Wayne: Storming Hell, Anthony Wayne's Fight	120
II. EUROPEAN SYMPATHIZERS	135
14. Baron Johann De Kalb	136
15. French General Lafayette	142
16. Baron De Steuben: To Forge An Army	153
17. Charles Gravier, Comte de Vergennes	163
III. BRITISH LOYALISTS	169
18. John André	170
19. Edward Bancroft: A Patriot No More	178
20. Sir Henry Clinton: Resignation Denied	190
21. General Charles Cornwallis: A War Within Heart and Mind	200
22. Captain Patrick Ferguson: Ferguson's Journey	209
23. General William Howe	216
24. King George III: America's Last King	223
25. Major Banastre Tarleton: Tarleton's Fight And Newly-found friend	233

ABOUT THE AUTHORS 242
EPIC PUBLISHING TEAMS 274

VIRTUAL EPIC PATRIOT CAMP

The Story Behind
*"The Epic Story of 1777-79:
Trials, Turning Points, and Triumphs"*

The book you hold in your hand is the work of the twenty-five campers from the second virtual Epic Patriot Camp 2023. They not only wrote the chapters, but they came up with the book title as well. We worked with each camper as they researched and wrote their chapter, highlighting as applicable seven key events: Battle of Brandywine, Battle of Saratoga, Valley Forge, Battle of Monmouth, Conway Cabal, Culper Spy Ring, and the French Alliance.

The point of camp is to encourage the next generation to learn America's epic history and to tell the story for generations to come. We taught them how crucial it is to get their research right, and to thoroughly study the good, the bad, and the ugly of history. Some campers were more thorough than others; of course, some are more mature than others, with more research and writing experience. You'll see their bibliographies, biographies, and acknowledgments in the back of the book. While we attempted to fact check their work, the scope of the project necessitated that we rely on their research. While researching in Valley Forge in May 2023, I discovered that references to Baron De Steuben as "De Steuben" did not begin until the early twentieth century, with the dedication of a statue at Valley Forge by a German delegation. Hence, we chose to use De Steuben for his most historically accurate reference in 1777-1779. We hope there are no historical errors, but we appreciate your understanding if any slipped into these pages.

One of the ways to get young people excited about history is to weave in fun storytelling with historical fiction. Some people will never pick up historical books like us history geeks, so stories are a way to teach while engaging the non-history loving (is there such a thing?) reader. We encouraged campers to flex their creative writing muscles to write historical fiction, and some even chose to incorporate fantasy as well with talking animals. The point is to make history FUN while learning. Some of these young writers had so much fun that they are continuing to write their own books with their assigned characters. That's a good sign that we've accomplished our mission with Epic Patriot Camp.

You will read many humorous scenes, and many tender, emotional scenes as well. The creativity of the campers blew us away! We're so very proud of each one of them, and we hope that history will come alive for you as you read this book. Please encourage our campers by leaving a review on Amazon, and by buying copies of this book for your local school, history group, library, and friends. We appreciate you helping to fuel the pens of the next generation, and we thank you in advance for your support. If you would like to learn more about Epic Patriot Camp, please visit www.epicorderoftheseven.com. For interviews or more information, please contact Jenny at jenny@epicorderoftheseven.com.

We are grateful to three gentlemen who gave their valuable time to our campers. Thank you to Bruce Mowday, author of numerous books, including *Lafayette at Brandywine: The Making of An American Hero,* for joining us online to discuss researching and writing about history. Our campers were so excited to interact with you and learned a great deal! Many thanks also to Mark Schneider for making a surprise appearance as the Marquis de Lafayette! It was the perfect ending to camp and left everyone smiling for days. Finally, we are grateful to Richard Schumann (Colonial Williamsburg's Patrick Henry) for lending his signature, powerful voice to the book trailers written and produced by our Marketing Team.

This book is what training up the next generation of historians and authors looks like in living, breathing red, white, and blue. May the lifeblood of patriotism continue to flow from our pens into the hearts of Americans through the relentless pursuit of our EPIC history.

HUZZAH!

Jenny L. Cote and Libby Carty McNamee

THE ORIGINAL EPIC PATRIOT CAMP

The Story Behind Epic Patriot Camp

It all started with my villain, Banastre Tarleton.

I am currently writing a series of books on the American Revolution and have traveled to most sites where the war unfolded, both politically and militarily. My focal protagonist characters for the series are Patrick Henry and the Marquis de Lafayette, but Banastre Tarleton is my antagonist. My endless research includes reading books and documents, making site visits to museums and battlefields, and talking to historical experts. One of those experts is military historian and re-enactor Mark Schneider who happens to portray two of my three characters: Lafayette and Tarleton. (He also portrays Napoleon all over the world, so to say he knows history well is a bit of an understatement.) I'm forever indebted to Mark for his tireless assistance with my research over the years, as well as his insightful critiques of my work.

In January 2015, Mark was scheduled to portray Banastre Tarleton for the 234th Anniversary of the Battle of Cowpens. I decided to make the trek from Atlanta for the event as I had not yet visited the NPS Cowpens National Battlefield. Reenactments bring history to life! While at Cowpens, Mark introduced me to John Slaughter who was the NPS Superintendent of the Revolutionary Parks of the Southern Campaign of the American Revolution. I asked John if he would be interested in having me do an event for kids at one of these NPS events, and he replied, "Could you do a whole week?" They had just received grant money to create a summer writing camp at Kings Mountain, and John immediately saw the opportunity to do something unique for June 2015 using my books and brand.

Our team met in March 2015 and developed Epic Patriot Camp, a creative writing day camp for kids 9-13 provided by the National Park Service. The goal of the camp was for participants to learn about the Overmountain Victory Trail leading to the Battle of Kings Mountain by researching a soldier and crafting a story about the soldier's battle experience. Kids spent time each day with me to learn new research and writing skills. They also put themselves in the shoes of those who fought in the battle through hands-on activities: colonial clothes, weapons demonstrations, militia drills, colonial trades and crafts, spending time on the battlefield, etc. The culminating experience was an overnight colonial style camp: canvas tents, open-fire cooking, lantern hikes, etc. On the final day the kids presented their stories from their soldier's point of view for family and friends. Epic

Patriot Camp 2015 was an immediate success and led to subsequent years and other locations including Cowpens and the Muster Grounds in Abingdon, Virginia.

Then came Covid. The world shut down, and Epic Patriot Camp was discontinued. Frustrated, in 2022 I decided to create a Virtual Epic Patriot Camp experience and asked my dear friend and fellow historical author Libby McNamee if she would partner with me. This online camp would be the same in terms of campers assuming the identity of a Patriot, British Loyalist or French ally to research and write a character story, but we decided to focus on one year: 1776. No, we couldn't provide an in-person experience of hands-on colonial activities, but we could provide an opportunity for budding writers to become published authors. At first, we retained the same age range of 9-13, but because we received numerous requests from older teens, we opened camp to all ages. Campers chose either a Tuesday or Wednesday group that met online for three hours each week for a month.

The result? We had twenty-five campers aged 10-19 from fourteen states, Washington D.C., and even one from Australia. Not only did they bond with their assignments, but they also bonded with each other. It was our hope that Epic Patriot Camp 2022 would foster friendships with kids who shared a mutual interest for history and writing. Our hopes were not only realized, but they were surpassed! Of course, Banastre Tarleton *had* to make an appearance before and during camp, giving us his lofty opinions while trying to make it all about him.

The ultimate outcome was our first published book: *The Epic Story of 1776: 25 People, 13 Colonies, and 1 War*. This book also surpassed our expectations, for not only was it released on Amazon, but was soon carried by stores and historical sites such as the American Revolution Museum in Yorktown, Mount Vernon, and the Boston Tea Party Ships and Museum. Our campers even held their first book signings during Victory at Yorktown Week 2022. We continued Epic Patriot Camp 2023 to focus on the years 1777-1779, and this book is the outcome of our second virtual year.

So, thank you, "Bloody Banastre Tarleton," for making Epic Patriot Camp possible. I hate to admit it, but it truly *is* all about you in a way, because it all started with you. Ah, but I know how the story *ends* in 1781, and I can't wait to chat with you then.

See you in my pages,

Jenny L. Cote

I. AMERICAN PATRIOTS

GENERAL BENEDICT ARNOLD: THE UNAPPRECIATED TURNCOAT

BY ELLA QUILL

GENERAL BENEDICT ARNOLD: THE UNAPPRECIATED TURNCOAT

PHILADELPHIA, PENNSYLVANIA
10 JULY 1777

A man sat at his desk, bent over a paper. The candle on the desk flickered, and the open window let in gusts of air. He did not notice the breeze playing with his wig, as he focused on the letter before him.

"It's not right," he muttered. "I deserved this promotion! This insult injures my character to its core." He dipped his quill into the ink, scratched a few words, then dipped again. He blew on the paper, then held it up to the flame. He grumbled while reading it. Then in a burst of rage, he crumpled it and tossed it across the room, yelling, "Those blasted men! What've they done? Did they capture Fort Ticonderoga? Did they invade Canada? Where's my promotion? No more! I'll work for this service no longer."

He slumped back at the desk again and pulled out a fresh sheet of paper. "I must let Congress know about my resignation..."

Brighton, Tennessee
Modern Day

"Kids, please shelve these books." Ella's mother, Grace, handed her daughter a stack. The family owned a library. No one else knew, though, about its magical nature. When you opened a book in this library, it transported you to that world of its subject.

"Sure, Mom." Ella took the stack and handed half to her twin brother, Jason. The teens sauntered down the long rows of bookshelves.

Ella nudged Jason. "I bet I can shelve mine faster than you."

"Yeah, right." He elbowed her back, rolling his eyes.

"Watch me!" She took off running. When he sprinted after her, he bumped into a shelf, and several books tumbled off with a thud.

She chuckled, but suddenly, everything went black.

The Streets of Philadelphia, Pennsylvania

THE EPIC STORY OF AMERICA 1777-1779

12 July 1777

Someone shook her shoulder. "Excuse me, miss, are you quite alright?"

Ella opened her eyes and looked up. A man in his thirties reached towards her. His dress was Colonial, complete with breeches, a loose-fitting shirt with a vest, and a tri-cornered hat. Alarmed, she scooted backwards, her back hitting the trunk of a tree.

She glanced behind the man. She was sitting next to a cobblestone road near some shops and taverns. *I must have fallen into a book on American Colonial History!*

She turned back to the man, took his outstretched hand, and stood up. "Well, yes, I'm okay. Where are we anyway?"

He stared at her for a moment. "We are in Philadelphia," he responded with a bit of scorn.

"Oh," she replied. *That makes sense. It was a big city during Colonial times.*

He adjusted his vest and extended his hand. "I am General Benedict Arnold at your service, m'lady."

Benedict Arnold... Why does that name sound familiar? Ella thought. "Oh, nice to meet you, Mr. Arnold. I am Elizabeth Matthews, but you may call me Ella."

"Very well, Miss Ella. What brought you here to Philadelphia?" he asked.

"Oh, I–um–was traveling, and I was-um-robbed! By a group of highwaymen, and then I found myself here," she explained, hoping her story sounded believable enough.

Arnold stroked his chin. "Interesting. That explains why I found you unconscious on the road."

"Oh, uh, yes, it does." She stared at her feet bashfully. *Now what am I going to do?*

"Very well, I take it you have nowhere to stay and no means to pay since you were robbed. Come with me, I know of a good place for young ladies." Arnold briskly started off, and she trotted to keep up.

She gazed around at the bustling Colonial city. "Why are you here in Philadelphia? Do you live here?"

He frowned. "No, I do not. I am here to submit my letter of resignation."

"Resignation from what?"

"The Continental Army! They don't know, much less care, how valuable I am!" Arnold snapped. Ella shrank back as he continued, "My character is deeply offended by the lack of respect I have been given. It wounds me."

She glanced at him. "I see. So...what did they do?"

He balled up his fist. "Listen, m'lady, I have taken many valuable actions for the freedom of this country, stories I may share later, but to whom did they give promotion? The lads under me in rank! That angers me terribly."

He feels underappreciated. The poor man. They were nearing an inn, and Arnold led Ella inside and strode over to the bar. "This young lady needs a room."

The bartender nodded. "How many nights?"

Arnold glanced over at Ella. "A fortnight or so 'til we figure out what she will do next."

He passed some paper money and a few coins to the man who nodded. "Right up the stairs to the left."

As Arnold thanked the man, she asked, "What year is it again? I, um, always lose track."

He smiled and winked at her. "It is the year 1777."

Ella smiled back. *The American Revolution! I am in the middle of the revolution!*

Arnold led her to her room, then tipped his hat and reached out his hand. "It was charming seeing you, Miss Ella, and I will be in contact."

Philadelphia, Pennsylvania
13 July 1777

The next day, Arnold showed up at the tavern and toured Ella around Philadelphia. He gestured towards the building on their right. "This is the court building, where I met with Congress to present my case."

"Your case about your promotion?"

"Yes, exactly. And if we walk a bit down this way..." Arnold led her down a few blocks and turned a corner. "Here is the postal office and the good Doctor Franklin's home."

"Wait, like Benjamin Franklin?" Ella asked, staring at the house. She sensed some movement at the window, and a black dog sat there, eyeing them. *Benjamin Franklin had a dog? Who knew?*

"Aye. Ben Franklin," Arnold replied, stepping into a nearby inn. "Care for supper?"

"Oh, sure!" Ella followed him as they sat down at a table, and Arnold ordered.

"I was always a wild lad..." he shared with a chuckle. "My poor mother didn't know what to do with me. I was always doing a dare or a prank." He paused and shared, "My father...he was a great merchant. He made the family name Arnold proud, until..." He placed his head in his hands for a moment, then looked up and sighed. "Until he was a drunkard and ruined the name Arnold, and I had to grow up with that name on my shoulders."

Ella looked sympathetically towards him as he kept talking. "Anyway, I apprenticed under some family friends who ran an apothecary business. Then, when I was old enough, I left them and joined the military."

At this moment, their food arrived, and Ella heard no more stories about Arnold's childhood as they ate their meal in silence.

Philadelphia, Pennsylvania
30 June 1777

"I don't believe that a young lady like yourself should come with me to a battlefield," Arnold said, fingering the letter he just received from General Washington.

Ella shrugged. "I have nowhere else to go. Please let me come. I can help the medics and the nurses. I can carry water, I mean, Adam's Ale," she said, using the new Colonial slang she learned.

Arnold bent and lifted her chin with one finger, so she was forced to look up at him. "There is a lot of carnage in war, m'lady. Are you sure you wish to come with me?"

Ella's breath quickened at his touch, but she nodded bravely. "I—I have to find my brother," she blurted out. "I haven't seen him since I left—on my journey, and he might have enlisted." *Speaking of, I wonder where Jason is anyways? No doubt he followed me in this book, but who is he here with? Where is he?*

Arnold nodded, folding up the letter and placing it in his pocket. "Very well. We shall leave first thing tomorrow morning for Fort Stanwix."

Saratoga, New York
7 October 1777

"That blasted Gates!" Arnold yelled, pacing around the tent. Ella sat nearby, quietly mending a soldier's trousers. By now, she was used to his rants. Ever since they arrived at Fort Stanwix a few weeks back, Arnold and General Horatio Gates clashed. Gates ordered Arnold to stay away from the battle, but Arnold strongly disagreed. So, Gates stripped Arnold of his command.

Ella could see that all he wanted was to fight and bravely lead men to victory. She heard his stories about capturing Fort Ticonderoga with Ethan Allan, creating America's first navy, and even invading Canada. She was certain this was the first time America invaded another country.

Deep down, after getting to know Arnold as an American hero, she was beginning to like him. He had gone through so much, all for his country's good. Why didn't the others see that?

"What did Gates do this time?" she asked. *Every day it's something about Gates...*

"I deserve honor! I deserve respect! I didn't come here just to sit back and watch those boys die on the battlefield! I came to lead them out there to victory and freedom!" Arnold yelled, pumping his fist in the air.

"Hmmm," Ella replied, the needle between her lips as she held up the trousers.

"I cannot obey his commands. I will not!" With a rush of fury, Arnold stormed out of the tent.

Ella shook her head. He had done this previously. He would return. But as the day went on, and Arnold did not come back, she began to wonder. She slipped out of the tent and asked around.

One man saw Arnold riding a horse to the battle. Ella scrambled up a rocky ledge nearby to watch.

And yes, there he was, lifting his sword and yelling battle cries. To Ella, he honestly looked like a hero atop his horse.

"Come on, men! Pull together! We can do this! Huzzah!" And they charged into the fight.

Ella watched with awe as Arnold fought. He was like a wild man, swinging his sword, dodging bullets, calling out encouragement.

Suddenly, his horse collapsed, falling over, and bringing Arnold down. There was a sickening scream of pain that ripped from Arnold's throat. Ella gasped in terror and looked to see if anyone noticed.

Several men saw Arnold fall, but there was nothing they could do. Ella watched as Arnold struggled to get out from under the horse. Then he passed out due to the pain.

She scrambled off the ledge and back to the camp. There, she waited anxiously as Arnold was brought to his tent and laid on the cot, still unconscious.

Ella gagged and looked away as the medics inspected the wound. He suffered a bullet wound, and several bones were broken. Arnold needed a place to rest.

Every day, Ella tended to Arnold, who remained in a feverish state. Some days he yelled in his sleep, and it rattled her. He sounded angry and bitter. And he was, especially since Gates took credit for the victory at Saratoga when Arnold deserved it.

Eventually, Arnold recovered. However while he was recuperating, he received a letter from General Washington requesting that he go back to Philadelphia and command the area.

So, in early 1778, Ella went with Arnold to Philadelphia. They moved into the fancy residence where General William Howe used to live. Arnold got himself an ornate carriage, and warmed up to being in charge. However, this caused some conflict, since a man named Joseph Reed did not approve of Arnold's command.

One day, they headed to the theater that Arnold often attended. Ella looked out the carriage window. "Looks like there's going to be a crowd tonight."

Arnold nodded absentmindedly. Ladies chatted outside, and he suddenly sat up straighter. "We've arrived."

The driver came out and opened the door. He then helped Arnold out and handed him his walking stick. Arnold took it and stumbled over to a lady. "Brigadier General Arnold, at your service. Who do I have the pleasure of meeting?"

The young lady rolled her eyes and laughed as he took her hand. "Peggy Shippen."

He then offered her his arm, and they walked together into the theater.

Ella stood there, blinking. The ladies nearby turned to her and giggled, "Did you see that? General Arnold likes Miss Shippen."

Ella nodded, wondering, *Aren't the Shippen family Loyalists?* She watched as Arnold helped Peggy into her chair, speaking eloquently.

Arnold Home, Philadelphia, Pennsylvania
5 May 1779

Ella was up late, thinking in bed. Peggy and Arnold talked down below. Just recently, the two married, and now stayed up late every night enjoying themselves. But tonight was different. They spoke in hushed tones, sounding worried. Ella strained to listen.

"Yes, we can. I will speak of the times we've spent in the past." It was Peggy. She sounded almost dreamy. "He was such a handsome gentleman. No one will suspect me by sending him a letter."

"Aye." Arnold whispered back. "And then I'll use the concoction to write between the lines using our new code."

Code? Concoction? Handsome gentleman? Ella got up and moved closer to the door, straining her ears.

"Clinton wants to know if I can get him at West Point. The Americans will be sorry now." Arnold chuckled as Peggy joined in.

Ella's heart skipped a beat as she recalled what she heard about Benedict Arnold.

Brighton, Tennessee
Modern Day

"Andrew? Do you know where the kids are?" Grace asked, wandering in to find her husband. "I told them to shelve some books but haven't seen them since."

Andrew, the twins' father, rounded the corner. "They probably fell into a book again. Look, here's one about the American Revolution on the floor." He picked it up, flipped it over and shook it.

The two teenagers tumbled headfirst from the pages, one yelling, "Traitor! He's a traitor!"

"Goodness, Ella! What on earth are you talking about?" Grace asked, helping her daughter up.

Ella breathed hard. "Benedict Arnold.... I've been with him for several months. He was so kind to me, and everyone undervalued him, but—but—he's a traitor!"

"Didn't you pay any attention in history class?" Jason snorted, getting up and dusting himself off.

Ella glared at him, and then threw her arms around him. "Jason, I fell into the book! Did you? Who did you meet?"

Jason shrugged. "John Andre..." he looked down at the floor, deep in thought.

"Who is he?" Ella asked, but her brother shrugged, avoiding eye contact.

Grace and Andrew looked at each other and raised their eyebrows. She took the book from him and placed it back on the shelf. "Sounds like a story for another time," she said, wrapping her arms around the twins.

GEORGE BLAKEY: THE UNTOLD STORY OF A RIFLEMAN

BY THORSTEN SCHOEN

GEORGE BLAKEY: THE UNTOLD STORY OF A RIFLEMAN

CULPEPER, VIRGINIA
JULY 1775 – FEBRUARY 1776

Winter is passing. Working outside on the family farm, George Blakey and his younger brother William relish seasonal changes. Trees start to grow their leaves, the sun and warmth of spring begin melting away the snow-covered ground, and Blakey relents to his growing desire to enlist.

I, George Blakey, currently stand at the enlisting post to join the army. My heart stops, stupefied, for standing in line to enlist is William.

"William, you mustn't enlist. You have a wife and a newborn," I pleaded and sat down beside him.

"George, why must *you* enlist?! Even if you are the oldest son, and unmarried, please tell me it's not just in defiance of our family's gentry status that sends you to war," sputtered William. He reflects, *What a privilege and curse it is to come from a Virginia family well positioned in the social hierarchy.*

"I know your worries. I can't deny the pressure from our uncle and cousins to ascend in governance, and to begin planting tobacco to prosper is burdensome. By enlisting, I hope to send a message to them that I do not think our land or freedom will be protected if we only sit back as planters and public servants. William, you know that I'm a gentle Christian man; all I ever yearned for was acreage and the freedom to till it," countered George.

William furrowed his brow. "Listen, I understand you're apprehensive to see me go to war, but if you're going to enlist, at least allow me to also fight for this country's freedom."

"But what would happen to your family if you—"

"If something were to happen to me, I trust that you would take care of my family." Putting on a brave face, I nodded and hugged my brother.

I signed my name to enlist, and William signed his name directly under mine. Soon thereafter, we separated, as directed, into different companies, and disheartened, my brother left to go to war. Gloomily, I think, *Already I have lost my brother.*

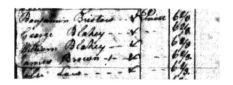

I enlisted in Captain Thomas Patterson's Company for two years with the promise of Sergeant. My service would begin in the 6th regiment of the Virginia Line commanded by Colonel Mordecai Buckner. Now it was my turn to head off to war.

Trenton to Princeton, New Jersey
24 December 1776 – 6 January 1777
Heroes in the News: The Battle of Princeton

In late October of 1776, Washington's Continental Army fought through New York before retreating across New Jersey. Early Christmas morning, they overtook the Hessians in Trenton. Following that surprise attack, Washington faced a second battle before advancing to Princeton.

On January 2, 1777, the Americans found themselves trapped with their backs up against the Assunpink Creek in Trenton. They could either retreat by water or battle the British line of march on land surrounding them. That evening, Major Edward Hand strategically positioned the riflemen in hopes of slowing British advancement. He ordered the riflemen to scatter around in ditches, behind trees, and in the curves of the Trenton to Princeton Road to counter any British attempting to cross the Assunpink.

The shadow of a barn cloaked four riflemen. One of them pointed to some stacked barrels. Nodding in unison, they made a run for it. Crack! Bam! I fell heavily to the ground, crawled behind the barrels with others, lowered his hands to the rifle, took aim, and fired.

This flagging continued until dusk when Cornwallis's advance guard neared the river. Hessians charged the riflemen with their bayonets, but the riflemen quickly retreated to safety. Three times the British charged Assunpink. The Patriots opened fire, intercepting with grapeshot, musket fire, and cannons. Following the success of the riflemen, it was a great liquidation of the British. Cornwallis appeared to have had this idea behind the attack: 'If at first, you don't succeed, fail, fail again.'

After enjoying a fabulous retreat from Cornwallis, despite still being cornered by the British, everyone in the encampment nestled in for a well-earned night of sleep. Everyone except for Washington, that is, for as the sun and colonial men settled down for the night, a fortuitous miracle fell upon them. Temperatures dropped, cold north winds blew in, and just as Washington had speculated and hoped, the mud-ice roads froze over to make ice-capable travel ground for his army. However, a successful exit meant marching out in the dead dark of night in complete silence.

"Hurry and get up," whispered an officer. "We are all marching."

"What is going on? I just fell asleep," I asked, yawning.

After many hours of quiet confusion, the whole encampment moved out as quietly and quickly as a colony of rabbits. As I staggered along constantly bumping into other rifles and riflemen in the dark, I thought, *Even the carriages are quietly moving. Oh, they're covered in cloth. That was smart. I wonder who did that?*

"Psst Blakey, why are all the fires still burning?" whispered Wilhem.

"I was just wondering that," I answered.

"A detachment of the New Jersey militia is keeping the campfires going to trick any British watching, should they try to follow our tracks at daybreak," murmured another rifleman.

British Camp Near Trenton

"General Cornwallis, if Washington is the General I take him to be, his army will not be found there in the morning."

"Lieutenant-General Erskine, we'll bag the old fox in the morning. He simply does not have enough boats to retreat, and when our reinforcements arrive from Princeton he will be outmanned and trapped."

Erskine turned away with a frown. *He knew how crafty Washington could be, called the "fox" by the British.* He knew better than to argue with Cornwallis, so he took his leave.

Washington's Army Marching to Princeton

During the night of January 3, 1777, Washington's army marched just under twenty miles. It was extremely cold, with unseen obstacles to stumble over in the dark, heavy wooded areas and icy streams.

"I'm so tired I can barely keep my eyes open," I muttered with heavy eyelids. "I could just fall asleep right here."

"Blakey, hey, you've been swaying at every halt. We have a long march still ahead, and my arms are tired of supporting you as you sleepwalk," whispered Wilhelm.

Suddenly, the complete silence of the dark night was followed by complete chaos. Our regiment marched right into British forces creating a colliding surprise. *'Talk about a wake-up call.'* My instincts took over, shifting his rifle, loading it, taking aim, and firing.

It ended with the British surrendering. There were around forty-five casualties, one hundred injured, and two hundred extra prisoners, as well as captured cargo. With this additional load to his already exhausted men, Washington angled north retreating to the Watchung Mountains around Morristown.

I spent the winter at Washington's Morristown encampment. Captain Patterson left the army after contracting smallpox. Washington then transferred me to a company under General Daniel Morgan.

Morristown, Trenton, Germantown, Maidenhead & Philadelphia
June 1777 – August 1777

In June 1777, General George Washington organized a special unit known as the Corps of Rangers. From June to August, I fight under Captain Morgan as part of his Ranger Force. Morgan reads direct orders from Washington for his Rangers to traverse ground as sharpshooters with orders to 'fall upon their flanks and gall them as much as possible' as they advance towards this town, that town, and lastly Brunswick.

I have never engaged in so many quick and hard marches while also fighting the British two or three fights a day. Captain Morgan's training is intense in the woods surrounding the small British outposts, I muse.

"Sharpshooters, today, disguised as Indians, we will carry out our hit-and-run tactic on the British. The distinguished British find the hit-and-run a disturbing tactic," Morgan explains. "We are moving into our positions now. Lennon, Temple, and Mill, you hit-and-run. Blakey and Wilhelm, see that gallant officer by the tent? I respect him, but it is necessary that he die. Take your place in the woods, and do your duty."

I find it challenging to understand Morgan, I think. *I can't believe he survived a musket ball that knocked out half his teeth on one side and exited through his neck. I understood his orders were for Wilhelm and me to take a British officer out.*

August 1777 to October 1777

*Freeman's Farm, Saratoga & Philadelphia Hospital
The Battle of Clouds & First Battle of Saratoga*

Our rifle force united with General Horatio Gates in opposing Burgoyne. On September 16th, we were engaged in battle when a hurricane-driven rainstorm poured heavily for twenty hours and became known as the Battle of Clouds. This took a toll on my body, as a cold dampness settled deep into my bones.

We then moved to settle around the outskirts of Saratoga Village. Just three days later on September 19th, General Morgan and General Benedict Arnold had us advance on the British vanguard at Freeman's Farm. We fought ferociously just as General Morgan trained us, concealing ourselves in the thick woods and dispatching British officers. We successfully hindered the British forces until the German reinforcements arrived. At dusk, we withdrew.

That night, I succumbed to my exhaustion. My unconscious body had to be lifted onto a cart that took me to a hospital in Philadelphia. Many of Morgan's riflemen fell ill at this time and were carted away. Not all returned.

I woke up in the hospital, confused but comfortable. The intense training and continuous fighting under Morgan for nearly three months had caught up to him. Being drenched by the Battle of the Clouds, the zealous fighting at Freeman's Farm, and the cold and exhaustion had finally overwhelmed me. Thankfully, I made a quick recovery and returned to fight with General Morgan in late October.

Valley Forge, Pennsylvania
Mid-November 1777 – Late February 1778
White Horse Encampment

I trudged through six-inch snow stained brown. It's only been a few months, but there is barely enough water or food to make it until February. Suddenly, out of nowhere, a hidden rock jumped out of the snow to meet my foot. This caused me to face-plant into nearby murky water. "WAAGUHUHUHUHUHU!" My nostrils flared as his throat filled up with water. There was a strange red tint to the water, which suspiciously smelled and tasted like decaying carcasses. I wiped away the residue. The suspicious stew was a wake-up call to me who, only moments ago had been sleepily trudging down the path.

"C'mon, stop playing in the snow. We have somewhere to be." Wilhelm lowered his hand to help him up.

"Thanks," I muttered as I spit out the foul water.

"Hurry, we must get our rations before they run out. Yesterday, I got spoiled and rotted meat. At least, I think it was meat. Maybe it was from the dead horse." Wilhelm suddenly stopped talking, too hungry and upset to even finish his sentence.

Valley Forge triggered a change for me, and I was suffocating from all the death and desertion surrounding me. Then, I bumped into a man while lining up for rations. "Sir, excuse me. I apologize, I didn't mean—" My heart stopped. I barely recognized this frail skeleton of a man. I couldn't, *didn't,* believe it. I stood frozen. So many emotions flooded me, but I remained in utter disbelief.

"George?" William whispered in a broken voice. He was shaking and quivering.

"WILLIAM, Lord, is it true, my brother, William?" I cried, sobbing as he gently embraced him for fear that he would break. *If I were hydrated, tears would be flowing like the James River into the Chesapeake Bay.*

Culpeper County, Virginia
Late August 1778

A man is hoeing crops on his farm but sits for a break. He looks a bit older than before and has deep wisdom in his eyes. He glanced over his friend Wilhelm beside him.

"Thanks for allowing me to reside here on my journey home. It's been an honor to serve by your side throughout this enduring war," thanked Wilhelm gratefully.

"The honor has been mine. I have learned plenty and changed quite a lot. I am thankful to have served beside you," answered Blakey.

"How have you changed, and what have you learned?" questioned Wilhelm.

"At first, when I joined this war, I thought I needed to prove something to my family. After all my battles though, I've learned much. Personally, experiencing others' hardships has changed me," began Blakey.

"I am still farming, and I boat flour down the James River for the army. I may not be using my rifle on the frontline anymore, but I am still serving my country by producing and delivering needed supplies to my Patriotic brothers still fighting in the field."

"The thing that I've learned the most though, is that sometimes a powerful position isn't the best. After watching others suffer for basic needs, I realize that the best position is one where you can help others in your own humble way," summarized Blakey.

"Those words are powerful and very true. I'll always be grateful for our fire-forged friendship," stated Wilhelm.

"WILHELM, WE NEED TO LEAVE," a voice interrupted them as Blakey looked over to see a few carriages laden with supplies. Thanking Blakey again, Wilhelm stood up and headed in their direction. Blakey watched them leave, reminiscing, and headed back inside for the night.

BENJAMIN FRANKLIN: SPIES, STRINGS ATTACHED, AND STAINED SECRETARIES

BY CHRISTOPHER J. WATT

THE EPIC STORY OF AMERICA 1777-1779

PROLOGUE

Great Britain shan't ever be defeated."

It was nearly a year since the peace conference with Admiral Richard Howe on Staten Island. Congress tasked Benjamin Franklin, along with John Adams and Edward Rutledge, to meet with the British admiral to discuss peace with the independent American colonies and Great Britain. After a few hours, it became clear that peace wasn't yet an option.

Franklin was later sent to France to collaborate with Silas Deane and discuss with the French Court the idea of an alliance and support for the Patriot cause. Things were progressing slowly, but progressing nonetheless. At least, it *seemed* like things were progressing.

CHAUMONT HOUSE, PASSY, FRANCE
4 JANUARY 1777

Benjamin Franklin leaned back in his chair as he read over the letter to the American Committee of Secret Correspondence. After he satisfied himself with rereading it a fifth time, he took the goose feather quill and, after dipping it into the ebony black inkwell, signed off.

I am, Gentlemen, Your most obedient, humble Servant,
B. Frankl

Before he could finish his name, his door swung open, sending a whoosh of air into the room and disrupting the loose papers, and a pitch black dog galumphed in. She bounded up to Franklin's left side, and lovingly knocked him hard enough to send his elbow into the inkwell, pouring it all over the desk.

"Shadow, for the love of liberty," Franklin grumbled with a laugh. "If only William knew the loving menace you can be sometimes. Now I must replace what you so enthusiastically overturned." He stood up with the empty inkwell in hand and left the room on a quest to end his epistle.

With that, Shadow pounced up onto the warm chair, her eyes darting back and forth as she read every word of the letter.

"Excellent work on that inkwell diversion," came the voice of a Eurasian magpie by the windowsill, who nudged the window ajar and hopped inside.

"Why thank you, Nimbus," Shadow replied. Since May of 1775, the animal spy team followed Benjamin Franklin, with Shadow posing as Franklin's son's black Newfoundland. After the failed peace conference on Staten Island, Shadow and Nimbus helped the British win the Landing of Kip's Bay and returned to London. Soon after Christmas, they ventured back to France for the next part of the mission.

"What do we have here?" Nimbus asked, scanning the letter. "Dr Franklin is telling the Committee of Secret Correspondence about his meeting with the Comte de Vergennes earlier last month."

"We must inform the British Secret Service," Shadow added. "We have three days until the next dead drop. The Americans won't form this alliance if we can help it!"

Tuileries Gardens, Paris, France
9:31am, 7 January 1777

"Another set of intelligence preventing the Americans from hiding from the British, huzzah!" Shadow cheered from behind the Horse Chestnut tree to Nimbus perched on the branch above. The two observed as Edward Bancroft, Franklin's secretary, stood up from kneeling by a tree and left the gardens. Once he was out of sight, the two animals raced over and pulled out the bottle from the hollow in the trunk. Little did any of the commissioners know that Edward Bancroft was a spy working for the British Secret Service and would communicate to the spymasters by dropping false love letters—with the real notes in invisible ink between the lines—in a bottle into the hollow of the tree every Tuesday.

"Here's our postscript note," Nimbus held a small, rolled piece of paper in his claws. Inside contained all the extra information Bancroft hadn't yet discovered that either Shadow or Nimbus had gathered.

With his beak he hooked the cork, opened the bottle, and slipped the note inside. "The irony is perfect: Britain expects us to leave our espionage with *strings* attached. *And* you have to 'read between the lines' to discover the truth," he chuckled, returning it to the hollow. Nimbus didn't just intend a pun, he meant literal strings, too—the spymasters required Bancroft to tie a string to the bottle to prove it was genuine.

"How poetic; loyalty to England comes with a catch!" Shadow laughed at his quip.

Chaumont House, Passy, France
3 March 1777

"Many thanks unto you, Dr Bancroft," Franklin acknowledged, nodding his head. "Your willingness to do this for us has not escaped me." Over the past month, he and Silas Deane sent Edward Bancroft to London to gather information on the British side of the war.

Bancroft smiled. "It is my pleasure; anything for the Patriots! I shall be sure to return with all things important," he reported.

Shadow sat by the window. "Are you all set?" she whispered to Nimbus on the sill.

"Indeed, I am. I'll report back to you as soon as I can," he replied. "These Americans believe Bancroft's going to London to gather intelligence. What they do not know is that he'll be *sharing* intelligence with the Brits and *planting* false intel for the Americans. Oh, the joys of doing espionage for England," he flapped his wings. "I will see you soon, my friend."

Chaumont House, Passy, France
16 March 1777

'Dr. Bancroft is arrested in London for corresponding with and assisting us.'

Franklin shook his head in dismay as Deane wrote his letter to Congress. The news arrived that morning. London authorities arrested Bancroft for conspiring with the American delegates in

France. This, of course, was no surprise to Shadow by the crackling fireplace. The whole plan was for Nimbus to get Bancroft arrested as a setup.

Deane added, *I feel more for Dr. Bancroft than I can express.*

"Serves him right," Arthur Lee sniffed with his arms crossed over his chest. "That so-called 'Patriot' was up to no good. In fact, if I didn't know any better, this arrest was a set-up! The scoundrel's tricking you, I have no doubt."

Shadow shifted her position. She didn't like Lee. His paranoia that anyone and everyone worked for the enemy made her espionage even trickier than usual. *His speculations are too accurate for my liking. Nimbus and I must find a way to convince him that Dr Bancroft is innocent.*

Versailles, France,
13 December 1777

"Consider America's future," Franklin proposed. With Deane in the middle of the group, they once again stood before the French minister of foreign affairs, Comte de Vergennes. They did so for the past year, with each meeting different from the last, but discussing the same purpose since their first meeting in December the previous year. "Consider the young ones who will be educated. You have the authority to decide whether they are taught about a war that failed, or a victory they achieved thanks to the heroic French aid that you, *Monsieur* Vergennes, authorised."

Vergennes nodded slowly but uttered nothing.

"I understand that you and the French Court are concerned about supporting a cause which has the objective of overthrowing its monarch. I hear that your reigning monarch, King Louis XVI, fears it 'contagious,' but surely your good people would know not to do such a thing when *their* king isn't a tyrant," Deane complimented the French.

"*Oui, Monsieur Deane,*" Vergennes agreed. "The good people of France would never overthrow their king! He is a *bon* leader, no? *Monsieur Franklin,* I appreciate your insight and wise words."

Franklin nodded.

Silas grinned.

Lee sighed.

"*Le Pacte de Famille* means we must wait for Spain's approval before making any final arrangements on this proposal," Vergennes admitted. The Bourbon family pact was a formal alliance between France and Spain to ensure cooperation between the two nations. "I shall send a letter to King Charles III of Spain. We will have our answer in three weeks."

Chaumont House, Passy, France
6 January 1778

"The Spanish king rejected the alliance. He won't recognise America as its own nation," Deane announced, walking into Franklin's office with Lee and Lee's secretary. "We have no hope."

Lying by the warm hearth, Shadow snapped her head towards Nimbus in a nearby tree and wagged her tail as the signal. Nimbus flew to perch close enough to eavesdrop.

"'No hope' is a little harsh," Franklin screwed his face, not flustered with the unfortunate news. "We are closer to Alliance than we realise. The French Court is impatient. And an impatient mind..." he wriggled his finger with a wink, as a grandfather does to his grandchildren, "is a mind which is quick to decide something that'll remove the impatience from thought."

Deane nodded and looked at Lee. "I understand, Dr Franklin. How excellent that you believe an alliance between America and France is close."

This has taken a dark turn! Shadow stood up and left the room reticently. *I must notify Paul Wentworth and the British spymasters immediately!*

Following more discussion, Lee, his secretary, and Deane left Franklin's office. Bancroft left when Shadow had, using the excuse that he thought he heard someone calling for him.

"Time to meet with Mr Wentworth," Franklin muttered.

Nimbus, still sitting near the window, took to the skies and flew in search of his canine companion.

Shadow and Nimbus stood in the elaborate gardens surrounding Chaumont House, hidden from any passers-by.

"They will reunite America in loyalty to the British Crown," Nimbus reported. "Dr Franklin made that clear: 'Time to meet with Mr Wentworth.'" The magpie imitated the ambassador almost perfectly in both voice and tone.

A servant walking from the house overheard the voice. Thinking it was Benjamin Franklin himself, he took off running down the road, shouting, "*Réunion de Franklin avec la Grande-Bretagne pour la paix! La paix!!*"

Benjamin Franklin sat in his cosy office, writing a letter. With the Frenchman's wild cries outside, he smiled. "My plan is falling into place rapidly."

Versailles, France
8 January 1778

Franklin played France and Great Britain into thinking that America was closer to an alliance with the other. Concerned that America would align with Britain, France suddenly made haste to meet again, this time over supper, with the American ambassadors. On behalf of Vergennes, his secretary now met with them two days after Franklin met with British emissary Paul Wentworth.

"I only have one question for you, *mes amis*," Vergennes' secretary declared. "It seems to me—and the French Court—that America is more intent on considering peace with England than it is forming an alliance with France. What is necessary to be done to give enough satisfaction to you commissioners so that you would not listen to *les propositions* from England for peace with them?"

Deane and Lee both turned to Franklin to respond. Although they knew the answer, the French would listen to Franklin more than anyone else.

Before he could answer, Shadow took a running leap onto the

dinner table in a blur of black fur. The crockery overturned, the food flew across the floor, and the elaborate tablecloth tore. An unfortunate wineglass toppled over and stained the burgundy liquid into the secretary's white uniform, who screamed.

"*Monsieur* Secretary, I apologise most humbly," Franklin gasped, remembering a similar event in 1776. "I ask for your most gracious forgiveness."

"*Accepté*," the horrified secretary grumbled. "Consider my question and return once you have an answer. Versailles is known for making memories—and I am *certain* that *nothing* shall tempt me to ever forget your Newfoundland dog."

Paris, France
6 December 1778

After over a year of debates and discussions with the French Court, a final decision had been made and it was time to sign the Treaty of French Alliance. Benjamin Franklin made it clear—in a diplomatic manner appealing to the French—that the immediate conclusion of a treaty between the nations would remove all thoughts of an alliance with England. On this day, the three American commissioners met with Comte de Vergennes and French diplomat Conrad Alexandre Gérard de Reyneval to sign the document.

Two animals hid outside the window as the signing took place. "We failed, Nimbus!" Shadow lamented. "Our attempts to prevent this alliance were to no avail!"

"We haven't failed," Nimbus affirmed with a confident nod. "Our mission was to conduct espionage for the British on the progression of the alliance. That's exactly what we did. *And* we did rather well at it."

"Here you go again making history," Silas Deane whispered to Benjamin Franklin, the most famous American in Europe. Unlike all other occasions when he met with the French Court, Franklin wore a cornflower-blue suit with gold buttons. He had set quite a fashion trend around France with his rustic brown attire. "Why, Dr Franklin, haven't you worn your usual wardrobe today?"

"To give this piece a little revenge," he replied with a wink. In 1774, Franklin turned from supporting England to become a Patriot. While he was in London, he appeared before the King's Privy Council where solicitor general Alexander Wedderburn utterly humiliated him. The following day he was stripped of his title as postmaster general. He wore the same blue suit on this day.

"*Mes amis*, the Treaty of French Alliance is signed," Vergennes announced once Arthur Lee completed his turn with the quill. "America and France are official allies!"

"Huzzah!" the Americans shouted. Their mission was complete. Their hard work had paid off and France would soon send aid to the independent American *states* to help win the war.

"I appreciate your consideration of America's future generations, *Monsieur* Vergennes," Franklin smiled and nodded to his grandson, Temple Franklin. "Signing this treaty will forever etch in the minds of America's children France's generosity."

"*Merci* to *you*, *Docteur* Franklin," Vergennes thanked. "The pleasure is all mine that such a daring act is carried out with such love for the children." With that, the men exited the office to celebrate, leaving Edward Bancroft alone with two other British spies at the window.

Versailles, France
20 March 1778

"*Vive Franklin!*" cried the throngs crowding the streets, hoping for a glimpse of Benjamin Franklin's coach entering the golden gates of Versailles. To make the signing of the Alliance official, King Louis XVI and his court of ministers, including the Queen of France, Marie Antoinette, were receiving the American commissioners.

After entering the courtyard, the rather impertinent and snobbish attendants who rented out the dazzling ceremonial swords, a required piece of attire when entering Versailles, met the commissioners. All but Franklin wore one, as well as other important items of court dress. The ex-postmaster general once again dressed in his simple brown garb and did not hold a sword. His only adornment was his spectacles. Of course, this inspired many fans of Franklin in the crowd. Many women wore their wigs in imitation of his fur cap.

When they entered the elaborate palace, the councilmen were escorted to the king's bedchamber, the custom in colonial France. The King of France kneeled in a position of prayer, facing the window.

I love this floor, Franklin marveled, brushing his feet over it.

"I hope that this will be for the good of both nations," came King Louis' voice as he opened his eyes and stood to face his guests. "I am exceedingly satisfied with your conduct since you arrived in my kingdom, *messieurs*."

"Your most Christian Majesty, it has truly been an honour to be working with and for you this past year," Deane bowed in respect.

The king nodded in acknowledgement before gesturing to Franklin. "*Docteur Franklin*, your name has appeared many times in this court for many reasons. I even had a chamber pot made bearing your likeness for the Comtesse Diane de Polignac."

Lee snorted back a guffaw at this news before trying to maintain a steady composure.

"News reached me of your unforgettable *chienne*, too," he chuckled and nodded at Shadow, invited to join the committee after her 'contribution' to the meeting with Vergennes' secretary.

Franklin grinned. "I am honoured to meet you and that my son's Newfoundland reached your ears. She is as unique as they come."

If only you knew how unique I really am, Shadow thought, wagging her tail.

"Come," King Louis XVI ordered. "Let us celebrate this achievement between our nations and enjoy ourselves before we immerse ourselves in more serious matters. The future of France and America awaits!"

The alliance with France was completed. The Patriots at home would soon receive reinforcements, artillery, and more. Benjamin Franklin and his brilliant mind had done it again, changing the course of history. With his witty thoughts and iconic nature, he won the French over and the coveted alliance signed *for the children*.

However, the war wasn't over yet. And neither was the espionage.

EPILOGUE

While the delegates celebrated at Versailles, two creatures stood outside, hidden within the sprawling gardens, discussing their next move.

"They could've had it all," Shadow lamented and shook her head. "Knighthoods, pardons, money, and jobs to any American who helps to secure peace and return loyalty back to England. Yet these so-called 'Patriots' squandered it, all for the cause of liberty!"

Nimbus shook his feathers in agreement. "Indeed—'tis rather odd how they threw away all their loyalty for *liberty* instead."

"Some loyalty comes with a price, and that price isn't worth paying when it takes away your freedom," she observed, remembering their conversation in 1777 about how loyalty to England comes with 'strings attached'. "The sentiment has the essence of being somewhat inspirational, don't you think, Nimbus?"

"Agreed," he replied. "The fact that these Americans are putting their very lives, fortunes, and honour on the line just for the sake of liberty and uprising against a supposedly tyrannical power. What do you believe is next?" he asked his Loyalist friend.

"Since the Alliance has been signed, we should endeavour to capture even the minutest detail in our espionage to help the British win the war." She shrugged off the revelation of liberty-versus-loyalty. "With our schemes, Great Britain shan't *ever* be defeated! HUZZAH!"

GENERAL HORATIO GATES: THE SPIES OF SARATOGA

BY ROXANNE MESSIER

GENERAL HORATIO GATES: THE SPIES OF SARATOGA

BAILEY TAVERN, ENGLAND
17 OCTOBER 1745

Horatio Gates entered Bailey Tavern, teeming with soldiers eating and drinking around tables. He took a seat at a table beside a handsome man gambling. He was clearly winning by the smug look on his face. Gates recognized him for they belonged to the same regiment. He had never met the man, but his reputation preceded him. His name was John Burgoyne.

Gates ordered a small beer as Burgoyne collected his money from the poor, beaten soldier. "Good day, Sir," Gates greeted him. "You are John Burgoyne, correct?"

Burgoyne confirmed this and Gates introduced himself. The two men talked and began to find much in common. Both were ambitious, and though neither liked to admit it, they were arrogant as well. Neither had wealthy parents but climbed the ladder of British society by becoming lieutenants. The men bonded, though they never met again. Until now—as enemies.

Near Freeman's Farm, Saratoga, New York
19 September 1777

A girl knelt on the ground, staring intently at the battle unfolding before her. Her hand was continually on a small lump concealed under her farm dress. She gasped and whirled around as she heard the crunching sounds of someone's footsteps behind her. A brown-haired boy holding a knapsack in his clenched fist was its source. "Please don't be scared," he pleaded.

"I'm not scared," she retorted. "I was just spooked for a second."

The boy sat down beside her. "What's your name?" he asked.

"Pleasant," the girl curtly answered.

"My name is Heinrich," the boy commented, "I think Pleasant is a strange name."

"Well, Heinrich is a strange name for an American," Pleasant snapped.

Heinrich's eyes widened slightly. "Well...Well...I'm from Hesse-Kassel," he admitted, "My parents wanted to give me a better opportunity to succeed in life. So, when our ruler, Friedrich II asked for servants for the ships that were carrying Hessian soldiers to fight the Americans, my parents sent me to be one of those servants. I arrived in Philadelphia, and learned from the men in Congress why America is fighting this war. They taught me English, and they taught me that the Patriot side is freedom's side. The side I knew my parents would want me to choose. But Philadelphia was taken, and my friends sent me to New York. I found out that the Patriot army was camping out in Albany, so I traveled here. I have no idea what's happening now, though."

"C'est incroyable!" Pleasant replied, stunned by Heinrich's tale. "And I can explain this battle, for I'm an expert on this war. This battle began when Lieutenant General John Burgoyne, who's the British commander in this battle, planned for him and Howe to march to Albany to cut off the Northern colonies from the rest of America. Burgoyne is capable, and not afraid to act; he won many of the battles fought in Canada and New York. After an American victory, the British headed to Albany, and camped at Saratoga. The Americans and British have been fighting for one hour here at Freeman's Farm."

Just then, a squawk came from above as a hawk who had been circling around Pleasant's general location noticed Heinrich. He dove down from the sky at the speed of a bullet, heading straight for him. In a split second, Pleasant jumped up and cawed at the hawk. It paused, then headed for a landing on Pleasant's gloved arm. "That bird tried to kill me!" Heinrich gasped.

"Don't worry, Courageux does this to everyone he doesn't know. His job is to keep me safe," Pleasant informed him, stroking the bird's feathered head. "I know how to speak hawk, so he doesn't hurt people that I trust."

Heinrich took a deep breath and exclaimed, "You speak hawk?!"

Pleasant didn't reply. She smiled at Courageux, then released him into the sky. The two noticed the battle came to a standstill. They waited for the battle to begin anew, unaware that from the bushes a short distance away, two pairs of eyes stared at them.

Gen. Horatio Gates' Headquarters,
Bemis Heights, Saratoga, New York
19 September 1777

Gunfire and shouts echoed throughout the area. The fight rapidly grew in ferocity as messengers informed Gates of the triumphs and troubles of his troops. He was in a quandary. Should he send much needed troops to Enoch Poor's brigade, or should he use those soldiers to protect against a possibility of an attack by German soldiers and British artillery that was near the river? He paced around his headquarters then summoned a messenger. "Tell my available troops to assemble close to the river to fight against the Germans," he ordered.

At supper, Gates tried to eat something, but the food tasted like sand in his mouth. Just then, Brigadier General Benedict Arnold rushed into headquarters. "What do you want, Arnold?" Gates snapped.

Arnold glared at him. "Sir, this is urgent," he informed Gates. "German troops are nearly destroying the New Hampshire continentals and Hull's detachment. We need reinforcements—desperately."

Gates offered Arnold a spot at his table. "Sit down and rest for a bit while I think."

"Sir, there is no time to waste—think quickly!" he urged Gates disrespectfully.

Gates rolled his eyes, sat down, and said, "I want you to tell Learned to send his brigade to the assistance of the New Hampshire continentals and Hull's detachment."

"But sir," Benedict protested. "Someone needs to accompany them that knows the lay of the land, or else they'll get lost."

Gates groaned. "Just do as I say!" he demanded.

As darkness fell, the battle ended, and the troops filed back to base. The generals lined up in Gates's headquarters and reported what occurred. "Sir, towards the end of the battle, we got word from General Benedict Arnold," was Learned's report. "He told us you had ordered my brigade to come rescue some troops from German soldiers. But we got lost in the woods. Thankfully, those troops-and my troops-are safe, but did you consider sending a guide with us?"

Gates glanced over at Benedict Arnold, who smirked at him. Since their argument that morning, when Gates had removed him from his place as second command, the two had become bitter rivals. And the arguments were only just beginning.

Near Freeman's Farm, Saratoga, New York
20 September 1777

Pleasant yawned and rubbed her back, sore from sleeping on the hard dirt ground. Then her eyes widened. *Why did I forget to write?* she chided herself. She pulled out a piece of parchment paper and writing utensils from a hidden pocket in her dress. The ink was in a little flask that she dipped the quill in, and using these things, she penned a letter.

"What are you writing?" Heinrich asked.

"A letter," Pleasant curtly replied.

"Okay...Why?" Heinrich asked. Pleasant pretended she didn't hear his words. "You said you trusted me, so trust me with this," Heinrich pleaded.

Pleasant sighed as she stared at Courageux, soaring through the air, free, like Heinrich's parents had wanted him to be. Free to know things. So, she decided to trust him with the information. "I'll tell you," Pleasant said. "But you must promise me you won't be scared."

"Why would I be scared?" Heinrich asked, confused.

"You'll see," Pleasant began. "My real name is Noemie Moreau. I can never reveal this, or else I will be killed by people who want my information. For you see, I am a spy for *sa majeste, Roi* Louis XVI, 'his majesty, King Louis XVI'." Noemie breathed deeply as she continued. "I spy on the Americans. Not for malicious purposes, of course, I do it so that the king can know if the Americans are succeeding. He doesn't want to officially support the losing side. For if the Americans lose the war, our country will be destroyed by the detestable British nation, if they know we have helped. So, the king sent me to America, along with my protector Courageux and this," Noemie explained, holding her clock locket.

With those words, she clutched the letter in one hand, the clock locket in the other, and disappeared. Heinrich collapsed to the ground in a faint. A few seconds later, Noemie reappeared, no longer clutching the letter. Heinrich was unconscious. With a gasp, Noemie rushed to his side and felt his pulse. Shakily, Heinrich sat up. "You're back?" he asked groggily. "Why don't you have the letter anymore?"

"Because I didn't just disappear, I teleported to King Louis' palace and gave him the letter," Noemie informed him.

"The clock locket—it teleports?" Heinrich wheezed.

"Yes, and it can also go back in time," Noemie reported.

"It g-goes back in time?" he stammered, his face pale. Noemie couldn't blame him for being scared. She had also been terrified when the king told her about the clock locket.

As Heinrich composed himself, he pondered this miraculous power. "Can I help spy?" he blurted.

Noemie shrugged. "Perhaps, I'll ask King Louis. Now, what's for breakfast?"

Over in the bushes, the eyes continued to stare, but they were wide with surprise. The figure behind the bushes fumed. He and his bloodhound, Mors, watched all that happened. "They have so many advantages!" he ranted, "Those dreadful 'Patriots' will surely win if they have those children on their side! But never fear Mors! I have the perfect plan to stop them.

Gen. Horatio Gates' Headquarters
Bemis Heights, Saratoga, New York
7 October 1777

Gates was looking out the window, a habit by now, and a

messenger from the advance guard burst into the room. "The British —are—very--near," he panted.

Horatio glanced at his aide, James Wilkinson. "James, go and investigate."

Horatio waited fifteen minutes until James came back. He breathlessly reported all he witnessed to Horatio. "The soldiers are sitting in the grain, with their firearms between their legs," he reported. "There are foragers cutting the wheat and placing it on horses, and the generals are climbing onto the farmhouse roof with their spy glasses."

Horatio puffed himself up, "Well, then, order on Morgan to begin the game," he announced dramatically.

Gen. Horatio Gates's Headquarters, Bemis Heights, Saratoga, New York
7 October 1777

Courageux flew over the British, gathering information for Noemie. He decided he should fly over Horatio Gates's headquarters. He wanted to gather some intelligence from the Americans. As he flew closer, he noticed that a suspicious man and his bloodhound were crouched outside of the headquarters. Courageux smelled trouble. He took off into the air, cawing as loud as he could and flying to Noemie and Heinrich.

Noemie wrapped her shawl closer around her. It became colder after the Battle of Freeman's Farm, and she was glad that she brought her shawl with her. Her eyes drifted to the sky. With her keen sense of sight, she spotted the tiny shape of Courageux as he barreled towards her. She heard his faint calls, and her heart froze at his words: "A bloodhound and his master are outside of Major General Horatio Gates's headquarters! Gates is in danger!"

Noemie scrambled to her feet and ran to find Heinrich, who was foraging for food. "Heinrich! We must get to the Major General's headquarters! Courageux says he's in danger!" she shrieked.

Heinrich burst from the bushes and held Noemie's hand as she clutched her clock locket tightly and muttered something under her breath. The two disappeared instantly.

As they reappeared beside the building, Noemie glanced around to make sure that the mysterious man and his bloodhound weren't close by. They peeked through the window, trying to spot Horatio Gates. But he wasn't there. Noemie and Heinrich glanced fearfully at each other. Were they too late? Courageux flew over them, yelling at the top of his lungs. Noemie deciphered his words and sighed in relief. "He's at the mess," she joyfully told Heinrich.

In an instant, they teleported to the mess. But someone had been watching them. The mysterious man cackled under his breath. "At the mess you say?" he muttered to Mors, "Why thank you for telling me."

Officer's Mess, Bemis Heights, Saratoga, New York
7 October 1777

Gates had never tasted better ox heart in his life. He raised his glass and toasted the chef for the delicious meal. The generals toasted. As Gates lowered his glass, the unmistakable sound of musket fire reached his ears. Arnold shot to his feet. "May I go investigate, sir?"

Gates stroked his chin in thought. "I'm afraid to trust you, Arnold." he replied hesitantly.

Arnold narrowed his eyes. "I will be cautious," he assured the general.

"Well, okay then, but take Benjamin Lincoln with you," Gates ordered.

Arnold and Lincoln obeyed. The men around the table grew quiet and forgot their appetites, waiting and waiting. Suddenly, the two men returned. "Sir, British troops are threatening our left flank; you must send reinforcements," Arnold urgently informed Gates.

"Then, I will send Morgan and Dearborn to outflank the British," Gates assured him.

Arnold's cold eyes scanned Gates's face. "That is nothing; you must send a stronger force," he insisted sharply.

Gates had no more patience left for Arnold. "General Arnold, I have nothing for you to do, you have no business here," he replied coldly.

Arnold's face fell, and he stalked out of the room, not looking back. Gates felt a little pang of guilt but shook it away. Lincoln shifted uncomfortably from foot to foot. "Perhaps you could send a strong force to help Morgan, maybe three regiments?" he suggested.

Gates nodded. "That's a good idea Lincoln, I will order it done."

Dinner ended, and Gates strolled out of the mess, heading to his headquarters. From behind, a huge weight landed on him, and he tumbled to the ground, claws raking his back. He tried to cry out in pain, but a hand clamped over his mouth. He looked up and saw a blonde-haired man smirking down at him. "Well Gates," The man chuckled in a crisp British accent, "it seems you are in a tight spot. In a second, my bloodhound could dig his claws deeper into your back and you would be, well," he drew his thumb across his throat, "dead."

Gates let out a muffled shriek, but no one heard his pitiful cries. Almost no one. Instantly, two children appeared before them. "You won't get away with this!" exclaimed the girl.

The boy glared at the man and leaped on him. The girl took this as affirmation that she could jump on the man too. She aimed for his legs and clung to them. The British man tottered and collapsed onto the ground. He struggled to his feet. "You can't outwit me," he sneered.

The girl smirked at him. "Well, if you don't surrender, this will happen," she screeched up at the sky, and a hawk sped down to earth, aiming at the man. His eyes widened.

"No, no! I surrender!" he held up his hands, and the bloodhound that had been on Horatio's back stumbled off him. But Gates still lay there, stunned.

The girl shook her head at the sky, and the hawk stopped in mid-air, and swooped down to land on the glove that the girl wore. "Now," the girl questioned, "why were you attempting to murder Horatio Gates? Are you a British assassin?"

"I'm a spy for the British. I was trying to stop the Americans from winning, so I decided the best way to do that was to kill the leader of their army. If I did that, then the British would surely win the battle. But you meddling kids destroyed my plans," he sulked.

"You'll be questioned further once you're imprisoned in the Bastille," the girl told him.

He groaned, as the girl grasped the boy's hand, and the boy reluctantly gripped the man's arm, and the man held his dog's collar. In the girl's other hand, she clasped a clock locket around her neck. She muttered something, then the strange group disappeared. Gates screamed weakly, hardly believing what had just happened. He stumbled to his feet, massaging his bleeding back as questions filled his mind.

As he arrived at his headquarters, he requested a jacket to hide his scratches, and then settled into his dreary battle routine. But all he could do was ponder his frightening encounter with near death. A messenger tapped him on the back, interrupting his thoughts. "Sir, General Arnold is acting quite strange. He rushed into the battle, and he's fighting fiercely."

Gates frowned. "Must be drunk; send Major Armstrong to bring him back to camp."

Soon, the messenger returned. "Sir, Armstrong couldn't catch Arnold, so he went to the troop's rear. Then, Arnold told three regiments to follow him to battle, which they did gladly."

He did WHAT? Gates thought. But to the messenger, he said, "As long as he is leading the regiments well, then leave him be." The messenger frowned but didn't comment.

As the battle wore on, Gates heard from more men that Arnold was a furious and skilled fighter, and the British seemed near surrender. Though Gates was jealous of Arnold's success, he was glad that the battle was reaching its end. That night, the battle came to a standstill. When morning came, he eagerly looked out the window, where the British camp used to be. It was gone. "The British are retreating!" he roared, banging his fists on his thin mattress.

Gates rushed to tell his generals to follow the British, ordering a detachment to cut the British off and spoil their escape. Gates came along with the troops to follow Burgoyne. He took his time, gathering numerous troops. As the days wore on, Gates and his soldiers followed the British troops, and each day, the cannon and gun fire grew more intense.

Gen. Horatio Gates's Headquarters, New York
17 October 1777

Gates puffed his chest as he and John Burgoyne encountered each other for the first time in exactly thirty-two years. Burgoyne yawned and smoothed his wrinkled coat as Wilkinson introduced the generals. Gates rolled his eyes. This was unnecessary; he had already met Burgoyne. Gates smiled. "I'm glad to see you," he told Burgoyne as Burgoyne reined in his horse.

"I'm not glad to see you. It's my fortune, sir, and not my fault that I'm here," Burgoyne replied. The two men dismounted from their horses and John reluctantly handed Horatio his sword in surrender. Gates handled the ornate sword, then returned it. His eyes wandered, and he spotted two children standing under a tree with a hawk on one child's shoulder. It was the two who rescued him. Gates waved, mouthing, "Thank you." They beamed, then disappeared.

GENERAL NATHANAEL GREENE: INTEGRITY FORGED BY FIRE

BY CAMERON GRAHAM

THE EPIC STORY OF AMERICA 1777-1779

NEW JERSEY, JUNE 1777

"Outrageous!" thirty-five-year-old Nathanael Greene fumed as he paced across the floor, his limp more prominent due to his agitation. "This old injury did not prevent me from becoming a major general, and I will not stand for Frenchmen taking positions that rightfully belong to hardworking Patriots who fought for our cause from the start. We all worked hard to earn our ranks. You doubly so, Knox. Then Philippe Charles Tronson du Coudray arrives from France and Congress wishes to replace you. We can only imagine what will happen as more French officers arrive every day. I am grateful for their guns, but these glory seeking foreigners are too much."

"It makes me furious how that Coudray fellow can waltz in and replace me," replied Knox. "I would rather resign than have Congress do away with me."

"I agree with you, Knox. Congress has made a terrible mistake in wanting to replace you. If you resign, I shall also," replied Greene.

Bethlehem, Pennsylvania
Summer 1777

Later that year, however, both Greene and Knox were able to enjoy a short and rare trip to the town of Bethlehem. Both had been missing their wives and were eager to purchase gifts for them and take their minds off Congress and the war. Their time in this 'singular happy place' would be short-lived, as they received news of British General William Howe's arrival at Chesapeake Bay.

Philadelphia, Pennsylvania
August 1777

The air filled with excitement as the Continental Army marched through the streets of Philadelphia on their way to fend off the British from capturing the city. Greene sat tall in his saddle with his chin held high, smiling. *How times have changed from the onset of the war*, he thought. *People openly support the cause rather than the days in my father's forge when talk was often heated but never resulted in action.*

The celebration soon faded away as the army approached the Schuylkill River. Once across, they slowly moved through the countryside trying to predict Howe's next move. Washington believed that Howe's ultimate goal was taking the city of Philadelphia. However, Washington also had to consider the large stores of food, weapons, clothing, and other supplies in the state's interior. As the long days went by, Greene spent his time writing letters, overseeing food rations and supplies for his soldiers. He missed his wife, Catherine, and was grateful for the company of his pet turtle, George. He had rescued the little turtle from the troops' cleaning water bucket and promptly named it after his friend and Commander in Chief back in 1776. *Was that only a year ago?* Greene sighed. *Maybe this war will end soon, and we both can head home.*

Finally, after weeks of anxious maneuvering the time had come for a pitched battle which both sides hoped would end the war in their favor. Howe marched his entire army towards the heart of Pennsylvania hoping to confuse Washington and ensure the British victory. The tactic worked as planned, but when Washington finally saw through the ruse, he immediately marched his army to the last point of defense.

Brandywine Creek, Pennsylvania
11 September 1777

Greene oversaw the 1st and 2nd Virginian and the 1st New York Brigades stationed in between Chadds Ford and Chadds Ferry. Throughout the day, Hessian and British troops could be seen preparing for battle on the other side. There were reports of British troops spotted on the Continental side of the river, however these reports were slow and unreliable. Reports were unconfirmed until later in the day which was too late to stop Cornwallis.

Around 3:30 p.m. shots were heard coming from the direction of Birmingham Meeting House. To the north, Stephen and Sterling's three-thousand men came under attack by the eighty-seven hundred troops under Cornwallis' command. The Patriots fell back, the Virginian troops made effective use of their rifles inflicting heavy casualties on the British as they shot from behind the trees. Greene brought his men into the action, acting as a rear guard allowing the rest of Washington's men to escape. After an hour of hard fighting, Greene's men, almost out of rounds, began to pull back.

After the battle, Washington ordered his troops back across the Schuylkill and took up fortifications north of the city at Valley Forge. This, however, allowed William Howe to march in unopposed and take Philadelphia. But supplying the British troops brought up new challenges. As the Patriot defenses along the Delaware River blocked the British fleet and French engineers helped build defenses on the river, this prevented the British from getting supplies to Philadelphia.

Germantown, Pennsylvania
October 1777

Ever since that pivotal day when Greene had witnessed Lord Sterling rush to Washington's headquarters there had been an unexplainable tension in the air. To everyone in camp, Washington continued as usual appearing to be unaffected by the visit, but Greene had a hunch that Conway was the subject of Sterling and Washington's conversation. The ever-ambitious Conway was known for his dislike of Washington and activity at his personal quarters had seen an increase in messengers and officers alike. With his suspicions, Greene made his way to consult Knox to determine the best course of action. What was not in question was their loyalty; no matter what the cost they would stand with Washington.

They did not have to wait long to discover the cost, facing open criticism for their loyalty to Washington, as rumors and letters began circulating throughout camp. Letters to Congress were not only concerning Washington but Greene and Knox as well. Greene received a letter from Joseph Reed disclosing that General Mifflin, a longtime critic of Greene, *claimed he did not oppose the Commander-in-Chief, but his favourites (yourself and Knox) who had undue influence over him*. This incident became known as the Conway Cabal.

Greene and Knox, on numerous occasions, met to vent over things said about them. Congress being distracted from addressing the critical issue of needed supplies troubled them both. At a time when Washington and the generals should be preparing for battle, Washington was having to deal with insubordination.

Valley Forge, Pennsylvania
19 December 1777

Twelve-thousand Continental soldiers marched into their new winter encampment, followed by over four-hundred women and children. Washington picked the spot because it was close enough to keep an eye on British troops sheltering in Philadelphia, yet far enough away to prevent a surprise attack.

Washington immediately set to work composing a letter of concern to Congress outlining the realities of their situation. If they did not send aid, the army was down to three choices—*starve, dissolve, or disperse*.

Work on structures began right away to prepare for the tough winter ahead. Work parties constructed earthworks for protection against enemy attacks, eventually constructing two miles of fortifications. Valley Forge, with fifteen-hundred huts for housing, became the fourth largest city in the colonies.

Greene walked to his quarters, passing the section of camp designated for Inspector General Thomas Conway's division. Greene could not argue the fact that Conway had distinguished himself at the Battle of Brandywine and Germantown, leading his brigade. Congress favored him despite his blatant disrespect for his superior officers. Greene shook his head at all the trouble that had come from this young general's pride. With that thought, Greene quickly checked his own pride and remembered he himself was not immune to such a fate, as pride often comes before a fall.

January 1778

Greene watched as snow blanketed the ground—winter was well underway at Valley Forge. The men's clothes were threadbare and many of them had rags wrapped around their feet instead of shoes. It angered Greene at the lack of supplies at such a critical time.

"Knox," Greene said, "the Quartermaster General, Commissary General and Clothier General Departments are in such a wretched condition that unless there are some very good alterations in those departments it will be impossible to prosecute another campaign. Our troops are naked, and the men are getting sickly in their huts."

Seeing his men cold and hungry was more than Greene could bear. He started to take matters into his own hands and began to lead foraging parties into the Pennsylvania countryside, commandeering needed food and supplies from nearby farms. Despite Washington's desire to maintain a friendly relationship with citizens, in Greene's eyes desperate times called for desperate measures; but he always made sure to promise future payment for the goods. During one such expedition, Greene had brought along his pet turtle, George, not wanting him to be missing upon his return. As his men approached a small barn nestled in a grove of trees, a farmer and his two sons appeared. The farmer was reluctant to give up his family's wheat stores. As the negotiations continued, George popped his head from Greene's satchel and the youngest boy moved closer in curiosity. A young captain handed a slip of paper to the boy that said Congress would compensate them for the wheat stores.

Greene frowned at the proceedings, as he knew the importance of friendship with the local people, but this foraging was necessary for the survival of his men and the efforts of the army. Catching the eye of the young boy looking at George, he had an idea. He lifted George from his pocket and approached the boy.

"Here, why don't you take my turtle? It is my promise that I will return," Greene said with a warm smile. "Would you take care of him for me?" The boy smiled and took hold of George.

Just then George caught sight of his friend in the forest, the much faster and crazy-spirited squirrel that longed to be part of the action. Hundley, who was out on a foraging expedition of his own, passed by and saw his friend being handed over to the boy. He thought to himself, *Oh good George has a new home and now the soldiers will stop looking at him so weird...oh wait what is that?* and he scampered off to investigate.

Upon his return, Washington sent for Greene. Suspecting he might be in trouble for the foraging, he began to prepare his defense. Rather than a reprimand, Washington expressed his great relief at the collapse of the Conway Cabal on the 19th of January as well as his eternal gratitude to Greene's loyalty. Returning to his quarters, Greene had another pleasant surprise as he discovered his wife, Catherine, had arrived and he was no longer alone.

February—March 1778

Things quieted down after Conway's resignation. However, the harsh realities of winter remained. *Is there new trouble on the horizon?* Greene wondered as he made his way to Washington's headquarters yet again.

"Your Excellency," Greene saluted.

"I called you here for a very special purpose," Washington answered, returning the salute. "More than anyone else, you possess the qualities necessary to organize and maintain this body of soldiers. This is why I recommended you to the post of the Quartermaster General."

"Thank you for your offer, sir" Greene replied, "but I am far more qualified as one who fights in the field rather than with pen and parchment."

Washington paused. "Greene, as one of my most trusted men, you are more than qualified for quartermaster general. Before the war, you ran a successful business *and, unless I am mistaken,* you took the initiative here at our winter encampment to supply your men." Greene held his breath, waiting for a reprimand. Instead, Washington continued, "You can assess and decipher any problem that might arise; I hope you will accept this position. You are now free to contemplate your decision on this matter." Greene set out in search of Knox to share this latest development.

"What am I going to do? Quartermaster is no job for a man of my standing," Greene ranted. "Nobody ever heard of a quartermaster in history." He sat down with a thud. "Oh, I suppose if one is going to complain about a situation then one must act to the best of his abilities when the opportunity presents itself. So, I, no more than anyone else, have a reason to complain about my station. All of you will be immortalizing yourself in the golden pages of history while I am confined to a series of drudgeries paving the way for it."

"I see you still want to serve our country on the battlefield, not behind a desk," Knox chuckled. "You haven't changed a bit, Greene. Maybe these will lighten your mood," Knox said, handing him several books on supply chain logistics.

Once Greene accepted the position, he worked hard to ensure that troops had necessary supplies including food, gunpowder, tents, wagons, horses, oxen, hay, oats, harnesses, and drivers. Greene, along with his assistants John Cox and Charles Pettit, established a series of supply depots and magazines all along the army's line of operation. As he struggled to figure out how to get provisions with no money, his thoughts turned to his turtle George. Greene wondered how the turtle was doing in the young boy's care and looked forward to being able to make good on the promissory note. *At least I can still confide in Caty on matters, especially when they weigh so heavy on my heart,* Greene thought, *but I miss George; I could tell him everything as all my secrets were safe with him.*

Since the arrival of Baron de Steuben, 23rd of February, troop discipline had improved. Greene smiled as he thought how Valley Forge was a fitting name as he observed the Continental Army taking shape as they were heated and formed on the anvil of hardships like the bars of iron in his father's forge. Greene's heart grew heavy as he wondered if they would break under the pressure before the work in progress was complete. The winter had been tough, and twenty-five hundred soldiers died of exposure, disease, or starvation despite Greene's best efforts to obtain the much-needed stores.

4 May 1778

As the weather warmed, Greene, Knox, and Washington were excited for the upcoming performance of Joseph Addison's play, *Cato*, in Valley Forge. Not only was it their favorite, but they hoped it would improve morale among the troops. Catherine and Martha, along with the other women at the camp, worked hard to make the play possible although Congress banned theatrical performances and extravagant expenses. Washington ignored this rule and insisted that the show must go on. Like Cato, each of these three generals were passionate Patriots, willing to give their lives to free their country from the tyranny of Great Britain.

Greene and Catherine watched from the audience. As the play progressed, Greene saw Cato's would-be murderers standing in shock as he unveiled their plot before their eyes and Greene could not help but remember when Washington rebuked Conway for his misconduct. As the play ended, Martha and Catherine, delighted with the performance, accompanied the men back to headquarters. Several of the men penned letters that evening sharing, *it was a great success attended by many.*

Martha, a few days later, hosted another fine celebration for the officers in honor of the recent alliance with the French. The presence of the women created a more relaxed ambiance relieving tensions once felt between the two groups. This alliance would prove critical in securing victory over the British for the remainder of the war.

Late May 1778

Greene celebrated along with Knox at the arrival of his wife, Lucy, and their 2-year-old daughter. He was happy that his friend would finally know the comforts of having his wife nearby but noticed that his wife, Catherine, seemed troubled. She had never enjoyed the same closeness with Lucy as with Martha. But missing their own children, she returned home at the end of May.

19 June 1778

The six months of encampment had been a testing ground for the army. They proved their organization and determination while facing unrelenting obstacles during a hard long winter. With questions of leadership, division among officers, and the lack of supplies behind them, the army was ready for what was next. The British were on the move once again, heading north to defend their stronghold in New York City and Washington's troops marched out of Valley Forge in hot pursuit. Washington, Greene, and Knox agreed a much more disciplined Continental Army emerged, and they were ready to face the British in battle.

Washington gathered his trusted officers to determine the best course of action against the enemy here in Monmouth. Greene stood with his arms crossed surveying the battle maps. He was not only across the table from Knox physically but also in opinion. Greene, along with Lafayette, felt an attack against the British forces would be the most effective strategy and would be the only way to ensure victory. On the contrary, Knox along with Charles Lee believed an attack would be foolish and urged Washington not to. During this heated discussion, Greene worried the war would cost him his friendship with Knox. They had never been on the opposite sides of the table.

Washington excused the council while he deliberated his choices. He decided to move forward with Greene and Lafayette's recommendation and attack the British in a head-on assault. He gave his orders to assemble the troops. As they prepared to move out under their commander's lead, Greene and Knox briefly passed by each other. Knox paused and extended his hand of friendship, and they wished each other Godspeed in the battle. Greene sighed, relieved their friendship would not be a casualty of this war.

Battle of Monmouth
28 June 1778

Washington and Lee attacked the rearguard of General Clinton. However, Lee after launching the initial attack, lost his confidence and ordered his troops to fall back. As Washington approached, he became infuriated by the chaos of troops fleeing the battlefield. In a rare burst of anger, he rode ahead and removed Lee from command. Washington then rallied the remaining men and continued the assault while waiting for the remainder of the Continental Army to arrive.

On arrival, he placed Greene on the right wing, Sterling to his left, Marquis de Lafayette took over Lee's troops, and Knox placed artillery on both flanks ready to fire upon the British. Greene's men soon faced an attack by Cornwallis, gaining support from artillery, Greene was able to repulse the attack. The battle swayed back and forth throughout the day; the extreme heat drained the men. As the sun set, the British withdrew having been repulsed over and over. Washington decided it best not to press, announcing that the men were "beat out and with heat and fatigue." The British withdrew to New York City under the cover of darkness while Washington and his army slept on the battlefield exhausted from the fight.

Newport, Rhode Island
29 July - August 1778

The war was returning to Greene's home state and his heart was troubled for his loved ones. He was grateful that Washington had dispatched him to join the fight as a consultant to John Sullivan and was eager to arrive. The objective was to recapture the key city of Newport. The battle would be the first major action with their French allies.

On July 29th, Sullivan held a war council with Greene, Lafayette, and French Admiral Comte d'Estaing. Newport had been a hot spot since the onset of the war in 1776. Sullivan decided to lift the siege and set up a defensive line across the north of the island to protect his rear from British General Pickett. Greene was at Turkey Hill with the 1st Rhode Island Infantry. Glovers took a defensive position behind stone walls near Quaker Hill. Pickett dispatched two detachments with orders not to engage in full combat but to hold position. The fighting Quaker was ready for action and was determined to defend his home.

The Patriots fought for every inch of ground and maintained their strong position, forcing Pickett to withdraw his troops. The Siege of Newport ended in a draw and although they were not able to capture and regain the city, they were able to regroup and continue their campaign in the area. The ability to retreat with most men and equipment showed the British the Continental Army was gaining momentum.

New Jersey

As quartermaster general, Greene worked hard to ensure that the army had necessary supplies. However, procuring all these supplies had cost an astronomical sum of money. The department had cost the Continental Congress over $37,000,000 in 1778. Mifflin, whom Greene replaced, and others convinced Congress to blame Greene for the overspending. When the projected cost of supplies came in at over $200,000,000 for 1779, Congress launched an official inquiry, much to his dismay.

It is my full determination to resign as soon as I can get out of the business without exposing myself to ruin or disgrace, Greene penned in response. And later when Congress banned purchasing any items on a line of credit Greene wrote to his assistant, Cox, *What to do or which way to turn, I know not. We can no longer support the army without cash than the Israelites could make bricks without straw. The Pharaoh brought death upon the firstborns of Egypt, and this Congress will have the same effect upon themselves.*

Pennsylvania Countryside
Winter 1779

Meanwhile in the Pennsylvania countryside, Hundley was sharing exciting news with his turtle friend, George.

"They can get messages even faster now George!" Hundley busily chattered about how he noticed news was getting to Washington and Greene faster and he saw increased activities near local spots he frequents in New York for nuts. "They're talking about something. Something BIG...I think?"

"That's interesting, Hundley," George slowly replied. "You better get ready. I have a feeling that things are going to happen fast...and that is just your speed."

"Yeah, George, and we have to get you to catch up, especially to Greene," replied Hundley.

George smiled. "It sounds like you're collecting a lot more than nuts. Greene has nothing to fear because Hundley's already on the case."

Arnold's Tavern
Morristown, New Jersey
Winter 1779

Greene looked through the ice-covered window into the icy whirlwind of snow that was now almost four feet deep. The weather was not what frustrated Greene, it was the lack of support from the civilians. *Morristown held such promise with plenty of timber, farms and mines*, Greene thought in disgust, *but it is a land overflowing with plenty, while the army starves.* He sat and penned a letter of frustration to Quartermaster Furman who was responsible for collecting the supplies in New Jersey and contemplated how to get food and shelter to keep these men alive.

His thoughts shifted to the other reason they selected Morristown, to keep a close eye on the British. Greene began going over recent reports coming from New York. The British were preparing for something big. *We are in for another hard winter,* Greene thought to himself. *What would the new year bring? What are the British up to? How much longer will this war last? Who else would turncoat or rise to take a leader's place?* Thoughts swirled in his mind like the blizzard outside. No matter what was to come, Greene knew he would stand true to the cause.

ALEXANDER HAMILTON: THE LIFE, THE STORY, AND THE LEGEND

BY ALEXANDRA ROBERSON

THE EPIC STORY OF AMERICA 1777-1779

CHARLESTON, NEVIS, BRITISH ISLANDS
11 JANUARY 1755

*I*n the month of January, a baby boy was born in the town of Charleston, on the island of Nevis. Alexander Hamilton grew up with his mother, Rachel Faucette, his brother, James Hamilton, and his father, James Hamilton Sr. Before the Hamilton brothers were born, Rachel Faucette was married to a different man by the name of John Michael Lavien. She fled her husband and met Alex's father in Charleston. In 1766, James Sr. abandoned the family and left Rachel to raise the brothers herself. Their mother died two years later. As an eleven-year-old, Alex got a job as a clerk for a trading company on St. Croix. Attention flooded into his life, from writing and publishing a passionate pamphlet about a hurricane that hit the island in 1772. The residents of the island raised money for Alexander to get to America. He arrived at New York as tensions rose in the colonies against its mother country.

Kings College, New York

"Man, in a state of nature may be considered, free from all restraints of act and power..." *No, this just does not sound right,* Alexander thought. He was in his chamber dorm room when a loud knock hit his door.

His friends William Becker, Christopher McNaught, and Isaac Darby had come to visit him.

"Hi Willy, Christopher, and Isaac," Alex says. "Is there something I can help you with?"

"Would you like to go to the tavern with us?" Willy asked.

Do I have the time? Alex wondered. *I must write my response to Samuel Seabury's 'A View of the Controversy Between Great-Britain and Her Colonies.'*

"I will come with you, just as long as we don't stay out too late," Alex responded.

"Great, let's go!" Isaac exclaimed.

As the college kids walked the streets of New York, Alex saw Fraunces Tavern.

"Hey, let's go there," Alex suggested.

"Why would we go there? All the English traitors drink there," Willy countered.

"Oh, right," Alex answered.

"We are going to Houndling's Tavern, the best tavern on this side of the Atlantic—well, at least in New York," Christopher interjected. "My father and his business partners go there all the time."

As the group started walking towards the Houndling's Tavern, numerous red military coats hung out to dry on lawns, and boisterous noises came from the kitchens of these occupied homes.

As the friends entered the tavern, wealthy Loyalists were drinking and talking about British traitors in the colonies, referred to as "Rebels." Alex and his friends sat at a rectangle bench on the side of the tavern with other college students and a few faculty members.

"Those insolent Rebels ruined my grandfather's British flag and my mother's flower bed two nights ago!" exclaimed a student named Thomas Clarkson. "These criminals must be punished for their crimes!"

Alex softly laughed. *I remember that! I did not realize it was Clarkson's house. I knew that it would cause trouble, but it was fun!*

"I cannot believe anyone would do that to a fellow citizen of the Crown. It is unreal how uncivilized people can be," Christopher asserted.

"I agree," Willy declared.

Late in the hour and after a few drinks, the students started talking about taxes.

"These taxes are going to help the East India Company and maybe squash the spark in these protesters," Christopher suggested.

"These taxes are wrong. Why tax someone with no representation in Parliament?" Alex retorted.

"Because the colonies first needed to be taxed for the Seven Years' War, then the Boston Tea Party," Christopher replied.

THE EPIC STORY OF AMERICA 1777-1779

"With the Seven Years' War, the taxes shouldn't have been so heavy, and without our consent!" Alex loudly announced.

Willy put a cautionary hand to Alexander's shoulder. "Alex, calm down. You are making a scene."

"NO!" Alex protested, "These taxes are wrong, and will forever be WRONG!!"

Alex then left the tavern, slamming the door. He walked the Loyalist streets thinking, *"Man, in a state of nature may be considered, as perfectly free from all restraints of law and government, and then, the weak must submit to the strong."*

James Vaux House, General Washington's Headquarters, New York
September 1777

"Now Hamilton," Washington began, "I know how much you love fighting on the field, but I need someone to fight on the backside. I need someone to help me with the army's needs and writing letters to Congress. I need you to be my aid-de-camp."

Alexander Hamilton stood speechless in front of the general.

"HAMILTON!" Alexander shook back to real time. "Alexander, Horatio Gates might run into some Redcoats. They might need backup, please tell me what we have," Washington asked Alex.

"Yes sir, sorry sir," Alexander apologized. "We have one rifle for each soldier, guns, cannons, and powder for the cannons."

"Thank you, we must make sure we have supplies if we need to go into battle," Washington explained.

"Hamilton," Washington asked.

"I am sorry sir, but I love the action and the heat of fighting," he told Washington. "I don't know if I would love to fight the war, without actually fighting it."

"You might if you were in my military family," Washington said.

Saratoga, New York
19 September 1777

"And then there *était comme un*-BAM, BOOM, BAM!" Snickers announced. *"J'ai vaincu le pigeon avec mon sang français!"*

"Snickers, we must speak anglas so we can fit in with the locals," Ollie replied.

"*BIEN, quoi que*," Snickers said angrily. "I mean, FINE, whatever."

Ollie and Snickers were young French eagle brothers, spying for Lafayette. He wanted to know strategies from the British, outcomes of battles from a bird's view, and to know if the Continental Army made any mistakes. Lafayette arrived in the former Colonies in the early summer. He brought Ollie and Snickers from his home to help him. Snickers was unconvinced, but Ollie was ecstatic. Since they were close, the pair went with Lafayette.

"Look at that battle!" Ollie exclaimed.

The brothers flew above the battlefield hoping to see American victory and British defeat at the end.

After the defeat at the Battle of Bennington, British General John Burgoyne marched his troops towards Saratoga. American General Horatio Gates and his troops built sturdy and intimidating defenses on Bemis Heights, south of Saratoga. American and British forces engaged in battle on Freeman's Farm. As the battle went on the British took heavy losses. Burgoyne's troops waited for reinforcements in their trenches, but no help came.

"I feel sorry for those *soldats* there in *les trancheess*," Ollie exclaimed.

When no reinforcements came, General Burgoyne launched another attack on American forces at Bemis Heights. Then he surrendered to General Gates.

"YAY! *VICTOIRE AMÉRICAINE!*" Ollie said.

"Ollie, *anglais* please," smirked Snickers.

"American victory!" Ollie exclaimed.

Valley Forge, New York
January 1778

"... eighty blankets, fifty uniforms, one hundred pairs of shoes, one hundred pounds of sugar, four hundred pounds of wood, eight horses, four cows, and three pigs. Lafayette, does that sound correct?" Hamilton asked.

"*Oui*, my friend," Lafayette replied.

"Good, Congress has to approve of these things if we are going to survive until spring," Hamilton added.

The winter of 1777 was not the worst winter, but it was brutal because of the limited supplies for the Continental army. Hamilton and Lafayette were in General Washington's headquarters, making lists of what the army needed.

As Hamilton walked down the hall, he noticed many soldiers outside sitting by the fire trying to keep warm, young soldiers trying to hunt squirrels to find something to eat, and old soldiers sharing stories of even colder winters.

"General Washington, sir," Hamilton said to Washington.

"Yes, Hamilton," Washington acknowledged.

"This list contains what we need from Congress," Hamilton started. "Is there anything else I should put on it?"

"The end of the war!" Washington said firmly. "My apologies, this winter weather is starting to take a toll on me. Even if we survive, the spring and summer will not be easy for battle… Two hundred pounds of flour should be the last item."

"Yes, sir," Hamilton responded.

Hamilton walked out of General Washington's office thinking, *If we do not get this army together this frosty winter, we will be losing this war.*

Head Quarters, Valley Forge
13 February 1778

Dear General Clinton,

There is a matter, which often obtrudes itself upon my mind, and which requires the attention of every person of sense and influence, among us. I mean a degeneracy of representation in the great council of America. It is a melancholy truth sir, and the effects of which we see daily and feel, that there is not so much wisdom in a certain body as there ought to be, and as the success of our affairs absolutely demands. Many members of it are no doubt men in every respect, fit for the trust, but this cannot be said of it as a body. Folly, caprice, a want foresight, comprehension, and dignity, characterize the general tenor of their actions. Of this I dare say, you are sensible, though you have not perhaps so many opportunities of knowing it as I have. Their conduct with respect to the army especially is feeble indecisive and improvident—insomuch, that we are reduced to a more terrible situation than you can conceive. False and contracted views of economy have prevented them, though repeatedly urged to it, from making that provision for officers which was requisite to interest them in the service, which has produced such carelessness and indifference to the service, as is subversive of every officer-like quality. They have disgusted the army by repeated instances of the most whimsical favoritism in their promotions, and by an absurd prodigality of rank to foreigners and to the meanest staff of the army. They have not been able to summon resolution enough to withstand the impudent importunity and vain boasting of foreign pretenders; but have manifested such a ductility and inconstancy in their proceedings, as will warrant the charge of suffering themselves to be bullied, by every petty rascal, who comes armed with ostentatious pretensions of military merit and experience. Would you believe it sir, it is become almost proverbial in the mouths of the French officers and other foreigners, that they have nothing more to do, to obtain whatever they please, than to assume a high tone and assert their own merit with confidence and perseverance?

By injudicious changes and arrangements in the Commissary's department, in the middle of a campaign, they have exposed the army frequently to temporary want, and to the danger of a dissolution, from absolute famine. On this very day there are complaints from the whole line, of having been three or four days without provisions; desertions have been immense, and strong features of mutiny begin to show themselves. It is indeed to be wondered at, that the soldiery have manifested so unparalleled a degree of patience, as they have. If effectual measures are not speedily adopted, I know not how we shall keep the army together or make another campaign.

I omit saying anything of the want of clothing for the army. It may be disputed whether more could have been done than has been done.

If you look into their conduct in the civil line, you will equally discover a deficiency of energy dignity and extensiveness of views; but of this you can better judge than myself, and it is unnecessary to particularize.

America once had a representation that would do honor to any age or nation. The present falling off is very alarming and dangerous. What is the cause? or How is it to be remedied? are questions that the welfare of these states requires should be well attended to. The great men who composed our first council; are they dead, have they deserted the cause, or what has become of them? Very few are dead and still fewer have deserted the cause;—they are all except the few who remain in Congress either in the field, or in the civil offices of their respective states; far the greater part are engaged in the latter. The only remedy then is to take them out of these employment positions and return them to the place where their presence is infinitely more important.

Each state in order to promote its own internal government and prosperity, has selected its best members to fill the offices within itself, and conduct its own affairs. Men have been fonder of the emoluments and conveniences, of being employed at home, and local attachment, falsely operating, has made them more provident for the particular interests of the states to which they belonged, than for the common interests of the confederacy...This is the object on which their eyes are fixed, hence it is America will derive its importance or insignificance, in their estimation.

I believe it unmasked its batteries too soon and begins to hide its head; but as I imagine it will only change the storm to a sap; all the true and sensible friends to their country, and of course to a certain great man, ought to be upon the watch, to counterplot the secret machinations of his enemies. Have you heard anything about Conway's history? He is one of the vermin bred in the entrails of this chimera dire, and there does not exist a more villainous calumniator and incendiary. He has gone to Albany on a certain expedition.

I am with great regard & respect, sir, your most obed. servant,
Alexander Hamilton

Valley Forge, New York
Late February 1778

Hamilton woke early to find the other aide-de-camps jumping and dancing. "What is with all the joy?" he asked sleepily.

"*La neige degele!*" Lafayette said.

"Lafayette, English please!" the other aide-de-camps exclaimed.

"Sorry, the snow is thawing! Spring is here!" Lafayette announced.

"Huzzah!" Hamilton proclaimed.

As Lafayette and Hamilton walked around Valley Forge, confident and enthusiastic soldiers marched and not a single scarred or weak one. "General von Steuven did an excellent job," Hamilton noticed.

"*Oui,*" Lafayette agreed.

In February, General De Steuben arrived at Valley Forge, took charge, and trained the Continental Army.

With General De Steuben's help this winter, the British are in for a shock, Hamilton reflected.

Monmouth, New York
28 June 1778

"Ollie," Snickers said. " *Il fait ridiculement chaud. Pouvons-nous s'il vous plaît voler à cet arbre là-bas?*"

"Snickers, remember, *anglais* please," Ollie replied.

"*Bien*, oh, I mean, fine. It is ridiculously hot. Can we please fly to that tree down there?" Snickers said, rolling his eyes.

"*Non*, it is a *beaucoup* better view if we see this battle from up here," Ollie answered. "Anyway, what will General Lafayette think when he asks what the British forces did during the *bataille*?"

The pair of eagles flew over to watch the battle closely. It began with General Charles Lee, but American forces were losing confidence and looking weak.

"Look, there's General Washington!" Snickers exclaimed.

Many Continental soldiers had already fled, but Washington continued to fight the battle. He put Nathanael Greene's soldiers to the right and William Alexander's to the left. Lee was replaced with Lafayette by Washington's orders, and Anthony Wayne took charge of the front with the rest of Lee's forces. Cannons and guns were placed to rain fire on the British! The fighting went on for hours, back and forth, trying to get the British to fall back, as the Continental army tightened their lines.

"It is five o'clock! Will this fight ever end?" Snickers murmured.

About an hour later, Washington declared his forces were exhausted, beat up, and drained. Under the cover of nightfall, the British stealthily retreated from the battle.

"Wake up, Snickers!" Ollie yelled.

"Wah?" Snickers asked sleepily. "*Qui* won? What happened? Who won?"

"Neither side," Ollie replied.

GOVERNOR PATRICK HENRY: SURPRISES AT EVERY TURN

BY EDAN MACNAUGHTON

THE EPIC STORY OF AMERICA 1777-1779

GOVERNOR'S PALACE, WILLIAMSBURG, VIRGINIA
DECEMBER 1777

Governor Patrick Henry strapped on his boots and stood, bracing himself to walk in the freezing weather. *While it might be quite frigid today, I desire to get outside before the sun goes down. Stretch the old legs a bit,* he thought with a chuckle. Right as he was about to step outside, someone pulled him back. "Where on God's green earth do you think you are going, Patrick?" his wife Dorothea shouted. "Do you not remember your physician telling you to avoid unnecessary time in the cold?" She shook her finger at him playfully.

"Ah, you are right, my dear, sorry," Henry replied. "I am currently feeling confused on how to handle several situations that require my attention as governor. I thought that taking a walk outside might help clear my head, but I shall heed your recommendation to stay inside."

"Well, if you need help clearing your head, let me assist you! Instead of getting lost in your own thoughts, share with me what is troubling you," Dorothea suggested.

"Yes, that would be most helpful. There are many things troubling my mind," Henry replied. "The Continental Army lacks supplies up near Philadelphia. The Virginia Militia's supply shortage worsened after two supply wagons broke down last week. Then today, I received word of a shortage of workers to undertake a project in north Williamsburg due to sickness. The words of our fellow Patriot Thomas Paine are quite true, 'These are the times that try men's souls.'" Henry let out a sigh.

"Patrick, while that all may be true, you must also remember the words of our Lord in 2 Corinthians 12:9, *My grace is sufficient for you. My power is perfected in weakness,*" Dorothea replied. "Our young nation, America, and home state of Virginia are assailed by trials on every side, but the Lord has raised up leaders like you to lead us in these challenging times. Always remember that I believe in you and have faith in the job you are doing."

"Thank you," Henry replied. "That is exactly what I needed to hear.

The timing of your encouragement could not be better. Do you recall meeting a young man named George Rogers Clark a few months ago?" Dorothea nodded her head. "Well, he is coming to present a plan to attack British forts in the west. I am intrigued by his zeal but want to hear more of what he has in mind. Attacking forts controlled by the strongest fighting force in the world is no small feat, so Mr. Clark's plan must be extremely convincing for me to give my approval."

"That certainly sounds promising, my love. I must go downstairs now to check on the children, but please remember that I love and believe in you!" Dorothea then kissed Patrick on the forehead and departed.

Moments later, there was a knock on the office door. "Governor Henry, George Rogers Clark has arrived. May I send him in?" His servant, William, called out.

"You may send him in, William. Thank you. I have been expecting him," Governor Henry replied. A young man with reddish blonde hair walked through the doorway.

"Greetings, Governor Henry! Many thanks for allowing me to come over. It is an honor to be in your presence," George Rogers Clark said.

"It's an honor to have you here," Henry replied. "I must admit, I was not sure if you'd be able to make it given the weather."

"Well, it is nothing compared to what our army brothers face in the northeast. It has been a brutal winter so far," Clark replied.

"Yes, we must remember and pray for our fellow countrymen in Valley Forge and Philadelphia. They are suffering from a lack of food and basic clothing, widespread disease, and Philadelphia's occupation by General Howe's troops. May the good Lord help them survive," Henry declared. "Shall we discuss your plan to take British forts out west?"

"Yes, I have all the details worked out for what I hope shall be a successful campaign. First, I was thinking…" George Rogers Clark's voice trailed off.

A pair of eyes watched them from above. *Yes, go on, I must hear every word.*

THE EPIC STORY OF AMERICA 1777-1779

4 February 1778

"Governor Henry, are you in there?" called William, the servant, outside of the governor's bedroom.

"Yes, I am, William. You may come in," Henry replied.

William entered the room to find the Governor resting in bed. "I didn't mean to intrude. This letter just arrived from an anonymous sender."

"You did not intrude at all," Henry replied. "Thank you for delivering this; I shall review it immediately." William then left the room so the 41-year-old governor could read the letter in private.

Henry opened the letter, furrowing his eyebrows as he tried to think of who would choose to write to him anonymously. *Perhaps it's classified information regarding the Continental Army or Virginia Militia?*

The common danger of our country first brought you and me together. I happily recollect on your influence and brilliance upon the opinions of this country in the beginning of the present war. You first taught us to shake off our idolatrous attachment to the British Crown, and to oppose its encroachments upon our liberties with our very lives. By these means you saved us from ruin. The Independence of America is the result of the kind of thinking and action that you displayed which followed the destructive rule of Kings and the mighty power of Great Britain.

"But sir, we have only passed the Red Sea. A dreary wilderness is still before us. Unless a Moses or a Joshua is raised up on our behalf, we will perish before we reach the promised land. We have nothing to fear from our enemies on the way. General Howe, it is true, has taken Philadelphia, but he has only changed his prison. His dominions are bounded passively on all sides by his troops. America can only be undone by herself. She looks up to her leaders, for protection, but alas! What are they? Her representation in Congress dwindled to only twenty-one members—Her Adams—Her Wilson—her Henry, are no more among them. Her counsels weak—and partial remedies applied constantly for universal diseases. Her army—what is it?

Mr. Henry took a moment to digest the letter. He was not yet sure why it was signed anonymously. *Let me read onto the end and see if I can ascertain what the writer is trying to tell me.*

Is our case desperate? By no means. We have wisdom, Virtue—& strength enough to save us if they could be called into action. The Northern Army has Shown us what Americans are capable of doing with a General at their head. The Spirit of the Southern Army is in no ways inferior to the Spirit of the northern. A Gates—a Lee, or a Conway would, in a few weeks render them an unstoppable body of men.

Henry's eyes widened. *Oh dear, this sounds like a plot to replace Washington as commander-in-chief!*

You may rest assured of each of the facts related in this letter. The Author of this letter is one of your Philadelphia friends. A hint of his name if found out by the handwriting, must not be mentioned to you by even your most trusted friend. Even the letter must be thrown in the fire. But some of its contents ought to be made public in order to awaken, enlighten, and alarm our country. I rely upon your prudence and am dear sir with my usual Attachment to you & to our beloved independence

Yours sincerely,

Henry finished the letter, flabbergasted. A certain pair of lines in particular jumped off the page at him and he read them again.

"The Northern army has shown us what Americans are capable of doing with a General at their head. The spirit of the Southern Army is in no way inferior to the Spirit of the Northern. A Gates— a Lee, or a Conway would, in a few weeks, render them an irresistible body of men."

A mixture of rage and fury burned inside Henry's belly. "Whoever wrote this letter is trying to convince me to join an attempt to usurp George Washington as commander-in-chief! The contents of this very letter are TREACHEROUS! AND THE FACT THE SENDER WISHES ME TO CAST THIS LETTER INTO THE FLAMES IS INSUFFERABLE! I SHALL DO JUST THE OPPOSITE! TOMORROW I WILL BE SENDING THIS ON TO GENERAL WASHINGTON HIMSELF. HE MUST BE ALERTED," he finished his fiery declaration by pounding his bed.

A pair of ears listened in as Henry vented his frustration.

Well, that did not go as I had hoped! So, the good old governor won't join the cabal against Washington, huh? Well then...I'll just have to make sure that he doesn't forward that letter to his fellow Virginian...

A tired Governor Patrick Henry looked around his desk for his special writing quill, but he could not find it anywhere. His mood was not helped by the fact that he did not sleep well the night before as he lay awake fuming about the plot against George Washington that he uncovered. What upset him most was the fact that the letter came to him from a fellow American supposedly committed to the same cause. The words of Dr. Benjamin Franklin from the day the Declaration of Independence was ratified echoed in Henry's head. *'We must all hang together, or we most assuredly will all hang separately.'*

Henry hit his desk. *Well, whoever wrote this letter is most assuredly working separately from the rest of us. How many more people have they written or spoken to with the intention of trying to get them to join this cabal? They did mention Horatio Gates, Thomas Conway, and Charles Lee. I suspect that those three could be on the wrong side of this incident.*

Shouts rang out. Henry ran downstairs as a crowd of people gathered at the front door. "Is everything all right?" he asked.

"No," his wife Dorothea said. "It's William, he fell off a ladder!"

Patrick and the others ran outside to check on the fallen servant. They found William lying on the ground outside in excruciating pain. "Good heavens! Are you alright, William?" Patrick asked, worried.

"Yesss, sirrr. Somethingg knocked me over from behindd. Not sureee but I think it could have been a birddd," a slurring and shaky William mumbled.

"Perfect, now that I distracted Mr. Henry by knocking William over, I shall make my way into his office and steal that letter before he can send it on to George Washington!" Charles the British crow said mischievously. As he flew into Patrick Henry's office, he was shocked to see another animal already on the governor's desk! It was Patrick's own cat Cato!

"Not so fast Charles! This letter is going to be forwarded on by my human to George Washington and you will not stop him! Come and get it from me!" Cato tauntingly replied. The cat then reached over to the desk and softly tucked the letter into his mouth, before running out of the room.

"Nooooo! You shan't do that, you crazy cat! That letter must be destroyed!!!!" Charles the crow squawked.

The two animals ran around the house without worrying about the humans noticing them since everyone had gone outside to check on William. Just then, Cato the cat sprinted for an open window. *I have an idea as to how I can shake this crow!* Cato jumped out of the window just before someone shut it. Charles the crow, however, was not so lucky. He was flying full speed when the window was slammed shut and as a result collided with it violently. He had failed in his mission to destroy the letter.

Cato calmly and confidently returned the letter to Patrick Henry's desk. This fight for liberty wasn't just for humans after all, it involved animals too.

It turned out that William had just bruised his head slightly, which was remarkable given the fact he fell down quite a distance. So, after making sure that his top servant got proper medical attention, Patrick Henry returned to his office and found everything just as he had left it. In fact, even the quill that he couldn't find earlier was back in its normal spot. Feeling the urgency of needing to forward the treacherous letter on, Patrick made sure to keep his accompanying note brief. Only a day before, he had had no knowledge of a dangerous cabal against General Washington; now he had made an effort to warn his friend of this threat. As he handed the packet of letters to his trusted courier, Patrick said a quick prayer for his friend's safety and that this plot against him would be exposed.

Valley Forge, Pennsylvania
19 March 1778

General George Washington sat in his tent reading messages and letters that he had received during the day. He got down to the last letter in his stack. He noted the name on the front, Patrick Henry. *Ah, a letter from my good friend down south. I wonder what he has to say.*

Washington ripped open the envelope, and two papers fell out. He read the first:

Williamsburg, Virginia, 20 February 1778
Dear Sir,
You will no doubt be surprised at seeing the enclosed letter, in which the affirmations bestowed on me are undeserved. The disrespect aimed at you is also unjust. I am sorry there should be one man who counts himself my friend, who is not yours.

Perhaps I give you needless trouble in handing you this paper. The writer of it may be too insignificant to deserve any notice. If I knew this to be the case, I should not have intruded on your time which is so precious. But there may possibly be some scheme or party forming against you. The enclosed leads to such a suspicion. Believe me Sir, I have too high a sense of the obligations America has to you to abet or countenance so unworthy a proceeding. The most exalted merit hath ever been found to attract envy. But I please myself with the hope, that the same fortitude & greatness of mind which have hitherto braved all the difficulties & dangers inseparable from your station, will rise superior to every attempt of the envious partisan.

I really cannot tell who is the writer of this letter, which not a little perplexes me. The handwriting is altogether strange to me.

To give you the trouble of this, gives me pain. It would suit me better to give you some assistance in the great business of the war. But I will not conceal anything from you, by which you may be affected. For I really think your personal welfare & the happiness of America are intimately connected. I beg you will be assured of that high regard & esteem with which I ever am Dear Sir your affectionate friend & very humble Servant
P. Henry

"Oh my, what could be in this other letter?" General Washington wondered. As he read it, his face burned with anger. "Lieutenant Colonel Hamilton, I request your presence in my tent this instant!" Washington's voice boomed from his tent. His 21-year-old aide-de-camp came running from a nearby tent.

"Yes, your Excellency?" Hamilton asked.

"Who have we received letters from in Philadelphia this week?" Washington asked.

"Every letter that you have received from Philadelphia this week has been from either Dr. Benjamin Rush, Henry Laurens, or Robert

Morris." Hamilton coughed. "Forgive me, Laurens and Morris wrote their letters not from Philadelphia but from Baltimore, as Congress is located there now. Pardon my prior mistake, General." Hamilton said in a slightly worried tone.

Washington's thoughts were elsewhere, so he hardly noticed Hamilton's mistake. "Very well, tomorrow bring me all the recent letters from Dr. Benjamin Rush as I wish to review them further," he ordered.

"Yes, General, I will get on that right away!" Hamilton declared.

Alone in his tent again, Washington processed all that happened. *I will thank Mr. Henry for alerting me of this cabal, but only after I find out the author of the original letter.*

TO PATRICK HENRY
Camp at Valley Forge, 28 March 1778
Dear Sir,
I can only thank you again, in the language of the most undissembled gratitude for your friendship; and assure you, the indulgent disposition, which Virginia in particular and the states in general entertain towards me, gives me the most sensible pleasure. The approbation of my country is what I wish, and as far as my abilities and opportunity will permit, I hope I shall endeavor to deserve it. It is the highest reward to a feeling mind, and happy are they, who so conduct themselves, as to merit it.

The Anonymous Letter, with which you were pleased to favor me, was written by Doctor Rush, so far as I can judge from a similitude of hands. This Man has been elaborate & studied in his professions of regard for me; and long since the Letter to you.

My caution to avoid anything that could injure the service, prevented me from communicating, but to very few of my friends, the intrigues of a faction which I know was formed against me. Since communicating it might serve to publish our internal dissensions But their own restless zeal to advance their views has too clearly betrayed them, and made concealment on my part fruitless. I cannot precisely mark the extent of their views, but it appeared in general, that General Gates was to be exalted, on the ruin of my reputation and influence. This I am authorized to say from undeniable facts, in my own possession, from publications, the evident scope of which, could not be mistaken, and from private detractions industriously circulated. General Mifflin, it is commonly supposed, bore the second part in the Cabal; and General Conway was a very active, and malignant partisan but I have good reasons to believe that their machinations have recoiled most sensibly upon themselves. With sentiments of great esteem and regard I am Dear Sir your Affectionate Humble servant.

Gen. George Washington

General Washington then called over his trusted courier and instructed him to deliver the letter to Virginia. *Thank you, Providence, for people in my life like Patrick Henry. It is truly an honor to call him my friend.*

End of Summer 1777

The Henry family had just sat down for supper when William (who recovered remarkably well from his fall) handed Patrick a letter. "Oh, look at this," he exclaimed. "A letter from George Rogers Clark! I hope all is well." Henry proceeded to open and read the letter. "Huzzah!" he exclaimed while raising his fist. "Clark's men have captured a fort out west. The previously British controlled Fort Kaskaskia is now under his control!" Mrs. Henry and the children clapped and cheered.

Then Patrick continued, "Clark said that though he and his men were outnumbered going into the battle it did not matter due to the valiant efforts of his troops! His plan worked almost to perfection, and the British were completely taken by surprise. They were in such a relaxed state that they were actually in the midst of throwing a ball when Clark and his men attacked! The fort was taken without one shot being fired!" Henry then read onto the end, "It keeps getting better! This great victory took place on July 4th, the two-year anniversary of America declaring her independence! Patrick Henry put down the letter and raised a glass as he and his family toasted the success of Clark's men and the American cause at large.

"Tonight, is a night of celebration!" Mrs. Henry shouted. "I shall bring out the apple pie for dessert as we rejoice!"

Later that night, after much celebrating with the children, Patrick and his wife Dorothea retired to their bedroom. Before he blew out the candles in the room for the night, he decided to take out his journal and make a new entry. As he picked it up, a slightly weathered letter fell out, one that he had written to himself a couple of years prior on New Year's Eve when discouraged. *Writing that letter back in 1776 truly boosted my spirits and helped me carry on in the middle of a tough time. Looking back on it now, it is remarkable to see how dejected I was.*

Patrick picked up the fallen letter and tucked it back inside his journal. He then sat down on his bed and wrote:

These last few months have most certainly been full of surprises. However, through it all I have seen the spirit of the American cause prevail. It is the same cause that every single human being has been born with since the beginning of time. Freedom. America's cause is the cause of freedom. Just imagine a land where every man, woman, and child, no matter the color of their skin or social status or background, can have the same opportunity and chance to pursue happiness. A land like that has never existed before in human history! However, if the dream that I and many others have of seeing a free America for all is to be fulfilled, she must survive this present conflict first. Just as these past few months have been full of surprises for me personally, I pray that these next few years may be full of happier surprises for America. I also hope that one day in the future I will be able to look back on this entry and remember the struggles and victories that led to America winning this war and becoming a truly free and independent nation. One nation under God, indivisible, with liberty and justice for all.

Patrick Henry

GENERAL HENRY KNOX

BY KIT PACENTRILLI

GENERAL HENRY KNOX

ASSUNPINK CREEK, NEW JERSEY
2 JANUARY 1777

*B*OOM! A cannon fired on the battlefield. *Oh no, not already,* I thought. I could barely make out the twinkling stars behind the dense clouds of pewter-colored smoke. A couple of days ago, General Washington put his men in a defensive line just South of Assunpink Creek. Last night, I brought the artillery here. Then the British General Cornwallis started to make his way over to fight us. Luckily, General Hand commanded some riflemen to slow him down.

"MEN!" I shouted. "Get down! Cornwallis is firing at us." Lieutenant General Cornwallis fired repeatedly but then moved on to another regiment.

"This is strange, this is much less involved than a battle should be. This is not going to end well," I said.

"Sir, what should we do?" a young rifleman named Elias Billingsley asked.

"We fire until they stop," I declared. "FIRE, MEN! FIRE YOUR RIFLES! FIRE THE CANNONS, TOO!!" I commanded. The artillery shot their weapons and soon the British firing ceased. "STOP!" I yelled, and the artillery ceased as well.

"They're retiring for the night, sir," Billingsley said.

"THANK YOU, MEN!" I shouted. All the people in the artillery looked at me. "PITCH THE TENTS AND GET A GOOD NIGHT'S REST! TOMORROW WILL BE A LONG DAY!"

"YESSSSIR!" they shouted, their words slurring together. As the men slept, I planned our attack. With some rustling outside my tent, I grabbed my rifle only to encounter General Washington.

"I need you to fire some cannons at the British throughout the night. Every hour or so, just to keep them on their toes," Washington said, and he walked out of the tent. *Now,* I thought, *I just need to get some of my men to assist me with the cannons.*

I snuck into a large tent where ten of my men slept. It was crowded, but I suppose sleeping ten people in a tent was better than sleeping outside. I woke five of them up and asked them if they would accompany me to the cannons. Even though they were tired, they followed me. When we got to the cannons, we loaded five of them and decided that every thirty minutes, we would set one off. I looked up at the moon just west of the middle of the sky.

"I'm guessing it's around 11:30 p.m. right now," I whispered. "Let's set a cannon off. Wait. Henry, William, if anybody from our troops wakes up after we fire, tell them to be quiet."

"Yes sir," they whispered back to me.

"Okay, Billingsley, James, are you ready to set the cannon off?" I whispered. They nodded, so I gave them permission. They lit the cannon, and we rushed back behind a rock in case there were some extra sparks. The cannon went off and launched the ball far into the distance. Every thirty minutes or so, we'd fire another cannon ball. At 1:00 a.m., General Washington came over to us.

"Knox," Washington said, "I need you to stop. You did exactly as I instructed, and you did it well. But now we must leave. The British will attack. I am going to leave five-hundred men and some cannons to make the British think we are still here, but before they get here, even those men will go."

I packed my things and saddled my horse. I got on my horse, and soon we're all moving. As we rode to our next location, I took out my journal to write a new entry. However, I got distracted and looked at my old entries instead.

11/16/75

Dear Journal,

My name is Henry Knox, and I am 25-years-old. The Revolutionary War between the States and Great Britain began just a few months ago with the first shots fired at Lexington and Concord. General George Washington and John Adams have recruited me to aid Richard Gridley, which makes me Colonel of the Regiment of Artillery. I am excited about this new job. I wonder where it will take me and what I will do.

I thought about the twinkle in my eye and the big smile on my face when I was first appointed. I remember thinking of all the places I was going to see and all the things I was going to do. Now, all of that has been replaced with seriousness. There was rarely a big smile on my face, if ever. I hardly feel excited, just weighed down by my responsibilities in charge of the artillery.

Eventually, we arrived at our destination. We got off our horses and prepared for battle at Princeton. I made sure all the cannons were functioning and ready, while the rest of my men got into place. The sun started to rise, and by the time it was fully up, our five-hundred men who stayed behind in Trenton joined us just as the British approached.

"FIRE!" yelled Washington, and we started to fire cannonballs and shoot our muskets at the British. The British retaliated but their offense wasn't half as powerful as ours. By midmorning, the British were defeated.

***

It has almost been a year since our victory at the Battle of Assunpink Creek. In that time, I had several arguments with people, trying to improve the artillery's manufacturing capability, but it accomplished little. I just returned to the artillery yesterday. I found Billingsley, and luckily, he hasn't changed much. He was overjoyed to see me again and asked how my months have been.

"Good," I answered. "How have yours been?"

"They've been good. I spent them with the artillery, so I've been doing the normal stuff," Billingsley replied.

"Billingsley!" a man with a French accent shouted *"Que fais-tu?"*

"Uhm," Billingsley answered.

"Il parle avec moi, je suis Henry Knox," I said to the French man.

"Who is this man?" I asked Billingsley.

"You were replaced. His name is Phillipe Charles Tronson du Coudray," he replied.

"D'accord. Je m'appelle Phillipe Charles Tronson du Coudray, et cet homme est un de mes hommes pour l'artillerie," Coudray proceeded to boast, telling me that he was in charge of the artillery. Even though Billingsley also told me this news, it still was a shock.

"*Quoi?*" I asked.

"*Oui, je suis responsable de l'artillerie,*" he replied.

"*Non, je suis responsable de l'artillerie,*" I argued. I knew arguing with him that I was in charge of the artillery would do nothing, but I figured I'd try anyway.

"*Comment t'appelles tu encore? Ah, oui, tu es Henry Knox, je vous remplacé,*" he explained to me.

"What is going on?" Billingsley whispered to me.

"He is telling me that he replaced me," I said to Billingsley. "*Ah, d'accord, je suis désolé pour la confusion,*" I replied to du Coudray, trying not to feel sad.

"*C'est d'accord,*" Coudray said, and walked away.

"I hate General Coudray. He's annoying and refuses to learn English. We never know what he's trying to tell us. We only know what he wants us to do because he waves his hand around to try to tell us what to do," Billingsley said.

"Well, I'll be leaving then," I said, not knowing what to do, since I wasn't in charge of the artillery anymore.

"Good day then, sir," Billingsley said, and I could tell he felt sad. I waved goodbye and then walked off into the distance.

***

Several weeks ago, I met up with Nathanael Greene and John Sullivan to discuss our threat of resignation to Congress. We are all vital to them, but they keep giving unimportant French men important jobs, and it isn't fair. We went to John's room in an inn. We sat around the small table with a quill and ink, and I wrote:

6 June 1777

To Congress,

We, Henry Knox, John Sullivan, and Nathanael Greene would like to warn you that if you keep giving command to inexperienced French men who volunteer to fight, we shall resign. We do not care if you say that we cannot resign, because we warned you, and we are experienced in these jobs and worked our way up to this position. We will not let you replace us with terri-

ble, inexperienced, French men that refuse to learn English and help us out, only letting us rely on their hand motions to tell us what to do. We hope you take these men down, or you will not like the consequences.

Respectfully,
Nathanael Greene, Henry Knox, John Sullivan
11 June 1777
To John Sullivan, Nathanael Greene, and Henry Knox,
We do not appreciate your threat to resign from the army, but in further speculation, we decided that you may be right. It may have been wrong to put some men with little experience in those positions. If it pleases you, we will give you your old positions back, and give them lower positions.
U.S. Congress

"We got our positions back!" I said to John.

"We succeeded! You two got your jobs back, and I got to help!" Nathanael said back.

"I have to go back to the artillery," I told them. "But how will we prove to the French men that we are now in charge, and they aren't when there is only one letter?"

"I think Congress thought of that." Nathanael pulled out a copy of the letter from the envelope.

"Yes!" John exclaimed. "No time to waste!"

"Goodbye, my friends, I will see you soon!" I said. We grabbed our bags and ran to where our respective sections of the army were. I ran all the way to the artillery. I found Billingsley, Henry, William, and James.

"General Knox!" they shouted. "Please tell us you've come to rid us of Coudray."

"I have," I said, and their jaws dropped. They smiled like they knew this day would come someday, but not this early. "Would you mind telling me where he is, so I can rid you of him immediately?"

"YES!" the four shouted. "He's over—."

"*Excusez-moi, que faites-vous maintenant?*" Du Coudray asked.

"Not again!" William gushed in exasperation.

"*Nous parlons ensemble. Tu as un problème avec ça?*" I asked.

"*Oui! J'ai un problème avec ça!*" Du Coudray shouted. "*Ces hommes travaillent, mais tu parles avec eux, et maintenant, ils ne travaillent pas!"* Du Coudray's face was red now. Knox had to act quickly, or else Du Coudray might attempt murder.

"Were you all supposed to be working? Coudray says he's mad because we're talking and you were supposed to be working," I said. *"Je suis très désolé, Monsieur, mais, le Congrès a envoyé une lettre à moi. La lettre dit ça je suis responsable de l'artillerie,"* I explained to him. This enraged Du Coudray even more.

"Non! Ça n'est pas possible!" Du Coudray shouted.

"Oui, c'est vrai. Je dis la vérité," I shot back. *"Voici la lettre, si vous avez un problème, vous pouvez aller au Congrès."* Du Coudray looked like he was going to explode; there was steam practically coming out of his ears, but he stalked off, likely insulting Congress under his breath.

"HUZZAH!" James shouted, "We got rid of Coudray!"

"It's a good thing he doesn't know English, because if he heard you say that you might not be standing right now," I said back to James.

"What did you say to him that made his face turn into a purple tomato?" Henry asked.

"I told him I had a letter from Congress that said I was in charge of the artillery and not him. He said that that wasn't possible, and I told him it was true. I handed him the letter and told him that if he had any problems, he could go to Congress," I explained.

"Wow," Elias said. "How did you say all that in French?"

"When I still worked in my bookstore, I taught myself French," I replied.

Brandywine Creek, Pennsylvania
11 September 1777

CRACK! I fired a musket, in the middle of a battle again. We were fighting at Brandywine, and General Greene, General Sullivan, and General Washington were with me. The British kept attacking, and we kept defending. Then, we sent our own attacks. Eventually it started to get dark out. Washington pulled Greene and me aside to the yard of a house. There were British troops approaching, and Washington told me he wanted the artillery to hold them off. I nodded my head, everything rushing by, and the two of them took off.

"ATTACK!" I screamed to my men. "FIRE! DON'T CEASE FIRING! KEEP FIRING! USE WHAT WE'VE GOT!" We ran out of bullets and cannonballs. I hoped that General Washington's plan was working, because if they didn't get to Dilworth to set up in time, then we were going to lose. There were five more cannonballs and one hundred more musket balls. With the number of men here, these would be gone in five minutes. I waited until the last second to call my troops off. As soon as the last few musket balls were gone, I ordered the last cannonball to fire.

"FIRE THE CANNONBALL!" I shouted, but as the cannonball was fired, it drowned out the rest of my sentence. "RUN!" I screamed, "FIGHT AND RUN!" We had nothing left and there was nothing we could do about it. "BRING AS MUCH OF THE SUPPLIES AS YOU CAN!" My men grabbed as much as their hands could carry and sprinted away as fast as they could. We soon made it back to the other troops.

"The—British—are—com—ing," I said, out of breath. "Hold—them—off. Send—help."

"It's okay, where's everyone?" Sullivan asked.

"Some. Are. Still. Running. Couldn't. Keep. Up," I replied.

"Very well," Washington said, and pointed to a group of men waiting for the British to come. "You ten men, get water for Knox's troops. They sprinted all the way here."

"Yes, sir!" the men shouted, hopping up from their rigid positions..

"THE REST OF YOU!" General Washington shouted, "PREPARE FOR BATTLE!" With that, he sent the generals back to their troops to prepare. I stayed to send the rest of the artillery soldiers where needed.

Eventually, almost all the artillery soldiers showed up, but our resources were depleted. General Washington gave us access to more bullets and cannonballs, and I lined up the artillery as a last defense. The British fired muskets and cannonballs at us.

"WASHINGTON! TAKE EVERYONE AND GET TO CHESTER!

WE'LL HOLD THEM OFF FOR A WHILE!" General Greene shouted. We gathered up our supplies yet again, but had to leave several cannons, because many horses were dead. We marched at a quick pace to Chester because we weren't sure how long General Greene could keep the British away. We arrived between midnight and two a.m. and collapsed on the ground. We knew that if General Greene and his troops came, they would wake us. However, we worried the British would reach us first, so we stood guard in shifts all night despite our exhaustion.

FRENCH GLOSSARY

À	to
Aller	to go
Au	to (going to a place)
Avec	with
C'est	it is
C'est vrai	it's true
Ça	that
Ça n'est pas	it isn't
Ces hommes travaillent	these men are working
Cet	this
Comment t'appelles tu	what is your name
D'accord	okay
De	of
Désolé	sorry
Encore	again
Ensemble	together
Est	is
Et	and
Eux	them (masculine)
Excusez-moi	excuse me
Homme	man
Il parle	he is talking
Ils ne travaillent pas	they are not working

J'ai………………………………………	I have
Je dis la verité…………………………	I am telling the truth
Je m'appelle……………………………	my name is
Je suis…………………………………	I am
Je vous remplacé………………………	I replaced you
L'artillerie……………………………	artillery
La confusion…………………………	confusion
La lettre dit…………………………	the letter says
Le Congrès a envoyé…………………	Congress sent
Maintenant……………………………	now
Mais……………………………………	but
Mes……………………………………	my (plural)
Moi……………………………………	me
Monsieur………………………………	sir/Mr.
Non……………………………………	no
Nous parlons…………………………	we are talking
Oui……………………………………	yes
Pour…………………………………	for
Un probleme…………………………	problem
Que fais-tu/Que faites-vous…………	what are you doing
Quoi?…………………………………	what?
Responsable…………………………	responsible/in charge of
Si………………………………………	if
Très…………………………………	very
Tu as/vous avez………………………	you have
Tu es…………………………………	you are
Tu parles……………………………	you are speaking
Une lettre……………………………	a letter
Voici…………………………………	here is
Vous pouvez…………………………	you can

GENERAL CHARLES LEE: PAPER, BULLETS, AND IMPULSIVITY

BY EMMA URRUTIA

GENERAL CHARLES LEE: PAPER, BULLETS, AND IMPULSIVITY

28 JUNE 1776

Jupiter observed as General Charles Lee observed maps and mumbled something regarding the Redcoats. His portion of the army was currently residing in Charleston, South Carolina. Their goal? Push the British forces, one of the biggest powers *ever*, out. This would require careful calculations. The man muttered a little more about the upcoming enemy, then strolled outside for some fresh air. She hopped onto the table and examined the work. Looked sound. She leaped off the table and scurried after Lee. She found him reviewing the battle plans with an officer. Her gaze darted to the fortifications surrounding the city. It appeared to be a sound structure. She nuzzled his leg as she settled around his leg. Just as she got herself comfortable, Lee was up and off again, returning to the plans. Jupiter lost her footing for a few moments before scampering after him.

Lee headed back inside. There wasn't much time before they would have to fend off the Redcoats. He shook his head. Why couldn't Britain just hear them out and avoid this whole conflict? He sighed, reviewed the plans one last time, then leaned back and closed his eyes. He was going to need the rest.

Jupiter crouched down low as she felt the palmetto logs shake as a cannonball struck. She knew what would happen. It had been happening for quite some time now.

Despite Lee's orders, the army was forbidden to evacuate the town when the British fleets arrived. The ships fired cannonball after cannonball, but the response was always the same. The palmetto would *repel* the cannonball, for some inexplicable reason. That didn't mean she didn't feel them strike though. They kept firing relentlessly, as if at some point they might break through. Jupiter darted over to Lee and smothered her ears with her paws. She just wished this would stop. The firing continued for what felt like forever. Cannons fired bullets and all Jupiter wished for was *PEACE*. Suddenly, her ears picked up a sound. Or rather, the absence of it. The British had stopped firing. They were leaving! Clinton had driven off his forces and they were leaving! They were victorious! The soldiers erupted in cheers as Jupiter picked up someone called Lee 'The Hero of Charleston.' Jupiter smiled. Now *THAT* she could get used to.

New Jersey
11 December 1776

Jupiter snuggled at the foot of the bed as Lee closed his eyes and fell asleep. The canine lifted her head, unable to stop herself from enjoying the view the window gave. Basking Ridge, New Jersey was truly a sight to behold. And to think this view came from a sleep-stay in a public tavern. Jupiter closed her eyes, smiling as things really seemed to be going right for once.

Jupiter was awoken to loud noises and someone kicking her trying to get out of bed. The sound of pounding on the door filled her ears, and she whimpered as she shrank from the sound. The door burst open the exact moment she shut her eyes tight. There was commotion and the sounds of pain, but Jupiter refused to open her eyes, resorting to covering them with her paws. Footsteps rang across the room, then receded.

"Grab the dog, will you?" A voice called, and before she knew it she was in the air. Jupiter lifted her paws and opened her eyes. It dawned on the dog someone was carrying her down to the entrance. Jupiter found herself face-to-face with a Redcoat. She snarled and squirmed, but the human had a tighter grip, leaving her defenseless. The canine was set down on the floor once they reached the entrance. Lee had his hands raised in the air, his head tilted to face a certain soldier on a horse. It was difficult to tell in the moonlight at first, but soon Jupiter recognized him. The worst Lobsterback of them all--*Banastre Tarleton*.

With a growl unlike anything she had emitted before, Jupiter leaped up to attack the soldier. Before she reached him though, she got snatched mid-air. A Redcoat held her paw in his filthy hands. She was flung through the air. Jupiter's head smacked directly into the wall, causing her consciousness to dwindle as she slumped on the grass, her head throbbing and her brain spinning. Darkness crept into her vision, a grinning Lobsterback filling her vision before everything went dark.

New York City
December 1776

Jupiter's vision slowly began to return as she blinked, her brain registering blurry figures and muffled sounds. As the hazy figures moved around and out of her line of sight, her eyes fell on a chair in the middle of the room. Something was on top of the chair. No, *someone*. As her foggy vision slowly began to clear, Jupiter managed to make out the person. It was Lee! She immediately got up, eager to reach him—

Only for her legs to buckle underneath her. She tried again, slower this time, and soon made it to Lee. She flopped on the ground next to him, the once-simple action now draining her. Her eyes closed again, but she didn't fall asleep fast enough. Her ears picked up a door opening and Lee speaking, giving vital information on how to take down the Continental Army. A pleased tone reached her ears, but that was the last she heard.

Sixteen Months Later, April 1778

Jupiter still couldn't believe it. After two long years, Washington had arranged a prisoner exchange. Lee (and Jupiter) would return to Washington, while the Continental Army would hand over a British prisoner of their own, General Richard Prescott. She remembered when she heard the news, making sure to keep her excitement down low, otherwise the humans would wonder what a dog was so happy about. She remembered when she had returned to her rightful army with Washington and Lafayette.

The thing she remembered the most though, was Lee's scowl and unimpressed expression. He didn't seem to care about the changes made during his time as a captive. Jupiter tried to make him happy, but it did little to cheer up the man. She knew where he wanted to be-

-with the British. Sharing plans, complaining about Washington, the ignorance regarding the army's improvements, she all knew what it meant. He didn't want to be here. Jupiter did have one idea that might help though. An upcoming battle would soon be upon them, taking place in Monmouth, New Jersey. Lee had taken the position of second-in-command for the fight. If they won, that would surely cheer him up! Jupiter settled down on the floor of the tent. *Yep,* she told herself happily, *everything is going according to plan.*

This is NOT going according to plan, Lee thought. The plans were confusing, no-one was listening to him, and these so-called 'Patriots' thought they were foolish enough to take on the BRITISH FLEET, and KING GEORGE III! His Majesty, who had once been his king, now was the person who was fighting against. How quickly things change. Lee sighed as his gaze drifted upwards to the roof of his tent. How he wished this awful, bloody mess was over already. He glanced down when Jupiter let out a whine and nuzzled at his feet before huddling next to the tent's entrance. He couldn't help but smile. At least the canine was someone predictable... to an extent. He shook his head to clear his thoughts before returning to work. He had a *lot* of work.

He was just grateful he took the second in command from the pompous Lafayette. Ugh. Just thinking of that *Frenchman* made his brain hurt and stomach squirm. If that man had taken the position, it might lead to some crazy ideas that the Americans preferred French leaders over Americans. Not yet him, of course, but some might. Despite the necessity of French forces, that man just got under his skin so easily! For now, he just needed to plan this fight. He stood up, left his tent, and mounted his horse to head to Monmouth.

War had arrived at Lee's door long ago, and he had no intention to close that door yet, no matter how much he wanted to do so.

Mayhem burst at the seams from every direction. Jupiter ducked next to Lee's horse as he struggled to regain control of his branch of soldiers. As the chaos ensued, one unidentifiable soldier shouted to retreat. And just like that, things went from bad to worse. Men began to fall back, darting away from the fight. Nobody was listening to Lee and the Americans were going to lose! Then, out of the corner of her vision, she spotted *Washington* heading over! The leader shouted for them to fight, and Jupiter felt a surge of excitement. *This* was the man chosen to lead, *this* was the man who would help them win. *This* was the man who would lead them all to freedom.

When Lee spotted Washington coming over, the angry look on the general's face caused Jupiter to cower behind Lee. Said human, however, seemed pleased with his order to retreat. What Washington said though caused the pleased expression to disappear within seconds.

"I want to know Lee, what caused all this chaos and confusion?" Jupiter let out a small whine, but neither man heard, as Lee tried to explain, blaming it on a lack of intelligence, his officers, and the fact that there were more Redcoats. But Washington was having none of it. The leader made his disappointment *painfully* clear, then rode off to help reinstate order to his troops, the troops *Lee* should've been leading. Lee shook his head in bewilderment, then got his horse to follow Washington with some distance between them.

When the battle was over, people were eyeing Lee as the villain.

4 July 1779

Despite everything that Lee did, Jupiter managed to still love Lee, even if some things he did were unnecessary. Some much had occurred. From Lee claiming his innocence to anyone willing to lend an ear, to sending a letter complaining about Washington, who responded calling it 'improper' and before you knew it, Lee took the matter to court. The canine found it to be a bit much. Weren't they all meant to work *together* to help the cause. Jupiter watched as the judge laid three charges onto Lee: Disobeying order, conducting a disorderly retreat, and speaking disrespectfully to the leader of the army, none other than Washington. When Lee was suspended from the army for a year though, he seemed to try even more to pin the blame on Washington. That led to De Steuben challenging him to a duel, and Lee was badly injured. Shortly after, Lee wrote an army resignation letter. Now, she stayed with him in Shenandoah, Virginia. Even after all of that, the dog couldn't help but love him. He was a human, and humans were born with mistakes and flaws. Jupiter didn't mind though, it wasn't a big deal to her that Lee wasn't perfect. She was content with this man, and that was all she wanted. Jupiter sighed, and nuzzled up next to Lee. Her human.

BENJAMIN TALLMADGE

BY ELLIOTT LAY

THE EPIC STORY OF AMERICA 1777-1779

NEAR GENERAL WASHINGTON'S HEADQUARTERS, FREDERICKSBURG, NEW YORK
SUMMER 1778

The oppressive sun beat down on his head as the heat searing the brick road beneath him. He urged his horse on, though they were both exhausted.

Finally, he reached his destination. Sweat rolled down his face, dampening his shirt. He dismounted, tied his horse to a tree, and slumped to the ground to take a short respite from the harsh heat. He wiped his brow with his sleeve.

Small wooden huts lined the land for as far as the eye could see, each crudely built. The walls were filled with holes, and the stick roofs seemed in perpetual danger of collapsing. Men dressed in rag-tag military uniforms roamed the dusty paths, performing various duties. Why was he here? Who were these people? What year was it? Unanswered questions filled his head as he sat under the protection of the maple leaves.

He stood. What was he doing? Why was he leaving the comfort of the tree? He tried to sit back down and lose himself under the tree, but his body would not obey him. He watched, dismayed, as one of his boots hit the ground in front of the other, then the other stepped in front of the first. Dimly, he realized he was walking deeper into the encampment, unable to command his body to halt. He heard a faint neigh from his horse, but it soon faded away.

The discordant noise of the camp rang in his ears. Men clamored about the latest news as boys ran around, thumping on their military drums. Women gossiped, washed laundry, and cooked the militia's midday meal. Meanwhile soldiers marched, some carrying messages throughout the camp. He understood none of it. It felt as if he were in a dream, floating within someone else's skin.

Presently, he found himself stopping in front of one particular hut. This was no hastily created construction. The walls were impeccably notched together, lacking any imperfections. An intricate cloth hung over the door. This roof was made of shingles, not sticks. Glass windows decorated the walls, providing its inhabitants with views of the camp without leaving the hut.

Without knowing why, he raised a fist and knocked on the door with three resounding thuds. The knocks echoed and rang in his ears.

Footsteps echoed, and then the door creaked. Suddenly, a man stood in the doorway, scrutinizing him.

"Can I help you?" he asked. He wore a proper military uniform, his blue coat and tan trousers lacking blemishes or tears.

Words spilled from his mouth, but they were not his own. "Are you Colonel John Chester?"

"That I am," the man replied. "Why have you come to my humble abode?"

He felt himself swallow hard. "I... I want to enlist."

"A fellow Patriot?" Chester chuckled. "Well, that's always a welcome sight."

Vaguely, he perceived himself following Chester into his home and sitting in front of his desk. The interior of the hut was just as appealing as the external side, furnished with rugs and fashionable furniture. Unlike all the others in the military encampment, this hut had two rooms. The first was embellished with bookshelves filled with tomes of knowledge and a luxurious fireplace with a stone chimney. The second was barely visible, but he noticed a second fireplace meant for cooking and a woman (Chester's wife?) bent over it, stirring a pot. Chester's desk was cluttered with papers and books, which the colonel hastily shoved aside, revealing a calendar buried under several books.

The date was 20 June 1776.

The colonel handed him several papers to sign, and he eagerly scrawled his name.

"You understand the dangers of enlisting?" Chester questioned.

"Yes," he responded, sounding sure of himself.

The colonel reached out and shook his hand. "Welcome to the Continental Army."

"Thank you, sir."

"You are dismissed."

He stood and strode briskly to the door.

When he stepped outside, he felt as if the world was whirling around him. Items from the colonel's home swirled around him menacingly.

The calendar, revolving around him, now read 27 August 1776.

***

When the whirlwind calmed, he found himself no longer in a Connecticut encampment, but on a battlefield. The moon shone overhead, far gentler than the sun that plagued him before he enlisted. He turned back, seeking the shelter of the colonel's home, but all that was behind him were soldiers engaged in warfare.

Something weighed heavy in his hands. He glanced down and realized he was holding a musket.

"Redcoats on our left flank!" someone shouted. "They're moving in!"

He found himself raising his musket and pulling the trigger, firing a bullet at the British soldiers. Faintly, a shout of pain pierced the night.

"Redcoats at the rear!" another soldier shouted. Cries of agony reached his ears from his fellow soldiers.

One of the voices was his own.

A sharp pain shot through his shoulder, and he fell to the ground. The world blurred, and he slumped to the ground, closing his eyes in search of rest.

***

He opened his eyes to find himself standing amidst a crowd. The people around him clamored and shouted, focusing their attention on a central area.

In the middle of the crowd stood a gallows. Its menacing wooden beams loomed over him.

A man on a horse was led to it. He wore clothing meant to blend in with the townspeople. His skin and hair were fair, and even from a distance, his eyes were a striking blue.

British soldiers looped a rope around the man's neck.

"This man has been caught, tried, and convicted for treason against the motherland, against Great Britain. For this offense, the penalty is death!" shouted a British officer.

Most of the crowd cheered. Others groaned. Many, such as him, remained quiet.

"Do you have any last words?" *the officer demanded.*

Sitting on the horse that would soon bring him to his death, the man spoke, his words resonating with the crowd.

"I am satisfied with the course in which I have engaged. If I had ten thousand lives, I would lay them all down, if called to it. I only regret that I have but one life to lose for my country."

Suddenly, vivid memories flooded his mind. He knew this man. He was a former classmate, a comrade, and a friend.

This man was Nathan Hale.

These events took place on 22 September 1776. Nathan Hale had been caught spying for General George Washington, commander-in-chief of the Continental Army. Hale was publicly hanged and made an example for any others with treasonous ideas.

He stared, transfixed, unable to look away. He tried to close his eyes, to leave, to run away. He did not want to relive these events again.

It was futile. He was trapped.

He watched, dread creeping through his thoughts, as the British soldiers shoved a sack onto Hale's head. The British officer raised his hand.

The moment had come. The officer slapped the horse on the rump. It bolted, and a resounding crack *sounded as Hale's neck snapped, and he hung limp from the gallows.*

A thousand emotions ran through his mind; shock that his friend was truly dead, anger that the British soldiers had killed him, and helplessness that he could do nothing to stop it, nor to stop things like this from happening again. His thoughts nearly drowned out the erupting cheer from the Loyalist audience, celebrating the death of a traitor.

He turned away and strode out of the crowd, shouldering people aside as he walked, feeling an emptiness inside. He did not care whether people stumbled or fell. He no longer felt any sympathy for those who cheered for his friend's death.

Suddenly, the world shifted again. Suddenly, he found himself sitting on a horse surrounded by British soldiers. Ahead, he perceived the gallows. One of the British soldiers carried a rope.

No, *he thought. He was taking Nathan Hale's place. He was riding to his death.*

The soldiers stopped the horse beneath the gallows.

"This man has been caught, tried, and convicted for treason against the motherland, against Great Britain. For this offense, the penalty is death!" shouted the British officer as the soldiers tied the rope around his neck.

He felt helpless, despairing, and confusion. How had he gotten here? What had he done to be hanged? He hadn't been caught spying like Hale.

Then came the demand for last words.

He tried to repeat what Hale had so confidently stated in the face of death but failed to remember. He found that he could not speak.

Vaguely, he saw the officer shrug and motion for the sack to go on. He felt the rough material of the gunny sack against his face. He felt the heat of his own breath and began to sweat. He heard the slap on the horse's rump, and death's cold fingers reached for him.

***

Benjamin Tallmadge sat up in bed, cold sweat running down his face. He was breathing hard, his heart pounding. The vivid nightmare covered actual events that had actually taken place, his enlistment into the Continental Army, the Battle of Long Island, and Nathan Hale's execution, to his own certain doom.

Those were the dangers of spying.

He glanced around frantically, making sure he wasn't still ensnared in another terrible scene of his nightmare.

What day is it? he thought, feverishly groping for anything to reassure him that he was no longer dreaming. His hands settled on his calendar, knocking over something that clattered to the floor.

He sighed in relief. It was mid-1778, not covered by his memories. He was no longer dreaming.

Benjamin sighed, lying back down, still breathing hard.

That's it, he thought. *I'm never going into spying.*

Feeling better, he rolled out of bed, dressed in his uniform, ate a quick breakfast, and strode out the door.

"Good morning, Major Tallmadge," a soldier greeted him, saluting. "General Washington would like to speak with you."

"Thank you, Private," Tallmadge responded, returning the salute. "I'm on my way."

What could General Washington possibly want from him? The question plagued him as he marched through the camp to Washington's hut.

"Good morning, General Washington," Tallmadge greeted him, saluting. "You requested me?"

"Yes, Tallmadge. Thank you for arriving at such short notice. Come, sit." Washington gestured to his hut, opening the door for him.

"How can I help you, sir?" Tallmadge asked respectfully.

"To put it simply, I want you to go into spying," replied General Washington.

An image of the gallows rushed into Tallmadge's mind. The memory of his friend Nathan Hale sitting on the horse with the rope tied around his neck, hopeless and despairing, filled his thoughts.

Spies were caught, tried, and hanged.

That was how it worked when you spied on the British.

But Nathan Hale's last words echoed in Tallmadge's mind.

I only regret that I have but one life to lose for my country.

Perhaps there was honor in dying for one's country.

Perhaps there were causes worth dying for.

Perhaps the liberty of his country was one of those causes.

But again, visions of the gallows filled his mind. The terror of that terrible death, mocked and ridiculed by the British in front of crowds, and hanged without dignity.

He shoved the image from his head.

"I'll do it," declared Tallmadge.

***

The summer heat struck Benjamin's face as he rode his horse through the town of Setauket. He gently pressed his knees into the horse's sides, urging the sweating animal on.

Finally, he halted his horse, dismounted, and tied it to a tree. He reached into the saddlebag and unfolded a rag, wiping the horse down. He leaned against the tree to take a brief rest in the shade before the upcoming encounter.

The town streets were lined with homes, their inhabitants tramping around to complete various tasks that contributed to the well-being of their families.

Since accepting his position as head of General Washington's spy organization, Benjamin had searched far and wide for the ideal individuals to add to his roster of members of Washington's spy ring. He had discovered several possible candidates, but most had fallen short upon closer investigation. However, the man he was about to approach, one Abraham Woodhull, had unknowingly survived Benjamin's scrutiny and fulfilled the criteria for a successful Patriot spy. Because of this, Benjamin was now sitting under a tree, preparing to approach his old friend and recruit him to the American cause.

He ran through his greeting in his head once more. He would have to test and verify Woodhull's allegiances. Was his old friend loyal to the British? Or was he as Benjamin hoped, sympathetic to the Patriots?

Once he initiated the conversation, he would have to improvise and hope events went as desired.

He rose, ready for the coming meeting. Slowly, almost dreamily, he strolled to the front door of a house and knocked firmly.

"Can I help you?" A man wearing common clothing opened the door.

Only then did Benjamin realize the similarity his world now held to his nightmare.

***

The next hour passed in a blur, as Benjamin and Abraham Woodhull reunited and spent the time immersed in conversation and pleasantries.

Finally, Benjamin realized that it was time to make his request. He now completely trusted Abraham, sure that his friend was loyal to the colonies. He only had to ask.

"Abraham, what would you think about spying for the Patriots?"

He found himself spilling the whole story as if in another dream. The words flowed from his mouth on their own. He told the story of his nightmare and his history fighting for the colonies. He told of his friend Nathan Hale, and how Hale was hung right before his eyes. He told how Washington recruited him to lead an espionage team, gathering information from the British.

"So far," Benjamin finished, "you're the only person I've found who is trustworthy and loyal to the Patriot cause. So, old friend, what do you say?"

"I'll do it," said Woodhull.

Right then and there, in the living room of a common townsperson, the Culper Spy Ring was formed.

***

The next year, Tallmadge provided diligent work in developing the Culper Spy Ring. He recruited multiple friends from his youth, while Tallmadge codenamed himself John Bolton. He devised a secure method of communication to prevent a repetition of Nathan Hale's death. Tallmadge himself wrote letters to General Washington detailing the findings of his spies.

One night, Benjamin lay awake in bed, thinking about the spy ring, whose members had grown to be some of his closest friends. What if one was caught? They were in British territory now, out of the sphere of protection conferred by General Washington's army. If one of them were to be caught, they would be as good as dead.

Benjamin sighed. He had done all he could. He had composed the best possible method of communication for them to use. He had and would do his best.

Perhaps it would not be enough.

But he knew there was honor in dying for one's country.

He knew there were causes worth dying for.
He was sure the liberty of their country was one of those causes.
Perhaps everything would turn out just fine.
Benjamin closed his eyes and plunged into another nightmare.

GENERAL GEORGE WASHINGTON

BY PERI JORDAN

THE EPIC STORY OF AMERICA 1777-1779

HARLEM HEIGHTS, NEW YORK
16 SEPTEMBER 1776

The soft scratching of a quill on parchment filled the tent. The writer sat erect at his desk, deep in thought. He was a tall man, broad-shouldered, and strong from years of manual labor. His face was impassive, but behind it, a turmoil of thoughts and emotions raged.

As footsteps approached, he set down his pen and turned toward the front of his tent, where a man ducked through the opening. The day was hot, and the man clearly had been out in it for too long. His face was flushed, and he leaned over slightly; clutching the tent pole and trying to catch his breath. Despite all this, a sense of urgency still lingered in the man's appearance. "General Washington, sir," he panted. "The British are advancing from the south."

The general hurried out of the tent, his face still calm. "General Reed and Lieutenant Knowlton, take 150 rangers and investigate. Relay your findings to me immediately." They could not afford yet another loss.

After several agonizing minutes of waiting, he could stand it no longer. He mounted his horse and was off. For two miles he rode, until he reached the southernmost point of the camp. As he surveyed his surroundings, General Reed galloped toward him, winded and panting.

"Sir, the lieutenant has entered into a bit of a skirmish with British forces just to the south." He pointed to a forest below, which echoed with shouting and gunshots. "I strongly recommend we send reinforcements immediately. They are advancing readily, and I would hate to disappoint our guests."

The general nodded his head and opened his mouth to speak as thunderous hoofbeats approached. Rangers raced toward the camp, with the British in hot pursuit.

"Fall back," the general ordered. "Retreat to camp!" However, to his astonishment, the British came to a halt instead of pursuing the rangers. The two generals watched as one of the officers lifted a bugle to his lips and blew. Washington's ears pricked up as he recognized the tune. It was one he was very familiar with, having played it himself countless times on his own hunting bugle at home.

"What is it, sir?"

"That bugler is playing *Gone Away*. A hunter plays it when he kills a fox, and the chase is over. They believe they have defeated us." As the two men listened to the song, Washington's face finally hardened. "Rally the troops. We're mounting a counterattack.

Benjamin Ring House
One Mile East of Brandywine Creek
Chadds Ford, Pennsylvania
11 September 1777

General Washington awoke with a start, the bugle still ringing in his ears. Sweat drenched his pillow, and his heart pounded like a drumbeat in his chest. *It was only a dream,* he reminded himself. *Only a dream.* They had won that battle, so it had turned out well, but even so, a year later, he could not erase that scene from his mind. The mockery, the piercing insult in that moment. The way those soldiers in their crimson coats stood, *laughing* at him. Calling *him* the hunted fox.

He forced himself to sit up, shove his feet into his boots, tug on his coat, and walk to the window. A light breeze whispered through the trees, painted silver in the moonlight. Nightbirds cooed and trilled, their lilting melodies filling his ears. Was he ready for this? Were his men ready for this? *Dear Lord, give me strength.* This would be the most important battle he had ever fought; it could decide if America would indeed be a free nation! Yes, of course they would emerge victorious. How could they not? He had painstakingly predicted every move the enemy would make; prepared all of his counterattacks.

Washington pulled out his pocket watch and checked the time. Thirteen minutes after four. "Wake up, men," he announced to the still room. "It's time to defend Philadelphia from the British."

THE EPIC STORY OF AMERICA 1777-1779

***

The sun was far from rising over the tops of the great trees as General Washington led his troops through the fields of Pennsylvania, but they were nearly there.

"Getting to this place is harder than actually fighting the British," remarked a soldier behind Washington.

"No doubt about it. I've tripped on stones and roots at least six times already! I've about broken both my ankles," another soldier replied.

"Don't get cocky, boys," a slightly older man reprimanded. "An attitude like that could get you killed or lose the battle altogether." The three men fell silent.

"Sure, but still, don't you think we've planned this out perfectly?" began the first soldier. "I mean, General Washington's planned out every move those Cat's Paws are going to make!"

The older man sighed. "Talk like that and *you'll* be the Cat's Paw, Williams, not the British. Savvy?"

"I agree," chimed in yet another soldier. "We can't afford to lose this battle. If the British take Philadelphia, they'll capture our Congress." Again, the group fell silent. What more was there to say?

Finally, they reached Chadds Ford, and everyone assumed their positions, waiting... waiting...waiting for the British to round the crest of the hills. At thirty-two minutes after five, every head turned west, every heart leapt, every mind began to race as the first gunshot exploded.

***

The afternoon sun was high in the sky as gunshots blasted in his ears, and dirt sprayed in all directions. With a piercing cry, another brave Patriot collapsed to the ground. The general painfully averted his gaze. Now was not the time to grieve. He urged his horse faster, but there was no escaping the pungent odor of gunpowder; the groans and cries of brother killing brother; the dozens of men strewn about on the ground like so many toy soldiers. War had seemed like a game as a child—nothing but little wooden men and little wooden cannons. Wooden men were expendable. Flesh-and-blood men had eternal souls.

He set his jaw and struggled to turn his mind from the grim thoughts. This was indeed a real battle, and his men needed him. "That's it, men," he shouted to his beloved band of soldiers. He said more, but it felt pathetic, even to his own ears. What do you say to husbands, fathers, sons, brothers, who will never return to their families? To the world, they were nothing more than wooden soldiers; knock them down, and more will fill their places. Who grieves the wooden soldier? His family? His fellows? The world gives them no names; they will not live on in history books; they are simply knocked down over and over, until there are none left to fight—but the canons keep on coming.

"Retreat!" No one heard. "RETREAT!" He bellowed again and again with all the force he could muster, but he could barely hear his own voice beneath all the chaos raging around him. The fighting had lasted all day, but there was no victory for the brave Americans. The only way to salvage anything was to retreat. Now.

He raced through the onslaught, shouting to his men. Finally, they turned and ran. Escaped. Fled. How pitiful it seemed; how weak. However, it was the best thing to do—was it not? Just then, it didn't seem like it. Many of those brave men, who fought so valiantly, would never see another victory. Would never see a free nation. Because they had been hunted down like foxes; crushed under the mighty blow of the hunter. He remembered again the lone bugler's song and those laughing, taunting voices. Washington, the fox, was caught again, snared in his own trap.

***

Later that night, Washington, bone-tired and discouraged, ventured into the camp hospital. Far too many men lay moaning, gasping for air, *dying*. No matter how many times he witnessed such scenes, they still wrenched his heart. Too many reminded him of his stepson, Jack.

He passed a cot where the young soldier—Williams, was his name?—was stretched out, a bandage wrapped tightly around his middle. His face was as white as the sheet he lay on, his chest rising and falling slowly. He would not survive the night. Washington paused. He knelt and gripped the young man's shoulder, but he didn't stir.

The general forced himself to move on. He was looking for someone in particular. A young man—hardly more than a boy, really—propped up against a tree, chatting jovially with another soldier. A bloodied bandage covered his leg, but the young Frenchman was in good spirits.

"My dear Marquis, how are you? I see you took a musket ball to the leg."

The young man's eyes lit up. "General! *Bonjour!* I am doing very well, I suppose, given the circumstances. How are you?"

"We lost the battle, and we have lost Philadelphia." Washington frowned. "So many men died for the cause, and we still lost Philadelphia." He still could not quite believe it was true.

"*Oui*, you could look at it that way," General Lafayette mused. "But look out there at the men who will see their families again! They thank you most heartily for saving their lives." He chuckled. "I should know! *Merci, merci, merci* for the command to retreat! If you hadn't, I would be on that hill," he pointed in the direction of the battlefield, "wondering what happens to British captives. I would never see my wife or sweet daughter again."

Washington nodded slowly. "I suppose you are correct, Marquis."

"And you live another day as well. You can lead us onto another victory! Even though we've lost this battle, doesn't mean we have lost the war."

Washington nodded again. "You are wise beyond your years." He turned to his assistant. "Fetch my personal surgeon," he commanded. "I want this man treated as if he were my son." He smiled at the astonished Marquis and declared, "America owes you a debt of gratitude."

"*Merci, mon* general."

As Washington turned to leave, he called over his shoulder, "Get some rest. We have a city to recover and a war to win."

MARTHA WASHINGTON: REVOLUTIONARY WINTERS

BY CHLOE FROST

MOUNT VERNON, VIRGINIA
DECEMBER 1777

*D*ear Diary,

This year has been anything but pleasant. In addition to the trials and turmoil of life, I lost my dearest sister, Anna Maria. Oh, how I will miss my sweet sister and our wonderful times together. I look back at playing as children on our parents' farm. I am saddened that I as the oldest child to my parents have lost someone who has known me my whole life. However, I am proud we overcame throughout the years. I grew up in a time when my people struggled to survive disease and starvation, which still affects some today. Not to mention the harsh winters we experience, for which, I am extremely anxious. Although my siblings and I were born to great wealth, we still were not strangers to the difficulties of the winters. Oh, although I am not a fan of the frigid conditions, I so miss my childhood at Chestnut Grove, our family home about 35 miles from Williamsburg.

I am not sure why I write a diary now at my age because I never wrote diaries or letters in my early years. My wish is to now record my feelings in the wake of the loss of my sister and record events. As I sit here and process my feelings on loss, I reflect on my childhood and the Pamunkey River which ran right by our home. Oh, the times we had playing in that river where Anna Maria was the best swimmer of all. She was fierce and courageous, and I hope to be just as courageous now in the wake of the times we are experiencing. This loss of my sister is bringing me back to the loss of my sweet daughter, who died at the age of 17 from seizures. She was also a great loss to me, not unlike my loss right now. George said the loss of Patsy reduced me to the "lowest ebb of my misery." I feel that now more than ever. Though, I am grateful to be comforted by the love of my son, Jacky, and his family who spend their time with me. Of course, my sweet Polly is by my side as well. She brightens my day whether by copying my words or just perching on my shoulder.

Back to the letter George wrote to me in 1775 when he informed me, he would become Commander in Chief of the Continental Army. Oh, the fear that overcame me but also the pride I felt at being a part of something bigger than myself. The latest loss of Philadelphia to the British has been on my mind recently and I am sure it weighs heavily on George as he was outmaneuvered when he was trying to defend against Sir William Howe's advance. Even more, George is probably anxious after dealing with the backlash and attempts by military officers and members of Congress to remove George from command of the Continental Army. Worse, they want to replace him with Horatio Gates. The tensions are high between George and Horatio following Saratoga. I hope we receive good news soon to boost George and the troops' morale. I love to lend a hand to help the troops when I can, so I have been quilting a good bit and managing the home while George is away. I hope I can be of further aid soon—I feel as though I should be doing more.

Oh, I hear someone calling me. It's time for my nightly chores: cleaning, turning down the beds, stoking the fire, and shutting everything down for the evening.

Mount Vernon, Virginia
Late December 1777

To: General George Washington, Winter Headquarters, Valley Forge

Dearest George,

My love, I am writing to you to express my sadness and loneliness during this time. I am aware of the trials and turmoil you and the troops are experiencing at Valley Forge as I have heard from you many of the awful conditions you have encountered. Not to mention, the great loss you were dealt in Philadelphia as well as the potential ousting by Horatio. I know you are doing great work and will be able to push through all the failures you have encountered thus far. I quilt and sew every day in hopes that my work will benefit you and the troops somehow. I have heard of the many soldiers who do not have adequate garments or footwear. My sincerest hope is that the items I will send to you will be of great use to you and the troops. I hope to see you soon and aid the efforts in a much greater way than I can from here in Mount Vernon.

Love,
Martha

Mount Vernon, Virginia
Late December 1777

To: Elizabeth Willing Powell
Dearest Elizabeth,

I apologize that I have not written to you in some time. Something terrible has happened, and it is my greatest despair that my dearest sister, Anna Maria, has passed away. As one of my closest friends and confidants I wanted to inform you as soon as possible. Alas, I have been in the pits of despair. Polly has tried her best to cheer me up, but I fear that even she is not able to bring me out of this pain and coldness I am feeling. Granted, the cold is presumably in a big part due to this once again harsh winter we are experiencing. Oh, you know how I despise winter and have my worst times in winter. Do you remember the letter I told you about where I informed Anna Maria of my deep depression back in 1762? As I am sitting here writing to you, Polly can tell I am upset. As the tears fall from my face, she tries her best to do her little dance she does that I so love, but all I can think about is the bad that is surrounding us.

George is in Valley Forge and I long to be with him. I long to feel as though I am helping and doing more than just managing his home. I hope the quilts I am making will do some good for the troops in this cold bitter time. I went outside for a bit today and noticed the huge piles of snow, all while it continues to come down. I stared at my garden for a while noticing the flowers and plants that have died. This also makes me sad, but I decided it's just a matter of nature and we must continue to move forward. After my short walk in the snow, I decided it was time to prepare dinner. I made a stew with potatoes, carrots, and beef to fill my stomach as well as the stomachs of my dear Jacky and his family.

The quilt I am currently working on is the fifth this month and this one has taken me a particularly long time. I am adding a little extra love into this one for someone who needs it. The troops are going through many more trying times than am I, and I hope that my efforts will ease some of the burdens and trials they are experiencing. I want so badly to help boost morale for George and the troops following the losses and missteps they have experienced with the loss of Philadelphia and the almost ousting of George by Horatio Gates. I have also heard of the terrible conditions which they face all while they are without adequate clothing and footwear. Many men are losing their limbs and even worse their lives. Things must change soon, or I fear we will lose everyone.

After dinner I was very anxious and wanted to take another walk outside before bed, however I know that I shouldn't go outside much because of the cold and the dangers of getting a sickness. Dearest Elizabeth, I know I have gone on far too long, but I miss you as well and I hope to see you soon when traveling conditions improve.

Love,
Martha

Mount Vernon, Virginia
Early January 1777

Dear Diary,

Winter has set in, but I will travel to Valley Forge at the end of the month to visit George and aid the effort at the Winter Quarters. This winter reminds me of the winter in 1762 that I recalled to Elizabeth in my most recent letter to her. That winter was very tough for me. I even wrote a letter to my dearest sister describing how unhappy I was with the bitter cold and the gloominess. I suffer from terrible depression during winters like this and with George away, it doesn't make things any easier. Although, I am sure I experience nothing compared to the great loss and bitterness the troops are dealing with right now. I received notice of a quote of the number of lives lost thus far, and the death toll is now up to nearly 2,000. So far this is the highest death toll of any Continental Army encampment. I am ready to see George, however I am anxious to arrive and see the conditions of Quarters when I arrive. I will write on my voyage to record the traveling conditions.

Between Mount Vernon and Valley Forge
Late January 1777

Dear Diary,
It has been five days and it is colder than ever. We have five more days to go, and I am not sure how much more we can endure. Sweet Polly of course is just chirping along and copying our every word with such joy that she warms my cold bones and heart. I didn't receive a letter from George before I left, so I am unaware of the current situation in Valley Forge which makes me anxious to see the state of the quarters. On one of our trails yesterday the horses were startled and stopped abruptly. Apparently, there were two foxes which were taunting them, and one almost bit my favorite horse's leg. Our driver, Joe got out to scare the foxes away by clapping his almost frostbitten hands. At that point, the foxes slipped away into the snowy forest, and we didn't see them again. They were rabid. When I told Joe I thought they were rabid, Polly piped up and kept saying, "rabid, rabid, rabid..." and wouldn't stop for almost an hour. Her antics give us something to laugh about during these times.

After the fox run-in, the sky got darker, so we set up camp to rest. Our camp was not comfortable, but it was in a safe area surrounded by a thick wood with room for a large fire to keep us warm. This morning, we resumed our travel again. This day was difficult as the wheels on our carriage are rickety and have trouble making it through the thick pillowy snow. I feel my worry growing stronger as we experience more issues traveling and as we get closer to Valley Forge. My comfort this morning comes from spending an hour reading the Bible and praying, it gives me such peace to know that God is with us. Of course, Polly as well!

Between Mount Vernon and Valley Forge
Early February 1777

Dear Diary,

The second half of our travel has been eventful. I am happier than ever to be able to see George tomorrow, even under the circumstances. I know that my visiting him is a result of the state of the war right now and my goal to help the cause. I hope that tomorrow after spending a short time visiting George that I will be able to hit the ground running with my chores in managing the Quarters and helping the soldiers keep warm. As far as the last few days go, it is hard to talk about because of the treacherous journey we had. In my last entry I spoke of the rickety wheels we have. Well, they are more than rickety—one was broken beyond repair and fell off the carriage.

We were stranded for a long while in a remote area before Joe went on foot for help. After several hours, Joe arrived in a stranger's wagon with a new wheel. Sometime later, Joe was able to fix and replace the part of the carriage that had broken down and we were on our way. As I waited for the work on the carriage to be complete, I saw a beautiful rabbit grazing in a field nearby and pointed it out to my travel companions. When I mentioned the animal, Polly thought I said rabid and started repeating "rabid, rabid, rabid..." repeatedly for the whole evening till we finally stopped for rest. Tomorrow will be a much better day, for we will arrive at the Winter Quarters, and I will see George and get started on my task to help the cause.

Valley Forge, Pennsylvania
March 1777

To Elizabeth Willing Powell
Dearest Elizabeth,
I arrived at the Winter Quarters in late February after a treach-

erous journey along unkempt roads and dangerous encounters with foxes. You would have laughed uncontrollably at Polly and her constant chirping, "rabid, rabid, rabid." She decided that since we spoke of the rabid-like nature of the foxes that it was now a word she wants to repeat constantly. She only does it because of the laughter she saw from us when she said it. We were not expecting something like that to come out of her beak! On to other news, the Quarters were in much more of a tragic state than I expected. There are many men who have lost limbs due to the frostbite in these bitter conditions, especially since they don't have proper attire in these conditions. I sew and make quilts and clothing, and it's not my best work, but time is of the essence in this situation. I have also been visiting the hospital. I feel that I have been of great help since I had some training as a child in herbs and natural remedies for diseases and conditions. Not to mention, my experience with my sick children. I was worried I wouldn't be of much use here, but I have been more helpful than I could have ever imagined. God is with us, and he is using me and many others during this time. My prayer time has grown from one hour to two hours and I read the Bible more now than ever. Dearest Elizabeth, I pray that I see you soon and George does as well. We miss your company as you are our dearest friend.

Valley Forge, Pennsylvania
Summer 1777

Dear Diary,

I have been at Valley Forge now for four months and it is almost my time to leave again. The other soldiers tell me that I have kept their spirits high during this time and I am glad to hear it, although they are most high spirited when Polly is around. She has a way of brightening the smile on everyone's faces and bringing some joy to this otherwise dark and scary time. It is now warming up here and my time spent making quilts was put to good use and helped many people from losing limbs and kept them from contracting sickness. During my time here I also organized many meals. God gave me these talents for a reason, and they were used well during my time here. I am excited to go back home for a while to spend time with Jacky and the grandchildren. Oh, how they put a smile on my face. Polly just saw me write Jacky's name and chirped– "Jacky, Jacky, Jacky."

"Yes, Polly we are going to see Jacky," I said. Oh, what a bittersweet time this is. I leave one person I love to see another. Hopefully we will all be together again soon.

GENERAL ANTHONY WAYNE: STORMING HELL, ANTHONY WAYNE'S FIGHT

BY CHASE ADAM

THE EPIC STORY OF AMERICA 1777-1779

PAOLI, PENNSYLVANIA
20 SEPTEMBER 1777, 10 pm

"*N*o quarter! No quarter!" A sea of Redcoats shouted their vicious battle cry, showing no mercy as they plunged bayonets into drowsy Continental soldiers.

Startled by the gory sounds of death and muskets firing into the night, Brigadier General Anthony Wayne looked to the north, horrified as the red wall of soldiers raced toward him.

"Fire! Fire at will!" he yelled, trying to suppress panic. Alas, it was already too late. The Continentals were deserting in full force, racing into the midnight forest for cover.

With hundreds of soldiers scrambling to escape the slaughter, General Wayne frantically counted the fighting men who remained. Fearful the death toll was too much to bear, he mounted his startled horse and galloped in the driving rain to the front lines to evacuate his men. He rounded up the courageous remaining soldiers, weary and bloodied and marched them two miles southwest to the White Horse Tavern, to await the anticipated and much needed reinforcements. Tragically the reinforcements never arrived. Little did Wayne know that His Excellency George Washington had sent the expected battalions to another location.

Continuing their battle-weary march to the safety of Fort Ticonderoga, General Wayne ordered the exhausted troops to set up camp and rest. Wearily, Wayne tied the canvas flaps of his own tent, and sat down at his worn makeshift desk. He dipped his quill in the black ink, and with a discouraged sigh, wrote to his beloved wife.

My Dear Polly,

I write in a time of great distress. His Excellency, General Washington, ordered me to attack the British General Howe. "Cutting off of the enemy's baggage would be of a great matter," he insisted.

So, fifteen hundred men and I, were sent marching to Paoli and Lancaster

GENERAL ANTHONY WAYNE: STORMING HELL, ANTHONY WAYNE'S FIGHT

Lane to fight the British. I was supposed to wait there in the hills under the cover of darkness for Colonel William Smallwood with his Maryland Line, and Generals Maxwell and Potter with their Pennsylvania Line.

I waited with great anxiety for them until nine o'clock when Morgan Jones, the father of Chaplain David Morgan told me some news of the utmost consequence. A neighborhood boy, captured by the British had returned home, claiming the British would attack us in the hills.

I chose not to believe this thoroughly unmilitary source. I would not abandon the position His Excellency ordered me to take.

Suddenly at ten p.m. the British pounced. The enemy removed their flints and used only their bayonets to avoid detection. Most men ran two miles to the White Horse Tavern. Colonel Richard Humpton and his 1st Regiment and Light Infantry with the artillery were the last to retreat even after being commanded by me to withdraw twice. We have now made camp to rest on our march to Fort Ticonderoga.

I was foolish tonight, my dearest Polly. I am vexed by my inexcusable oversight. The death of those brave soldiers; their families... they will miss them—oh how they will miss them! I immediately wrote to His Excellency for a Military Court of Inquiry to defend myself. Even though the whole disaster is my fault, I do not believe I should be charged with treason for it.

I hope this letter finds you in good health, my Polly.

Ant'y

GENERAL WAYNE WAS COURT-MARTIALED. Although convicted of a tactical error, the panel decided he acted with honor. During the grueling winter of 1777-78, the mighty British Army conquered Philadelphia, the American capital. Defeated, General Washington retreated to Valley Forge. Prussian General Baron de Steuben and French General Lafayette helped train the Continental Army. During the frigid and shoeless winter, the two European generals whipped the soldiers into shape.

Continental Camp, New Jersey
24 June 1778

On 17 June, British General Henry Clinton, General Howe's replacement, moved his troops from Philadelphia to New York, while the Rebels followed them. A week later, the Continental War Council held a tense meeting.

"We've been shadowing the British for nearly a week," noted General Washington.

"What should we do now?" General Charles Lee was first to speak up.

"Nothing!" Lee exclaimed in authoritative confidence, bordering cockiness. As second only to Washington in rank, Lee frequently took advantage of his position. "It would be better to wait and then attack once the enemy reaches New York." Other senior officers nodded their agreement.

Wayne was not satisfied with this idea. He did not like Lee and believed the Continental Army was ready to fight the British as soon as possible. He turned to Washington and asserted, "This could be our last chance to defeat the enemy! We've been training at Valley Forge all winter. We can fight them and win! Take 2,500-3,000 men led by either one major general or two brigadiers who will lead the attack on the rear column against the British. Then at the time of your choosing, Sir, you will reinforce them." Generals Lafayette, Steuben, and Greene all agreed with Wayne's plan.

General Washington nodded his approval. "General Greene, General Lafayette, and Colonel Hamilton, take 3,000 men under General Lee."

"But sir! This idea is madness!" General Lee objected angrily, raising his voice, "I strongly urge something else!" He finished desperately as he saw his authority slipping away.

Washington glanced at the angry Lee and said calmly, "Then I'll replace you with General Lafayette."

"But Sir!" Lee protested a second time, "If anyone should lead the men, in this foolish attack, it should be me!" Silence followed this arrogant declaration.

General Washington sighed. "Very well, then. But you have to work with General Lafayette and Brigadier Wayne to lead the five-thousand men. You are dismissed." There was a quiet murmur of consent as the commanding officers stood and exited the meeting.

Wayne's heart sank at his commander's orders. *Tensions are going to erupt,* he stewed, stomping out of the tent. *If Lee makes one wrong step... Cannon won't be the only thing exploding.*

Near Monmouth, New Jersey
27 June 1778

"We need to attack now, before it is too late!" General Wayne slammed his fist on the mahogany table to punctuate his point.

Three days had passed since Washington ordered Wayne's plan to be executed, and Generals Greene, Lafayette, Wayne, Lee, and Colonel Hamilton had gathered in a Council of War not far from the British baggage train.

"I strongly disagree, Mr. Wayne," General Lee retorted arrogantly. "General Washington has given me full authority over this expedition, and I believe we are not ready, especially if we're outnumbered against the finest troops of the British empire!" Lee still believed that he should rightfully oversee the operation, despite the explicit directions of the Commander-in- Chief. He irrationally continued his condescension, "I don't trust you at all Wayne. Not after the disaster caused by your arrogant, uneducated decisions at Paoli."

Wayne leapt from his chair, knocking the table over, maps scattering everywhere. He charged Lee with readied fists, eyes blazing. Lafayette intercepted the mad Wayne in the nick of time, catching the angry general before his fists flew. His nostrils flared as Wayne struggled in the strong Frenchman's grip.

"I do believe it is lunchtime now," Wayne seethed, tempering the heat in his voice. "We'll meet after lunch and take it to a vote." He glared at Lee with fiery eyes that shot out a warning: next time Lafayette won't be here.

The next day found Anthony Wayne marching with his brigade alongside the main army. The council had come to the decision that they would launch a surprise attack against the British at Monmouth Courthouse.

Wayne smiled, his back straight, eyes sharp, calloused hands gipping the reigns tightly. He anticipated the upcoming battle. It had been some time since his last face to face combat. He was ready. He dug his heels into his ride, urging the animal faster. One last check on the battalion. The soldiers looked ready and eager to fight. That was good, he knew. Lack of morale could be more devastating in battle than anything else and Wayne worked hard to make sure that his soldiers had what they needed. For that reason, Wayne was well loved and popular among his troops. On many occasions when food and boots were in short supply, especially in Valley Forge, he would buy the much-needed necessities in bulk out of his own pocket.

After three hard and tedious hours of marching, the weary soldiers, dusty and hungry, finally reached the position where they would ambush their hated enemy.

Just as he was about to give the order to get set for battle, the unmistakable sound of gunshots and panicked horses rang through his ears. His own horse reared up in fright, and he nearly fell off. He located the sound of the commotion at Colonel Butler's regiment and raced over on his anxious horse.

"Load muskets! Fire! Charge with bayonets!" Orders rang out to execute the exact drill General Steuben taught them during the unforgettable winter at Valley Forge. With practiced ease, the soldiers loaded and reloaded their weapons, rapid firing and reloading again. The time spent over the agonizing winter had paid off as the British fell back momentarily. Wayne knew however, that the superior numbers of the British would soon overwhelm the Continentals. They needed reinforcements. He spotted a soldier in the back lines, no more than twenty years of age, waiting for the men in front to fall so that he could take their place.

"You there! Come over here!" General Wayne called over the chaos of the battlefield, "Go to General Lee and request reinforcements."

"Yes, sir!" the young soldier replied crisply, racing off to fulfill this important job.

The soldier soon returned with the catastrophic news that General Lee would not send reinforcements. Wayne cursed Lee's incompetence. *That man is the worst possible choice for a commander,* he thought as he analyzed the situation of his men without reinforcements. Nonetheless, Lee eventually came through and a couple scores of men arrived at his right, ready to fight. With this new hope, Wayne ordered Brigadier General Charles Scott to move up on his left. Now that the rest of Wayne's forces were also marching against the Queen's Rangers, victory was very real and near.

Elsewhere on the battlefield, General Lee viewed victory as an impossibility. Lee noticed that the Queen's Rangers, a military unit of trained Loyalists, attacked the front lines where Wayne was positioned. But those were just civilians. Lee surmised that better trained troops were circling around them and forming lines to attack. When they attacked, they would annihilate the army long before Washington arrived. Believing the odds were not in their favor, he gave the cowardly order to fall back.

Wayne did not get the order to retreat. He urged his men to keep fighting. Seeing his forces were single-handedly fighting the enemy, he gave the order to fall back.

Down Monmouth Road, General Washington was surprised when hundreds of men flooded past him, racing away from the battlefield. The general finally tracked down Lee seeking an answer for the fleeing troops. "What is the meaning of this, Sir? I mean to know the meaning of this disaster and confusion," General Washington demanded.

Lee answered hotly, "By all means Sir, American soldiers cannot fight British grenadiers!"

Washington shook his head in disgust. "For now, I relieve you of your command," he decreed. "Now where are Wayne's forces?" Washington looked around for the distinguished general.

"He did not retreat, Sir," Lee spat.

"I pray that he is all right," Washington muttered as he looked nervously down the road. He knew the general was reckless at times and would fight to accomplish the goal—even without reinforcements.

General Wayne now stationed his men at Point of the Woods, a neck of trees not far from Monmouth. Sitting on his horse, he faced the intimidating wall of his Majesty's Troops. His heart skipped a few beats at the cadence of the British drums, realizing that his men were outnumbered at least three to one. He called his troops to fall back again, while the Redcoats chased them in hot pursuit. The Continentals pressed on and came upon a sight that drove them on just a little faster: General Greene's forces—a beacon of hope! They happily greeted their fellow Continental troops and reformed their ranks in preparation for the next attack.

The day hurried on and now well past noon, General Knox ordered for the artillery barrage on the British to begin. The British returned fire and the show of cannon fire and flying dirt continued until 4 o'clock.

With the heat climbing to nearly one hundred degrees, and cannonballs whizzing past in all directions, Wayne maneuvered his troops to the middle of the combined Continental Army. The men, exhausted and hot, quietly slipped away one by one to find refreshment from the disgusting, dirty, mosquito infested swamp nearby.

Multiple times the British General Clinton attacked the Continental lines and every time they were driven back by the passionate Americans. The cannon fire continued into the evening. Washington sent two brigades around to attack the British rear. Back and forth fighting ensued, but the British swiftly retreated from the persistent American forces.

"Sir! We need to press on! We can crush them!" Wayne exclaimed, galloping over to Washington, who was overlooking the battlefield.

A sweaty, tired Washington responded, "No. It is not wise. The men are beat out with heat and fatigue." Wayne started to protest but looked around at the exhausted soldiers gathering what little strength they had left to reform ranks. They needed rest. General Washington's word went out and the weary soldiers gratefully began to set up camp.

GENERAL ANTHONY WAYNE: STORMING HELL, ANTHONY WAYNE'S FIGHT

Continental Camp
5 July 1778

General Wayne gazed at the orange rays of the setting sun shooting out over the Continental camp. He sat down at his desk, his belly full of the evening meal. Picking up the quill pen once again on the writing desk in the corner of his tent, he began penning a letter about the events of the past fortnight.

My Dear Polly,

Exactly eight days ago, His Excellency brought it upon us to attack the British baggage train. We marched for three hours at dawn, and we were ready to ambush them. Then, before we could pounce, the Queen's Rangers attacked us first. When success and victory was at hand, General Lee retreated.

It was a foolish move. I cannot decide if Lee is a coward or just completely insane.

I wonder if he was for the worse cause—was he secretly working with the British?

It was later when I retreated, dear Polly, and I stationed my men at the Point of the Woods. We had just taken post when the enemy began their attack with horse, foot, and artillery. I called to fall back once again, and when we reached the main army, we started pounding with the artillery. It was terribly hot; the men drank from filthy water. One brave lass, Mary Ludwig Hayes, got clean water for her husband's artillery brigade and when he fell, she took over his position, even braving the cannon fire of the enemy.

Attack after attack and the British could not break our lines, and the Redcoats retreated.

Washington decided not to engage as they retreated, and in the morning, they left swiftly to escape to another battle.

Later, on the fourth of July, the caitiff Lee was rightfully court-martialed and drummed out of the army. The slimy liar then had the audacity to blame me for the loss at Monmouth. This might surprise you, my dear Polly, for I don't do this ever, but I challenged him to a duel. The coward declined on the grounds that he was already wounded from a different draw.

Despite the fact that I have been working diligently for His Excellency, I have not been promoted yet. I have not been pleased with Madame Fortune lately.

May this letter find you in good health.
Ant'y

A Sandy Beach, New York
Early July 1779

As the bright noon sun glistened off the turquoise waters of the Hudson, Anthony Wayne galloped along the burning sand on his brown stallion, pondering over the events of the last year.

He was getting weary of military life and Washington knew it. His Excellency had informed him that if he would press the state assembly for more food and clothing for the Pennsylvania Line, then he would receive a temporary discharge for the winter in Philadelphia. He had agreed and had so impressed the state assembly with his wit and logic that they recommended a promotion. Madame Fortune did not look upon the matter right away. With the deed done, Wayne headed off to Philadelphia to drink the winter away. He then traveled to Waynesborough, his lavish estate outside of Philadelphia. He smiled as he recalled how much he enjoyed the time with his family, especially his wife Polly, so much so that he had contemplated making his leave permanent.

His horse slowed to a trot as Wayne's thoughts then turned to the beginning of his military career, when he marched off hoping for great adventures beyond the horizon. He shook away the memories from the battle of Monmouth. The death and dying was taking its toll and he longed for the peace he had found at Waynesborough. But the glory of the battlefield still called to him, he remembered, and he had returned to the service of General Washington. His Excellency promoted him to oversee a light infantry corps, a total of two thousand men. Once again seeking to please Madame Fortune, Wayne urged his ride on looking for a battle to win for His Excellency.

And that he did. About fourteen miles from the camp at West Point, General Wayne rode his tawny stallion onto an emerald hill and looked across the glittering water of the Hudson. There he spotted a rock outcropping; he guessed about one hundred-fifty feet high. Perched on top was a small fort occupied by the British, and down below were gun boats, cannons gleaming.

Wayne smiled, his excitement mounting. He reigned his horse around swiftly, and raced away, a plan forming in his head.

Continental Camp, West Point, New York
One Week Later

Back at the camp, General Wayne and General Washington mapped out a plan to take Stony Point, the Fort upon the 150-foot cliff. For the past week, Wayne had sent scout after scout to check out the fort. He even sent Captain Allen McLane with a white flag of surrender to the fort. McLane was taken in and interrogated. The fort's commander, Colonel William Johnston, was so sure that the fort was impenetrable, that he did not even blindfold McLane and let him go afterwards. Wayne now had vivid details of the inside of the fort. Stony Point lived up to its name, for it was indeed a point made of stone. At the bottom of the cliff were abatis and redoubts defending the main fort high above. Inside was a wall with cannon lined up and facing out, threatening all invaders with a grim glare. Barracks and commanders' quarters completed the fortress. Captain McLane also learned that Colonel Johnston had not yet completed the western wall. Wayne looked forward to taking advantage of that fact.

A local further informed Wayne that a sandbar became visible around midnight across the river to Stony Point, which was crucial news.

With the plan set, Washington told Wayne, "These are my general ideas for a surprise attack, but you are at liberty to depart from them at any instance where you think they may be improved or changed for the better." And thinking again he added, "Remember, you don't have to go through with this. It is very risky."

Wayne looked his commander in the eye and committed adamantly, "Sir, give me permission, and I will storm hell itself for you."

Washington chuckled slightly at the persistence and loyalty of this General. "Let's just start with Stony Point first."

Near Stony Point
15 July 1779, 11 pm

Wayne sat down at his writing desk and buried his head in his hands. He desperately wanted to write to Polly but was so preoccupied with the upcoming attack and the thought of his possible death that he believed Polly wouldn't recover from hearing such news. He instead wrote to his good friend, Sharp Delany.

DEAR MR. DELANY,

This will not meet your eye until the writer is no more. I am waiting near the hour and scene of carnage. I have died in defense of the country. This would not have happened if Congress had supported the Continental Army. If ever any prediction was true, it is this, and if ever a great or good man was surrounded with a choice of difficulties, it is General Washington. For if I die, Washington may take more dangerous risks, and if he fails, Congress will dismiss him. That, by all means, should not happen. But, even if I live or die, America will triumph. Please take care of the education of my children Isaac and Margretta, and please see to the care of Polly, who may not survive the news of my death.

I am called to supper, but where to breakfast, either within the enemy's line in triumph or in the other world!

Ant'y Wayne

General Wayne rose unsure from the chair, the questions swirling in his head, almost taunting him. He glanced at his pocket-watch. It was time to march.

Wayne strode through the ranks dividing the light corps into three columns. Colonel Butler was to take 500 men on the left, attacking from the north, and Colonel Febiger would take the right with 600 men, creating the crucial distraction for the attack. Colonel Hardy with Wayne was to take the middle with the rest of the troops. The men were to fix bayonets with no gunpowder in their muskets, for this was to be a complete surprise attack, just like British General Grey on the horrendous night of Paoli.

Anthony's heart sat in his throat, sweat dripping off his forehead. He tried desperately to wipe it off without anyone noticing, willing himself to calm down. He was going to win the fort for His Excellency, and he would survive as well. As the men marched silently in the darkness, he recalled the words of his letter. "But even if I live or die, America will triumph!"

This is why he was doing this. He recalled the sweaty, bloody battlefields of summer and the agonizing drill camps of winter. America was a dream worth fighting for—for his children, for all the children of Patriots, for freedom and security. Tonight, he would win not only for his country, but for Polly and his children as well.

It was time. He gave the signal. Twenty men silently raced across the dark sandbar to dismantle the wooden abatis blocking their path. Following these were 120 hand-selected soldiers, carrying spontoons which resemble a pike and spear. Sprinting through the abatis debris, they charged into the redoubts to take out the sentries stationed there. They then started the treacherous climb, racing up the 150-foot rock face, sharp edges cutting into their hands. Not one cried out. They pressed on, eager to surprise the enemy. *One hundred feet left, 75 feet, 50 feet,* they counted as they swarmed up the moonlit cliff.

Up on the fort, British Colonel Johnston woke to yelling and firing flintlocks. He raced from his quarters. "Shoot south!" he ordered, wildly pointing toward Wayne's main force.

As the musket balls flew, a British soldier by the name of John Doe took aim and shot. His bullet raced through the air toward the light infantry corps below.

General Wayne surveyed his advancing army and glanced up, none too soon. Doe's shot was streaking towards him. He ducked just as the bullet grazed the top of his head. His eyes glazed over in agony, and he passed out.

The sharp pain at the top of his head woke Wayne like a gunshot. He called to the soldiers standing near him. "March on, boys. Carry me into the fort! For should the wound be mortal, I will die at the head of the column." The soldiers lifted their dedicated leader to his feet.

At the same time, Colonel Louis Fleury, a French engineer in Febiger's regiment, climbed over the wall, stabbing with his bayonet while dodging the blunt thrusts of his enemy, and reached the British flag at the center of the fort.

"THE FORT IS OURS!" Fleury yelled in his thick French accent. He ripped down the Union Jack as the Continental troops poured into the fort.

"HUZZAH!" yelled the soldiers outside, the resounding cheers rejuvenating them as they pressed harder to the fort with renewed spirits. British Colonel Johnston realized he had met his match and surrendered the post.

With the fort taken, General Anthony Wayne then ordered the cannon turned onto the British below at King's Ferry. The message was soon received by the startled gunboats. They sailed away as the cannonballs once used by their own splashed into the water beside them in attack.

After the battle, Wayne ordered the storehouse opened, exclaiming, "Why take a fort if you cannot enjoy the bounty?" With a cheer, the soldiers gladly obeyed, gathering the spoils to feast.

The next morning, Anthony Wayne reclined at the table with his senior officers already having enjoyed their looted breakfast of dried meat, pickles, bread, and hot chocolate, an expensive drink most had never tasted. They now savored the sweet drink as they rejoiced over their victory.

Wayne lifted his glass in toast, "To all the brave men who fought and died in the name of liberty, for the future of our children, and for America!"

"To America!" The echo resounded off the surrounding walls and into the morning. They took a long drink.

Wayne sat back. *To America,* he thought and took another swig.

II. EUROPEAN SYMPATHIZERS

BARON JOHANN DE KALB

BY HANNAH SCHNEIDER

THE EPIC STORY OF AMERICA 1777-1779

LA VICTOIRE, ATLANTIC OCEAN
30 APRIL 1777

I need to confide in someone, and a journal makes the best listener.
We find ourselves at sea now, the 'we' being myself, Baron Johann de Kalb of German descent, with an idealistic French aristocrat, the Marquis de Lafayette. We are heading to America, the former British Colonies now in rebellion.

Perhaps I should explain why I am on this ship, La Victoire. The young Marquis desires to join the Patriot army and fight against the British, as do I. We were promised commissions in their army as major generals by an American diplomat named Silas Deane. He came to France to secure French aid to help his fellow Americans. Alas, King Louis XVI is not yet prepared to fight the British and so must make the enemy believe that France wants peace while preparing for war. To keep up appearances with the British, he even forbade French soldiers from joining the Continental Army. As such, we snuck away.

I have no doubt the French king has discovered our flight by now, and I imagine his fury. He already forbade the Marquis from embarking, but my young friend is both wealthy and creative. When no one would take him, he purchased a ship to take himself! I applaud his ingenuity. It will serve him well on the field of battle.

The reason I wish to fight alongside the Americans is because I am no stranger to this land. A few years back, when the war known to the Patriots as the French and Indian War raged, I visited them in disguise on behalf of the French army to determine their mood toward their mother country. It was difficult to see, but it was there—resentment. When England goaded them on with that nasty little taxing business, I predicted their tempers would flare. And here we are. The former colonies are in full-blown rebellion.

Now I must turn my attention from the past and focus on the present. The clouds look a bit angry; I pray they pass over us, so we can make good time. At present, we are scheduled to land in South Carolina in twelve days, if the wind stays fair.

De Kalb's Cabin, Valley Forge, Pennsylvania

BARON JOHANN DE KALB

1 January 1778

I'm afraid I have been neglecting my journal lately. It has been so busy around here, getting supplies and recruiting soldiers, it's impossible to keep up a steady writing habit.

Lafayette and I made it safely to the colonies, and on time, too. At first their Congress was suspicious of us and denied us our commissions. Apparently, Silas Deane was handing out too many commissions to European soldiers, and many were lying about their capabilities. Eventually we both became major generals, though mine took a bit longer than the Marquis's. My strongly worded letter helped.

The colonists are most certainly losing, though none say it aloud. The British have taken the Patriot capital, Philadelphia, and keep beating us back. Now that winter is upon us, both armies have broken away. At first, I was grateful for the respite, but now I am not!

We are wintering at Valley Forge, a position near Philadelphia but not too close. The troops have erected two-thousand log cabins, stripping the surrounding land of trees. Each cabin houses twelve people. In such close quarters, disease in one man means his bunkmates become infected too, even though they mightn't show it right away. Typhoid, influenza, and dysentery run rampant.

And if those weren't bad enough, Mother Nature has inflicted smallpox on us as well! Smallpox is a ruthless killer. It tears its way through the camp, caring not for the poor victims with wives and children. Smallpox has only recently been introduced to the colonies, so the colonists have not yet developed immunity. One in three of those infected perish. More than one thousand have lost their lives already.

General Washington, thankfully, is immune. He already had a mild case of smallpox as a youth in Barbados. At least I know smallpox will not take him! Now he wishes to make his army immune as well. It is a gamble, but it may be the key to ending this outbreak. He has called doctors to Valley Forge to inoculate the soldiers. Inoculation will expose a soldier to just a few smallpox germs. If their body works fast enough, it can kill the smallpox and defeat the vile disease. Of course, if their body does not work fast enough, we could lose them.

According to figures, about one in fifty patients have died from inoculation. Risky, but it is better than taking a bout with the real thing. I might ask to be inoculated myself. I would be out of commission for a while but seeing how the British have not tried to attack us up here, it would be worth it.

I believe the army is so sick because of our location. Valley Forge may be a strategic position, but the housing is poor. We had to construct these two thousand huts ourselves, and furthermore, the foraging opportunities are lacking. The men survive on baked flour and water; they call it 'fire cake'. It tastes terrible.

We are lacking in everything. At least half of the army is unfit for duty for lack of shoes and proper winter coats. Their feet are cut and sore, and many have frostbite. They have invented a sorrowful chant. 'No meat, no soldier.' Some have added on more phrases, chanting 'no coat' or 'no shoe.'

I must go now. The soldiers are complaining again.

De Kalb's Cabin, Valley Forge, Pennsylvania
10 March 1778

It seems I forgot about my journal again. Despite it being winter, I have certainly been kept on my toes.

Another general named Thomas Conway proposed an attack on Canada, to liberate it from British hands. He reasoned that taking Canada would prevent the British from invading from the north and provide us with more supplies.

My friend Lafayette was appointed to lead the invasion, and he insisted on having me as his second-in-command. We began to put together the operation, but it was no good. It was obvious we couldn't take Canada with the measly group of soldiers the army could spare. And the gunpowder supply was even worse. There was no way our men could fire off more than three rounds of bullets. If we had gone ahead anyway... It was doomed to fail.

I sometimes wonder why Conway suggested it. Gates also strongly pushed for an invasion. They both also highly recommended Lafayette... And when Lafayette asked for me to accompany him, they were so on board it was suspicious. I wonder if they're up to something. Promotions, maybe?

Anyway, the hour is late. I should go to sleep for another day tomorrow. I'll try to write again soon, but you never know what turmoil will arise.

Drill Field, Valley Forge, Pennsylvania
31 March 1778

Well, I tried. So much for once a week. I write this entry not in my cabin, but on a hill overlooking the drill field. A group of soldiers is marching, or at least trying to. One of them just stumbled, throwing the whole line out of order.

Baron De Steuben has yelled himself hoarse; he is from Prussia and is now the drillmaster for the army. He arrived in Valley Forge on 23 February. Immediately he set to straightening the camp. He is a man after my own heart; this army needs some organization.

De Steuben had the soldiers first clean their cabins, inside and out. He changed the position of the latrines to point downhill and moved the kitchens uphill. And of course, he drilled the troops in maneuvers nonstop.

The quicker-learning units can now march in unison, load, and fire muskets efficiently, and quickly affix bayonets to charge without breaking rank. The other units are still attempting to charge in an even line. Currently, this unit is the only one struggling. De Steuben is spending increased time trying to whip them into shape.

He's moved from yelling in English to ranting in German, but only I can understand him. He is a native speaker of German, but he knows little English; I will translate a conversation from a few days back into English.

"This army is a disaster," De Steuben complained. "There is no order. How can they defeat the enemy if they scatter at the first gunshots?"

"They have much spirit," I offered. "At least they are trying to rebel. Anyone with less courage would let the British lion take their money and freedoms."

"Courage and spirit are well and good, but courage does not win the battle. Skill wins the battle. And here I see none." De Steuben waved his arms to illustrate the soldiers milling around the fires. "If they organize themselves, skill will follow. If they put spirit into that, they shall have no problems!"

I tried to defend the army, but I could see De Steuben's point. This ragtag army would need a miracle to survive the year. They would need a miracle to survive each battle! Hopefully, De Steuben's changes will be that needed miracle.

Valley Forge, Pennsylvania
6 May 1778

Welcome news has arrived today! I simply must jot this down before General Washington calls me. We have an alliance with France! Finally! The American agents over the ocean have been working hard, and they have succeeded! The French are coming! The Continental Army is jubilant!

Washington called for a parade to celebrate. The whole army will gather for it. I will be commanding the second line on the left.

The snow is thawing, and the birds are singing, the French are coming to help us, we have more supplies and recruits, and our army is professionally trained. Our miracle has come!

This year is looking up. The British need to look out because the Americans are coming after them! We might actually pull this revolution off.

I pray that we win this impossible war, striking down the British tyranny and establishing a free nation. I pray that it will be a great country, where everyone will have liberty. I pray that everyone will have the freedom of speech and religion as well as fair trial and representation. I pray that everyone in this future nation can be heard. I pray for a united nation, one nation, under God, with liberty and justice for all.

I fear it is too much to hope, but there is always a chance. Maybe if I write it, it will become true.

FRENCH GENERAL LAFAYETTE

BY JOY ELIZABETH TARDY

THE EPIC STORY OF AMERICA 1777-1779

*B*onjour! My name is Ophelie, the Golden Retriever of Marie-Joseph-Paul-Yves- Roch-Gilbert du Motier, le Marquis de Lafayette. I shall refer to my master as Lafayette. Now let us travel to the years 1777-1779.

The Docks, London, England
February 1777

Lafayette's family was *furieux because* of his strong desire to help the American Colonists gain their independence. However, they supported his *beau-frère*, Louis Vicomte de Noailles, in serving under General George Washington. In hopes of getting the seemingly foolish idea out of Lafayette's head, his in-laws told him to go visit the *grand-oncle* Emmanuel Marie Louis de Noailles, the newly appointed French ambassador in England.

Grand-oncle Emmanuel's Mansion, London, England
February 1777

When Lafayette walked into his *grand-oncle's* parlor, I was waiting patiently by the door. For weeks *grand-oncle* Emmanuel said my new owner was coming. At last I would finally have a permanent home. When the humans greeted each other with a kiss on each cheek, I thought, "Ewww!" *Grand-oncle* Emmanuel told Lafayette about the upcoming events while he stayed in London getting acquainted with the lords and ladies.

Windsor Palace, London, England
February 1777

For two weeks Lafayette bowed and smiled to the courtiers of the King's Court. When he came back to the house exhausted, he was bored of this lifestyle, but a hilarious thing happened when Lafayette was presented to King George III. Several days later came the night of the big ball thrown in his honor. Then a note arrived from his friend, Baron de Kalb. *La Victoire* was ready to set sail. When Lafayette left at once, his *pauvre grand-oncle* had to explain why the guest of honor did not attend his ball.

Baron de Kalb's Home, Chaillot, France
April 1777

My master and I took the next boat back to France, where we went to the village of Chaillot to hide. Lafayette's friend Baron de Kalb arranged for us to live in the gardener's house. Lafayette wrote letters to his family that he was going to America. Now he was not just going against family wishes, but also against King Louis XVI's new law banning noblemen from going to America.

Bordeaux, France
1-20 April 1777

La Victoire set sail today, despite the fact that the king forbade Lafayette from leaving. He sent a messenger in pursuit of Lafayette, to bring him back to France. Lafayette and I arrived in Marseille. Lafayette sent a letter to the prime minister begging to continue to America. While waiting for a reply, Comte de Broglie sent Vicomte de Mauroy to convince Lafayette that the king was only pretending to be mad because of the law. When the driver stopped to change the horses, Lafayette snuck away disguised as a courier and bought a Thoroughbred horse, which he named *Questa Gloire* meaning "one who seeks glory."

Major Benjamin Huger's Home, South Carolina
13 June-1 July 1777

After almost two months at sea, we finally landed in South Carolina. Our group walked or rode with the assistance of slaves to Major Benjamin Huger's house. Everyone was delighted to be on land again. When we arrived, I was delighted to find that the major also had dogs. After Mr. Huger made sure all the French officers were friends, the men were invited to come in, eat, and spend the night. I slept and ate with the other dogs. The next day a pilot was hired to sail the *La Victoire* around the British blockade and into a port. The major gave the men three horses, which the men took turns riding on the 300-mile journey to Philadelphia. We traveled through swamps and woods. On 1 July, I received a message from Nelly the bulldog in France with Adrienne, Lafayette's wife. Jolie the bald eagle delivered the note. Lafayette and Adrienne had a new daughter, Anastasi. When Lafayette got the letter, he was overjoyed at the birth of a new child, but disappointed it was not a son.

Philadelphia, City Tavern
27-31 July 1777

Today we reached the city of Philadelphia! The men hope to serve in the army soon. However, when the French officers visited Congress, they were surprised by their reception. The men of Congress were in no mood to accept any more French officers, because most of the men that had come previously were there only to seek fame and fortune. Lafayette was not so easily deterred from his dream, so he proposed that because he had financed the whole journey to America.

Congress owed him two favors. The first was to serve at his own expense and the second was that he be a volunteer officer. Congress allowed him to serve, and the title of Major General was honorary of the commission Silas Deane had given him. On July 31, Lafayette met General George Washington at the City Tavern in Philadelphia. To Lafayette, Washington appeared tired and stressed. Congress was annoyed that Washington hadn't yet attacked the British, and his counsel and reasoning was falling on deaf ears. Washington was annoyed that there was another French officer, because his experience with the current officers from France was that they were snobby and refused to comply with his orders.

Because Lafayette was of noble birth, Washington realized that being kind might improve the relationship with France. So, he invited Lafayette on a tour of the camp. Washington said, "We are shy to show ourselves to an officer who has just left the French army."

Lafayette replied, "I am here to learn, not teach."

Washington then offered to let him and me stay in his quarters.

Battle of Brandywine, Outer Philadelphia
11 September 1777

The battle wasn't going well. The British had crossed the rushing ford, but the American army was still trying to hold their ground. Then the British pushed forward with such force the American lines were broken and the retreat was starting in the most unorderly fashion. Lafayette rode Questa in the battle trying to halt the retreat. He jumped off to rally the troops while holding his sword and shouting, "Forward, men!"

As he ran forward, he was hit in the leg by a bullet, but he didn't notice until an aide told him his boot was full of blood. The aide grabbed the nearby Questa and lifted Lafayette onto the horse. Just then General Washington galloped up and got the men into an orderly retreat headed for the bridge at Chester Creek.

Sun Inn, Bethlehem, Pennsylvania
September 12-November 1777

Lafayette started the day by writing to his wife.
Chere Adrienne,
I was wounded in the Battle of Brandywine. The American army stood their ground nobly. The worst part was that we lost the battle. Don't be too worried about my injury. Please kiss my baby girls hundreds of times for me.
Affectueux,
Gilbert

He also sent letters to the officials in France, risky because he had disobeyed orders to stay in Paris. On 3 October 1777, Jolie flew from

France to Bethlehem. Adrienne and Lafayette's first daughter Henriette died. Only Questa and I would know. Sadly, it would be some months before Lafayette would find out. He was impatient to help General Washington especially after the loss at German Town.

Gloucester, New Jersey
November 1777

Lafayette volunteered to go with General Greene on a surprise raid, leading 400 men. He wanted to get a closer look at the British camp to estimate the people, guns and cannons, and fortifications. After he saw the size of Cornwallis's army and weaponry, he was ready. The attack caught the Hessian soldiers off guard. Lafayette's men pursued for a mile, capturing sixty Hessians before General Cornwallis sent his grenadiers. When Lafayette and his men regrouped with General Greene, one man died and five were wounded. Greene sent a glowing report about Lafayette and the attack to General Washington.

1 December 1777

Major General Lafayette is the new title, but most people called him "our Marquis." The victory from the surprise attack took away all prejudice General Washington had against foreign officers. Washington then wrote a letter to Congress urging them to give Lafayette a command. Once Lafayette was appointed as a Major General, Washington gave him the pick of any regiment to command. Out of all the regiments Lafayette chose the Virginia regiment because he loved General Washington so much. Sadly, he also got a letter from Adrienne telling him their daughter passed away

January 1778

Much has already happened in this new year. General Gates and Conway are determined to exploit Lafayette's determination to gain glory and his hatred towards England. As an insult to General Washington the Board of War appointed Lafayette the Commander of the Northern Forces. The rank was equal to General Washington's, which meant Lafayette would no longer answer to Washington, but to Congress and the Board of War. It named General Conway as his second in command and chief adviser. Indignantly Gilbert told the Board of War he would never accept an appointment that made him independent from his beloved General Washington and furthermore he would rather have the title of aide de camp to General Washington.

Even though Washington was deeply hurt at this betrayal by his men, he wrote a letter to Lafayette telling him he would rather have him in that title than any other man. Reluctantly Lafayette accepted the command unaware of the men's real motives for giving him that position. Lafayette requested the specifics on the invasion to Canada such as how many men he would be commanding and written details on the invasion plan. He also made two important demands. The first was that he got to pick all his officers and the second was the most shocking. He wanted to remain under the command of General Washington, which made no sense because his command was independent of Washington. Congress and the Board of War agreed to do this even though it insulted General Conway and Gates, but they didn't want to risk France not joining in an alliance. Lafayette worried about the invasion in Canada during the dead of winter, but General Gates says the British will never see it coming.

Albany, New York, and Canada
3 February- 10 March 1778

Today the company headed out to meet the rest of the men we have been promised. It has been bitterly cold, and it only gets worse as we head north. In a letter Lafayette wrote to General Washington, "I go on very slowly, sometimes drenched by rain, sometimes covered in snow, and not entertaining handsome thoughts about the projected incursion into Canada." When they arrived at the spot the troops were *supposed to be*, no one was there Lafayette realized he had been tricked.

He wrote an enraged letter to President Laurens of the Board of War demanding new instructions. He then looked around to see where he could set camp. He received new orders and he and his officers settled outside of Albany. They discovered twelve-thousand more troops living near anarchy.

Albany, Canada, and Johnson Town, New York
11 March-22 April 1778

Lafayette tired of waiting for new orders about Canada and sent a letter to the Board of War essentially challenging General Gates. Soon after General Philip Schuyler was asked to go and negotiate with the native tribes. Congress asked General Lafayette to accompany him because the tribes had once been loyal to France. Many still had a high esteem for the French, so bringing Lafayette was a political move. The Board of War hoped that having a high-ranking French Officer would encourage the Indians to join in freeing the colonies. General Schuyler and Lafayette and some other officers traveled four hundred miles to get to Johnson Town where the six Indian tribes were waiting by the Mohawk River. From the Senecas, Cayuga, Oneidas, Onondagas, Mohawks, and Tuscarora five hundred men, women, and children attended the meeting. The tribes were excited that there was a French general with them. The negotiations were extremely successful, the tribes signed a paper promising to be loyal to the colonists as well as presenting gifts of mirrors, brandy, rum, and French gold coins. They also adopted Lafayette as a warrior named *Kayewala*.

Lafayette then returned to Albany. While he had been away, two letters were delivered; one letter from President Laurens and the other from General Gates. President Laurens apologized for the issue that had happened and assured Lafayette that his reputation would not be marred. The letter from General Gates said that Lafayette would be transferred back to General Washington's regiment and General Conway would become the Commander-in-Chief of the Northern Forces. Lafayette sent a threatening letter to President Laurens and Congress that he did not believe Conway competent of leading the army. And if they allowed him to take over, he would look upon himself as ill-used. Lafayette's letter also implied he had more influence over France than he did. Shortly after that letter Congress sent a message that the Northern Force Command was no longer needed.

18-20 May 1778
Battle of Barren Hill, Pennsylvania

Lafayette rode swiftly from Valley Forge to Barren Hill to get strategic information about the British position. Washington gave him instructions to keep moving and never camp in the same place twice, so that the British wouldn't have the chance to capture or kill him. He and Colonel John Laurens camped on Barren Hill, which was halfway between Valley Forge and Philadelphia. Lafayette then made an almost fatal mistake of camping two nights on Barren Hill. A deserter from Gilbert's regiment went to General William Howe and told him where General Lafayette and Colonel Laurens camped. Howe was excited to learn that they were nearby and being the prideful man, he was determined to win back the favor of the Crown, plotting to capture the Marquis. Lafayette was oblivious to the plan but was rescued by a local physician who happened to hear the British Army go by his home. He hurried to warn Lafayette and help him escape. When General Howe and Clinton arrived at Barren Hill it was empty. Lafayette and his men made it back safely to Washington out of breath and a bit sheepish. Instead of scolding the embarrassed Lafayette, Washington praised him for cleverly escaping capture.

1 January-11 February 1779
North Sea

Before Lafayette and I could return to France, he became extremely ill. We thought he was going to die, but George Washington and his personal physician attended to him and declared he would live. On 11 January 1778, we boarded the *USS Alliance* and set sail for

France! We encountered several storms that shook the ship. Lafayette became so violently seasick that he thought he would die. Once the storms passed, we all thought that danger would be averted, but some men on board plotted mutiny. The ship was near England, and King George III had offered a large reward for the capture of the Marquis and anybody who helped the colonies.

The men planned to put all the men returning to France in irons and sail the ship into an English port and collect the reward for all the men. Their mistake was telling an Irish man about the plan when he was a loyal Patriot. The man told Lafayette who then told the captain of the ship. That night several men were clapped into the irons that they had plotted to put the Patriots into. Several days later the USS *Alliance* sailed into the French harbor and the mutineers were put into prison. Lafayette then rode to the Palace of Versailles. He went to his cousin the *Prince de Poix de Noailles'* house and he was having a *carnival*. When he entered the room, Lafayette instantly became the center of attention.

Palace of Versailles and Hôtel Noaille, France
12 February-April 1779

The *prince de Poix* escorted Lafayette to the Palace to visit Prime Minister Maurepas. The Prime Minister debriefed Lafayette on what had happened while he was gone, then ordered him to stay at the Hôtel Noailles under house arrest. When Lafayette walked in the door *cher* Adrienne came running and collapsed into his arms. It was so sweet to see them together. While waiting to be forgiven by the Crown, Lafayette and the Duc d'Ayen composed a letter suitable to send to King Louis XVI begging his forgiveness. The King enjoyed the letter so much he invited Lafayette to see him for a personal audience. Lafayette had been forgiven and now used his influence to help the colonies get supplies that they were in desperate need of. When Benjamin Franklin arrived in France, he took a strong liking to the Marquis de Lafayette. As the colonies began to struggle more, Franklin and Lafayette pressed the king and prime minister more urgently to help the colonies. By now Lafayette deeply missed his best friend, General Washington. He started to plan his return to help the American cause. The happy news—Adrienne is pregnant!

June-24 December 1779
Hôtel Noailles and Palace of Versailles, France

Lafayette paced around his room for hours. He is so eager to return to America. He is also waiting for the French Navy to come to the aid of the Americans. The rest of the summer and fall was a blur for Lafayette. Now it is Christmas Eve, and he is still planning to return to America. Adrienne sent a letter by Nelly the bulldog that a healthy baby boy was born. "The occupation of paternity is so sweet. Give in to them. They can only be good." Lafayette was so excited for an heir to the Lafayette and Noailles fortune. He spent a few days with the family and named the boy George Washington du Motier de Lafayette. Then he went back to planning his triumphant return to America.

FRENCH GLOSSARY

AFFECTUEUX- LOVING
cher- dearest, dear
furieux- furious
beau-frère- brother-in-law
grand-oncle- great uncle
jolie- pretty
gentil-gentile- kind
Opheli - help, aid
pauvre- poor
Questa Gloria- one who seeks glory

BARON DE STEUBEN: TO FORGE AN ARMY

BY MIKAYLA BADENHORST

Prussia, January 1777

Snowflakes drifted down and fell on my outstretched tongue. Oh, how I love it here. I never wanted to leave glorious Prussia. I sighed as my owner interrupted my serene moment.

"Azor!" he called. "Come here!"

I wasn't about to move. This was my favorite spot, and he was forcing me to leave for a foreign land.

"Azor!" the voice boomed again. "Come here!"

Lamenting, I turned as my master, Friedrich Wilhelm Ludolf Gerhard Augustin de Steuben, hopped in the carriage. I couldn't believe he was so relaxed about leaving Prussia, formerly called Germania by Julius Caesar. He petted me and smiled, a rarity these days.

"How *dare* he smile while I'm so depressed," I sulked.

I already missed Prussia, and we hadn't even left yet. Just because *he* couldn't find a stable military job didn't mean that *I* should be forced to leave *my* home and go to a strange country I'm sure I won't like. Ugh!! Sometimes I wish I was a human.

Beaumarchais House, Paris, France
June 1777

The Baron and I strolled through the gardens at our lodgings, admiring the gorgeous fountain, luxurious foliage, and myriad of birds. As we walked along the cobblestone pathway, despite my initial misgivings, my already large middle had happily expanded from eating the rich cuisine. I *liked* France. However, it was too expensive for my master's meager income, and Queen Antoinette's wigs looked like ships sailing on the ocean wearing French colors.

We entered a small courtyard, and I barked as a large man approached. He wore a beaver's tail on top of his long, stringy hair, as well as a long, brown coat over his breeches. He introduced himself as Benjamin Franklin. My master introduced himself in Prussian, but

Dr. Franklin couldn't understand him. So, my master will have to speak in French.

I liked the beaver tail, but noticed Dr. Franklin was quiet and reserved, as if he had been approached one too many times for a military post that he was unable to fund. A second man appeared, introducing himself. I liked Silas Deane immediately. He smiled at the Baron, offering refreshments before starting the interview. Noting my fine physique, Deane called for a servant to bring me a plate of food. I happily settled in, gulping the voracious amount of meat set before me, listening as the interview commenced.

"How do you do, sir?" interrupted the soft voice of a black Newfoundland. "My name is Shadow."

"*Gutentag*, I'm Azor." I whispered, looking up from my plate as she smiled. "You're British!"

"Yes, we are!" interjected a magpie, chattering excitedly. "I'm Nimbus, bird of His Majesty King George III."

"Benjamin Franklin is *my* master," Shadow proudly interjected.

Nodding, I turned my attention back to the Baron and Dr. Franklin, remaining on guard in case they were spying for King George. All was going well until Benjamin Franklin refused to pay for the Baron's passage to America.

"Congress has not authorized me to release money to fund any trips for foreign officers seeking to gain employment by the Americans," he informed the Baron.

Deane sucked in his breath. The Baron's eyes narrowed. I knew what was going to happen, so I quickly gobbled up the rest of my meal.

"I'm not asking for any pay, just travel expenses to America. Good grief, sir! How dare you refuse me this small request." With that, he turned on his heel and marched away with the air of an offended Prussian officer. I hesitated to follow, looking at my master's unfinished plate still on the table.

"Azor!"

Whining, I shrugged to Shadow and Nimbus, reluctantly following my master out the door.

"Ach, these humans. They are so complicated," I muttered.

Atlantic Ocean
October 1777

The ship rocked back and forth as another wave rolled over us. Thunder cracked overhead and lightning lit up the sky. For the first time in my life, I lost my appetite. I nestled close to my master, noting that he looked as scared as I felt. This treacherous trans-Atlantic voyage had already produced two fires and a previous storm. Not a good scenario for a ship ladened with cannons, muskets, mortars, gun powder, and carbines for the Rebels while in British waters.

"Why, oh why, did the Baron have to accept funds for this journey from Mr. Deane and Beaumarchais?" I moaned and rested my seasick head on my paws. "They even lied about my master's pedigree to make him look enticing to the American Congress. From a dog's point of view, I feel that we are barking up the wrong tree."

My stomach settled as the storm abated. Unfortunately, the captain started singing. I howled in protest as he yowled, trying to drown out the hopelessly off-key notes

Portsmouth, New Hampshire
1 December 1777

I've never been so happy to see land than after enduring the long, French-funded voyage across the Atlantic. I jumped overboard and swam to the dock, shivering in the cold water. My master laughed with his aide-de-camp and military secretary but sobered as we were apprehended by shabbily dressed civilians. They mistook the Baron for a Redcoat because of his scarlet jacket, chosen to make an impression.

"How dare someone touch my collar!" I barked as a young lad on the dock grabbed me.

My owner yelled at his aides to stay back while he straightened out this misunderstanding. I looked up at my captor, a skinny boy of about sixteen, wearing a threadbare shirt and breeches. I gazed down at his feet and almost gasped. His shoes were held together by a piece of dirty, knotted string. The dock went silent. My master frowned.

"*Wo ist die Arme?*" The men looked at each other and blushed. They couldn't understand the Baron's thick Prussian accent.

"Uh-oh, this can't be good," I thought.

After the Baron settled the mix-up, we proceeded to our room at a small tavern in Portsmouth. The Baron looked at the portrait of the King of England on the wall, took it down, and replaced it with his godfather, King Frederick I of Prussia. We both welcomed the sight of a familiar face.

Boston, Massachusetts
Mid-December 1777

The Baron was frustrated. General Washington nor Congress had responded to either of his letters seeking employment. Furthermore, no offers of hospitality were extended despite us being extravagantly entertained by Boston's elite. Thus, we are sharing two small rooms never meant to house four grown men and a substantially built Italian greyhound sometimes mistaken for an Irish wolfhound or mastiff.

"Azor, *meine hund!*" he exclaimed in shock, looking at the bill from the landlady. "You've somehow eaten us into debt!"

I looked away, pretending to be intrigued by dust bunnies under the bed. The Baron motioned for me to accompany him, striding to his carriage. I trotted alongside the carriage in the muddy road. Tiring, I jumped through the door of the carriage, landing with a thump on my master and his aide, leaving paw prints on their white breeches. Expecting chastisement, I was pleasantly surprised when he laughed, ruffled my fur, and called me a rascal. I settled in his lap, sighing as arrangements were made to leave Boston

Lancaster and York, Pennsylvania
1 February 1778

The Baron's hands shook as he nervously searched for something to wear to Congress, anxious to define his role within the Continental Army. Finally, after about an hour, he chose a simple blue cloak and black breeches with a white shirt. I laid my head on my front paws to show my approval. I never knew how *long* it could take a human to get dressed. Ha, now I prefer my fur even more.

I followed my master and twenty minutes later we reached Congress. Whining, I nudged my owner's leg, so he ruffled my fur.

"*Ach,* Azor," he said, tapping his fingers against his leg, "I have never been more anxious..."

My owner? Anxious? Never! I whined as we climbed the steps of Congress. My master told me to stay outside. A low growl entered my throat, but I obeyed. I waited in the cold until he burst through the doors with a huge smile.

"*Ach, Azor! Ich bin so glucklich!* I'm so happy! They're letting me volunteer with the Continental Army!"

I smiled as much as a dog could.

Valley Forge, Pennsylvania
23 February 1778

I awoke to the sound of the cook rattling around in the kitchen, preparing the Baron's favorite meal of beef and sauerkraut. Today we were to meet the commander-in-chief of the Continental Army, General Washington. The Baron couldn't eat his breakfast. I was more than happy to help him out.

"Azor, let's go," declared my owner.

I looked up. There he was, resplendent in a thick, black greyhound fur cape. Wait a minute. Greyhound fur? So *that's* where my beloved mother went. I'll think about that later.

After a successful meeting with General Washington, we toured Valley Forge. Suddenly, my owner halted the carriage. The Baron and I walked up to a cabin, and he knocked on a terribly constructed wall. The occupant who answered the blanket-door was none other than my captor from the dock! John Laurens, our translator, told us that his name was Private Joseph Plumb Martin.

"The morale of the army is terrible, and we barely have enough to eat," Laurens translated for Private Martin.

"How is the health of the men? And please tell me that you have uniforms," the Baron asked the private via Laurens.

Private Martin's face dropped.

"Almost 1,500 men have died and, well, our uniforms are the clothes on our backs," explained the private.

The Baron's eyes looked moist, and he struggled to collect himself. I whined and nudged him. He was thinking of his own men in Prussia.

"Danke, mein Sohn. Thank you, son." He left the cabin to continue making his rounds.

The environment was terrible. I saw bloody footprints in the snow, indicating that some men didn't even have shoes. The hospital was horrifying with men lying on the bare floor, most of them appearing practically dead.

My master turned his attention to John Laurens and peppered him with questions. Apparently, the army was severely underfunded. Suddenly, a snowball came flying from around the corner of a cabin and hit the Baron in the shoulder. I froze, expecting him to explode with anger. Surprisingly, he laughed, scooped some snow, and fired a snowball back at the young lad. Other men came out to participate in the fun, welcoming a moment of lightheartedness. John Laurens got nailed by six different snowballs, and a snowball exploded in my face as Private Martin ducked in front of me.

Later, back in our lodgings, I could see that the impromptu snowball fight reminded my master that we were dealing with young men from as young as 15 to as old as 30. Teenage boys who should be at home, not here at war. I thought of the young private, Joseph Plumb Martin. He couldn't have been more than 16 or 17, and I felt sobered. I saw my master climb into bed. For the first time in a while, he prayed.

"Dear God, help me. There's so much to do and so little time. Please, help." Turning over, he fell asleep.

"Lord, help my master, please," I prayed. "He needs it."

The next morning, the Baron began assessing the troops, deciding who to train first. I trotted alongside him as he made his rounds, shivering in the cold. The men peeked their heads out of their cabins as he marched past. At times he would motion to Laurens to translate after asking the men questions.

"Das ist sehr interessant. This is interesting," I remarked to Wilhelm, the Baron's horse.

"Indeed it is," he replied. "I never knew the Baron could survive this cold."

I laughed, remembering the frigid winters in Prussia. "But the camp is so confusing!" I exclaimed, surveying the hodgepodge of cabins randomly laid out.

"Ach, ja. Ich habe kopfschmerzin. I have a headache from traipsing around in circles," replied Wilhelm. I chuckled.

"Azor, let's go!" my master barked as I followed him back to our lodging for the night.

I woke up to footsteps and voices. Today we would begin training the Continental Army. We quickly made our way to General Washington at his headquarters. He smiled and motioned to a young man, Alexander Hamilton. He and John Laurens would translate.

We rallied the men and began their training. I settled in for what would become our routine. Around three hours each day were spent having the men march and march and march. When bored, I played with soldiers waiting for training. Unfortunately, the Baron ordered the men to rearrange the camp in a more orderly manner. There went my playtime.

The training was working. The Baron spent less time on simple things like marching and turned to more important things like commands and keeping order in the troops when under fire. I was surprised when he joked to the troops that the pointy thing on the muskets were used for killing the enemy, not for roasting squirrels on a skewer. Hmmm, roasted squirrel. I needed a snack.

Valley Forge, Pennsylvania

THE EPIC STORY OF AMERICA 1777-1779

One Month Later

"The Continental Army has come far in the past month," I noted to Wilhelm, glancing at my equestrian friend.

"The hospitals have had fewer patients, and the camp environment has gotten better," Wilhelm remarked.

"Our morale has improved even though Congress *still* refuses to give us proper funds," I sighed. "Luckily, my master is recording everything he has been teaching the troops so that a standard can be set."

Valley Forge, Pennsylvania
5 May 1778

"Baron De Steuben is being promoted to Major General," announced General Washington proudly to the troops.

I thought the Baron was going to erupt with happiness and pride as he was attacked with bear hugs from all sides and a cheer went up from the troops. I could relate as my chest swelled with loving pride for my drillmaster.

Monmouth Courthouse, Pennsylvania
June 28, 1778

It was a hot day at Monmouth Courthouse, and the *worst* possible day to have a battle. Men were fainting from the heat. THAT General Charles Lee!! Noticing we were in trouble; he ordered a retreat. I sprinted through the lines of soldiers, biting at their heels as they retreated. Looking up from nipping at yet another soldier's heel, I saw General Washington riding up to General Lee with a fierce look on his face. General Washington had decided to attack the British enroute to New York, exhibiting confidence in his rabble-in-arms-now-turned-professional-army. Retreat was not an option. Psychologically, these soldiers needed a win, a chance to test their newly acquired military skills gained from hour upon hour of drilling in the snow.

Wait! I couldn't find my master! Panicked, I tore through the battlefield, dodging bullets, and bayonets in order to find him.

"Where did *this* professional army come from?" a British officer exclaimed.

Pausing my frantic search, I looked up, seeing an amazing and beautiful sight. The Continental Army had rallied! Spotting De Steuben, I sat on my haunches. Where *did* this come from? Of course, I knew the answer. Knowing how hard they could fight, I believed we would march out as a serious fighting army. In that moment, I *knew* my Baron was the best officer. Of course, I may have some bias.

Congress, Philadelphia, Pennsylvania
March 29, 1779

"Huzzah, three cheers for Major General De Steuben," cried the men as their beloved drillmaster received word of the official adoption of his military recommendations in his book, Regulations for the Order and Discipline of the Troops of the United States, known as The Blue Book. Maybe this book would set a military standard for generations to come.

Ach, the last few years had been *sehr schwierig*, difficult. But with hard work, discipline, and a determined Baron, we managed to forge an army.

CHARLES GRAVIER, COMTE DE VERGENNES

BY ANNA KATE ROBERSON

CHARLES GRAVIER, COMTE DE VERGENNES

Quai d'Orsay, Ministry of Foreign Affairs
Paris, France

The Quai d'Orsay wasn't just a beautiful building in Paris housing France's Ministry of Foreign Affairs. It was the epicenter of trading, alliances, and relations with other countries. On this occasion, it changed the revolution raging half a world away.

A heated discussion took place in a side room between a regal and a rather familiar face. Ministry workers stood outside the door. "Why is he here?" one whispered. "Wasn't he relieved of duty a year ago?" questioned another. They dared not enter, risking the wrath of the king.

"But, but, but Your Majesty!" exclaimed the sophisticated Frenchman. The former Minister of Finance, Anne-Robert-Jacques Turgot, was of short stature and rotund shape with a curled and puffed-up wig. His formal attire suited his status as Baron d'Aulne. "This alliance against the British could result in economic ruin," he exclaimed.

"Indeed, Turgot, it could," said the king, but then he paused. "Or provide an ally—an ally who could provide positive changes for us."

"King Louis, I insist you reconsider making this alliance at once," he argued. "If we enter into this war, it could have devastating consequences on the French economy. In addition, innocent civilians could lose their lives."

"Those are valid concerns, Turgot," King Louis replied. "However, I have news from America." He stood up from his velvet chair and called toward the door. "Comte de Vergennes, please do join us if you don't mind." The door cracked, but no one entered. Then, it flung open, revealing the workers crowded together, eavesdropping on the conversation. At once, they scattered with the exception of a man carrying some books with papers on top.

"Bonjour, Votre Majesté." Charles Gravier, Comte de Vergennes, bowed as he entered the tense high office. Turgot's face turned chili-pepper red, but he refused to acknowledge Gravier.

Turgot turned to the king. "Your Majesty, may I ask why *he* is here?"

"The situation has changed. Mr. Gravier, if you don't mind, please share the letter we received." King Louis gestured with his right hand.

"Thank you, Your Majesty," Gravier replied. "We received news from America inviting us to join the revolution." Though Turgot was relieved of his duties as Minister of Finance in May, Gravier asked King Louis to include him at the meeting. Gravier wanted to prove the same point he made many times since America started the revolution.

"Preposterous!" Turgot exclaimed scornfully. "They haven't been able to defeat Britain in a great battle!"

"That is where you are wrong, my friend," Gravier said with a grin. "The Americans can surely defeat the British. Here is the latest news on the Battle of Saratoga." He laid out a letter sealed with wax before the Monarch.

King Louis opened it and pulled out a parchment. "My, this is remarkable work!" he remarked.

"Well, what does it say?" Turgot asked with a sharp tongue.

"Read it to us," King Louis demanded, thrusting the letter at him.

To the Ministry of Foreign Affairs, Paris, France:

Greatness is not achieved easily, not even freedom too. Freedom is a word, a word people long to hear. But each and every soldier has a desire to have their country gain this freedom in this army. Which is why I am pleased to write this letter of significant news from America. We have gained ground from the British, although the Hessians arrived in New York 15 January 1776. Nonetheless, we have incredible victories to share.

During the Battle of Trenton, General George Washington led his troops to victory against 1,500 Hessians. This occurred on 26 December 1776. The General only lost two men, while the Hessians lost twenty-two men, including their commander, Colonel Johann Rall.

The Battle of Saratoga has now shifted the war in America's favor. The Continental Army, led by General Benedict Arnold, defeated the British and Hessians with at least 8,000 soldiers making up the enemy's ranks. The general and his men surrounded the enemies and forced them to surrender. Those remaining tried to flee but were caught. This battle has now completely boosted American morale of the men fighting, instilling them with every confidence to gain the freedom they so desire.

Wishing great health and prosperity to whomever reads this.

As Turgot folded the letter, the king listed the major American victories over the past year. Then he announced, "This is when we shall begin our alliance with them—now."

"Sire! Once again, I respectfully urge you not to do it," Turgot exclaimed.

"May I remind you, the only reason you are here is because I insisted," interrupted the Comte de Vergennes.

"And why should that be?" Turgot glared at him.

"We need to show people like you that there are things worth fighting for," Mr. Gravier said. "If we can help one gain their freedom, we can provide for many more."

"There are several ways, but we can always leave them to the British, and claim the land west of the former Colonies," Turgot argued.

"Or the British can get it, and they gain more power, and then we could be led back into war with them," Mr. Gravier replied.

"Correct," King Louis said, nodding. "That is why I am announcing our partnership with America." Without hesitation, King Louis hailed the guard to remove Turgot.

"You are leading them to their deaths! The war will come here!" Turgot bellowed as the guard pulled him out the door. The hallway echoed with his shouts as he was marched him away.

Once calm returned to the room, King Louis vowed, "Now then, since the main issue is out the door, let us heed these American cries for our assistance."

French Residence of Benjamin Franklin
Paris, France
March 1778

A cool breeze of early spring could revive any old soul. Charles Gravier, Comte de Vergennes, wore an officer's uniform but removed some layers. He and Benjamin Franklin gathered at Franklin's home in Paris, since Franklin was exiled from Britain. Each prepared a cup of tea with some apple pie, one of Franklin's favorite foods. Then they sat on the velvet chairs.

"So, Dr. Franklin, how is the pie?" Comte de Vergennes asked.

"It is good, though the best do contain whipped cream." Dr. Franklin replied. "Or as people call it here, *crème fraîche*."

"Ah, that would have been a good idea," Comte de Vergennes noted. "I shall do that next time."

"Now," Dr. Franklin said, sitting up straight. "What has been the news from America?"

"Where to begin?" Comte de Vergennes asked.

"Well, I know one thing," Dr. Franklin said with a laugh. "The Americans are giving the British a run for their money."

"Very true, especially since our soldiers should be in or already are in America," Comte de Vergennes said, sipping his tea.

"General Washington is incredibly grateful for all the support. Ammunition, cannons, and manpower are all necessary to defeat Britain," Dr. Franklin replied.

"But of all the things, we must make sure America wins," Comte de Vergennes declared. "If we don't, everything we have worked so hard for will be gone."

"I completely agree with you. General Washington needs to find a future battle to end all battles, cornering the British general and forcing him to surrender," Dr. Franklin replied.

"Wouldn't that be a dream for him, to make it easy to win," Comte de Vergennes said. "Alas, this is life we are discussing."

"Fair, what is the number of troops and supplies heading to America?" Dr. Franklin asked.

"Well, we sent over 44,000 in total," Comte de Vergennes replied. "Mostly sailors, but many soldiers as well."

"My, my!" exclaimed Dr. Franklin. "That is incredible!"

"The alliance will send more artillery as well," Comte de Vergennes added.

"Charles, we have a chance," Dr. Franklin said, his voice shaking. "We have a chance for the Americans to break free."

"Dr. Franklin, there has always been a chance," Comte de Vergennes said. "It is mathematical. You had a chance, but a low percentage. Now you have raised the bar."

"America can become a new nation, with its children as the seeds. These seeds can spread everywhere and conquer the weeds," Dr. Franklin declared, speaking in metaphors.

"Dr. Franklin, are you well?" Comte de Vergennes asked.

"Physically yes, but mentally I am in shock," Dr. Franklin replied.

"I am glad you are well now," Comte de Vergennes replied.

"Thank you, but now we must head to the Ministry," Dr. Franklin said.

"Agreed, if we are to keep this alliance up, we need to work together and persuade for more supplies too," Comte de Vergennes said.

"Well done is better than well said," Dr. Franklin said. The two men headed to the Ministry of Foreign Affairs to fight for freedom abroad.

III. BRITISH LOYALISTS

JOHN ANDRÉ

BY JACOB WALTER

THE EPIC STORY OF AMERICA 1777-1779

Brighton, Tennessee
Modern Day

As I was sneaking from my parents' library and heading outside, Mom shouted, "Kids, will you shelve these books for me right now?"

Aww man, maybe I can't get outside without her noticing, I thought, but then my twin sister Ella shouted back, "Sure, Mom."

Okay, I guess I can shelve them. I rounded the corner of the shelf and then my sister Ella challenged me, "I bet I can shelve these faster than you, Jason."

"Yeah, right," I responded. I've been faster than her since the third grade, but I still enjoyed the race.

"Watch me!" she exclaimed and took off. I ran down the shelves toward the cart with the books to shelve. Once I started running, though, there was a huge thunk and a crash. I looked up just as a book swallowed Ella. Since our Matthews family library is magical, the books allow us to travel anywhere in the world by stepping or falling into them. So, I wasn't freaked out when the book swallowed Ella, since this was normal in our house. I ran over to see which book she'd fallen into. The book was about 1777 to 1779. *Well, I can't let Ella have all the fun.* Then without any further thought I jumped into an open page on the floor.

Head of Elk, Maryland
15 August 1777

"Why, hello young man. You look awfully young to roam these streets by yourself. Do you have family or friends in town?"

I swiveled my head around to a young, handsomely dressed gentleman. I could tell that this was in the early colonial years, because of the way he dressed. He wore white pants, a white shirt, black boots, and a deep blue jacket with a long tail and buttons on the end. He also had an exceptionally large pendant around his neck

JOHN ANDRÉ

bearing the British coat of arms. This pendant and the posh sounds of his spoken English led me to believe that he was British.

"Greetings to you as well. I don't have anyone in town. I got separated from my family, and then they left me here." This was a good excuse for now, since I had no genuine answer to this question. "Also, where are we? I've been wandering for a while and don't know where I am."

"You don't know where you are?" exclaimed the man. "Well, I won't hold that against you. We are in Head of Elk, Maryland."

"Head of Elk? Hmmmm. I have never heard of this place," I muttered. "What year is it?"

"What year is it?" exclaimed an alarmed André. "Are you really that lost?"

"Well, I am curious if a new year had happened while I was lost," I timidly explained. *A new year? I felt like slapping myself. I should have thought of a better excuse than that; he will never believe me.*

"Oh, sorry, I see that I have scared you with my outburst," André apologized, while still looking at me as though I had three heads. "It is not every day that people forget what year it is. The year is 1777, and we live under the glorious reign of His Majesty King George the III."

I must have fallen into a book that takes place during the American Revolution in America! This will be so exciting! I wonder who this man is. What if he is Nathan Hale, John Adams, or Patrick Henry?

"Yes, few have heard of Head of Elk. It is close to the border of Delaware and forty miles northeast of Baltimore. Also, we haven't been properly introduced, I am John André, head of His Majesty's 26th Foot. Who are you?"

"Jason Matthews. It's a pleasure to meet you," I answered. *John André? Really? I wish I could have found someone cooler. I've never even heard of him. I bet Ella got a cool character, like Washington, King George the III, or Benjamin Franklin.* "Mr. André, I was curious if I could go back to your house with you. I have no place to spend the night."

"Jason," André said, deep in thought. "I've always liked that name. If I had a son, I would have named him Jason, which means 'Healer,' and 'the Lord is Salvation.' Of course, you can stay with me; I've plenty of room. I have been very lonely recently. I could really use someone to talk to, and you seem like you have time on your hands while you are waiting for your parents to return. Come on, I'll show you the way. It is just around the block."

"Thanks so much, Mr. André. I greatly appreciate it. I can cook and clean as well if you need me to," I said, trying to sound helpful.

"Don't worry, you won't have to do women's work," André laughed. "We should only be here for a few days, and then we'll move out. Come on, I will get you dinner at the inn, then

As the innkeeper set down our meal, I peppered him with questions so he wouldn't ask *me* any. "Please tell me about yourself, Mr. André. Who were your parents, and where did you grow up?"

"Ahhhh, an inquisitive one, are we?" André chuckled. "I was born to Protestant parents who raised me well in the faith. My mother was from France, and my father was from Switzerland, but I grew up in England."

"Fascinating. Why did you choose military life?" I asked, trying to keep the questions flowing.

"As for the military, it is a long story." André sighed. "My father died in 1769, and in the same year the girl who I loved, Honora Sneyd, denied my feelings for her and broke my heart." André gazed off into the distance for a spell then continued. "Both of these sad events plus the fact that I needed to care for my family led to me to go into the military. I wasn't rich enough to buy my promotion, so I have worked my way to my current position. I am proud of my job and happy that I chose military life."

As the night went on André told me more about himself, about his passions for art, music, and poetry, and his training at renowned schools. He even knew four languages! He kept going all night until he realized how late it was and declared that it was time for bed. As I lay in bed that night I was amazed by André, and all the unique and amazing things about him. I was puzzled, the more I thought about this historical character. I had never heard of him before this adventure, and although he was fascinating there was nothing extraordinary about him. I kept thinking, *What did André do to get in this book? What did he do to impact American history?* Soon after, I fell asleep, but the next morning the questions still troubled me.

Brandywine Creek, Pennsylvania
11 September 1777

"André, you look awful! Are you hurt? There is blood all over your uniform!" I shouted. André had just returned from the Battle of Brandywine at 10:00 p.m. I stayed in André's tent in the British camp all day, listening to the furious battle a couple of miles away. What incredible sounds!

"Today was one of the worst battles in this revolution. Both sides lost so many good men that didn't deserve to die. It was awful. Men were lying dead everywhere, their blood staining the grass." André sat down on his cot, looking fatigued both mentally and physically. He sighed with tears in his eyes, then he looked up and said, "Sorry, I shouldn't have started talking to you that way. Let me tell you what happened from the beginning. Our plan was to split the army into two distinct parts. One under the command of Lord Cornwallis and the other under the command of General Knyphausen. Both parts of the armies would march up to where the Brandywine split. Once they reached the fork one army went up to Chadds Ford Road. The other would cross a hidden ford that the Americans forgot to block from British crossing. This would put the army that crossed the river on the enemy's right flank, and the army that took the road would be directly opposite of the enemy. I was with General Knyphausen and his troops, who were going to cross the ford."

André stood up and started pacing back and forth across his tent, his feet making rhythmic thumps on the earthen floor. "This plan would have worked, too, but with either some amazing spying or luck, Washington foiled our plans. On top of one of the hills overlooking the ford the Americans set up two twelve pounders and then three howitzers at the base. This made passing the Americans almost impossible without the loss of a massive number of lives." André sat back down on his bed.

"General Knyphausen pushed his troops across the river and met with fierce opposition. General Grey came over the top of the hill with perfect timing. The American couldn't fight two armies attacking from opposite sides, and the garrisons were sent running. Grey gave our troops the update that the main battle was underway, and we needed to hurry to help them." André started to pace again, this time slower. With tears in his eyes, he continued, "We rushed to the hill, fought for a long time, and came out victorious. We were so exhausted, though, that we couldn't even chase the Americans. The tally of arms taken is still coming in. Currently, we have seized five French brass guns, a brass six-pounder, and a howitzer, but there is still much unaccounted for."

André stared at me for what felt like a long time, then finally muttered, "Jason, I saw so many dead people out on that field. So many died for what they believed in. So many fought bravely and will never see their loved ones again."

"This is war. People die, people who don't expect to. It is okay," I responded. I put my arm around him. "I'm glad that you survived, though."

New York, New York
5 May 1779

"Jason, where are you?" shouted André from the dining room.

"Coming," I shouted back. I bounded down the stairs to see my good friend. It was late and André had been out all evening at a local tavern. André told me that he was meeting some friends. The way he said friends, though, I could tell that he wasn't spending time together with just *any* friends. The way he had been for the past month as well was strange too. He was always less forthcoming with what he was doing, and he was always watching his back. Yesterday he couldn't sit still. He went and checked the windows four times, and then when I walked in on him at his desk, he jumped sky-high as I set the mail down next to him. André's breathing was quicker, like he had run a marathon, and he was constantly sweating as though he were nervous.

I was uncertain why, but I knew one thing was for sure—something was up.

"Hello, Jason!" André said while taking off his coat and gloves.

"Hi, Mr. André. Oh, an officer from the British forces came while you were away. He gave me a letter from a Peggy Shippen and her friend. Do you know who they are?" I asked innocently. I was testing André to see if either person had anything to do with André's strange behavior.

"Ahhhh. Those are my, uh, friends at the tavern," he stated as though it were the end of the conversation. He couldn't hide a flinch though when I asked him my question.

André flinched and had to make an excuse. I knew it! These two people cannot be just friends from the tavern. Tonight, I will find out who they are.

"Okay, then, I will go back upstairs and read for a little while. I feel very tired," I responded as I began to walk up the stairs. Then I stopped and looked directly at André and said, "Mr. André, you are a great and noble person. I am glad I can look up to you, and that you chose to take me in."

André simply responded with a curt nod, then put his head into his hands. However, as I went to sleep, the sound of him sobbing drifted into my ears.

André must be asleep by now. The last time he moved was an hour and a half ago. I hopped out of bed and snuck downstairs to his office desk. Inside his secret drawer, I found the letter, but certain words were covered by a cut-out picture in the shape of a squash. The area that the paper didn't cover contained a message. So, I laid the sheet over the letter and read.

Dear John André,

It has come to my attention that the British army would much like to take West Point. I will be the commander of West Point soon, and I can hand it over to you. For my services I want 20,000 pounds in cash or jewels. Please discuss with General Clinton. We can communicate through a mutual correspondent, Peggy. You know her from your younger years, so she makes the perfect go-between. No one is suspicious of one of His Majesty's officers out with a fine-looking girl at a tavern. As I close this letter I leave you with one piece of advice—be safe and watch your back.

Benedict Arnold

Benedict Arnold! But he's with the Americans, so André is trying to turn him! André will be on the losing side of the war and he's British, but he isn't bad! I must talk André out of this underhanded scheme. He is a better man than this.

It was late, but it didn't stop me from running back up the stairs. On the way up, though, I slipped and hit my head with a crack. Then the world went black.

Brighton, Tennessee
Modern Day

I blinked in the blinding lights, and then I heard my sister Ella yelling, "Traitor! He's a traitor!"

"Goodness, Ella! What on earth are you talking about?" exclaimed my mother worriedly.

"Benedict Arnold.... I've been with him for several months. He was so kind to me, and everyone undervalued him, and—and—he's a traitor!" Ella vented through anger and confusion.

"Didn't you pay attention to history class?" I commented.

"Jason! Where have you been?" Ella exclaimed while hugging me.

I shrugged. "With John André..." *It sounds like our characters were similar. Both kind, noble gentlemen that did something for which no one will ever forgive them. They don't deserve that judgment though. They made one wrong decision, and they are forever scorned no matter what they do. The people who hate them don't even bother to investigate the real feelings, heart, and character of the person to judge them appropriately. It is so unjust!*

"Who is that?" questioned Ella.

I shrugged. I was still in shock on discovering what André was planning to do. I saw my parents look at one another and share a knowing glance. "Sounds like a story...," said my mother softly while hugging Ella and me ".... for another time."

EDWARD BANCROFT: A PATRIOT NO MORE

BY NAOMI HAYES

THE EPIC STORY OF AMERICA 1777-1779

Edward Bancroft's Home, London, England
8 August 1776

As I sealed the letter addressed to Paris, I thought back to my conversation two weeks ago with Silas Deane.

"Edward, I trust you. I brought you here to Paris for a reason," said Deane, my dear friend and former school teacher. "The diplomatic delegation has called me to represent the colonies to France so that I, or we, may affirm French negotiations. That is, to ally against Britain."

Deane's voice held so much hope as I frowned inwardly, *an alliance against Britain.*

"Oh! That's wonderful, Silas. What can I do?" I maintained my tone.

"Yes, well, first, I ask that you attend the negotiations, but perhaps you could become my assistant and interpret for me?" Deane concluded.

"Hmm. I'm sad to say I cannot attend the negotiations, but I would be pleased to assist you and interpret." I prayed silently, hoping he would not request a reason for my refusal.

"Thank you, Edward! I will be pleased to have your aid."

The thought faded as reality appeared. Why had I refused to attend the negotiations? For I did not agree with the thought of a Franco-American war against Britain, or the thought of American independence for that matter. Still, I served faithfully as Deane's assistant and interpreter. Eventually, Deane implored I should stay back in London so I could collect valuable information. Spying, I should call it. I agreed.

Spying was something I could manage well. My job was minor overall, but slightly effective at the moment. In every letter to Deane, I would attach a couple of newspaper clippings or short pamphlets about England's most recent dealings. Usually, I would send longer letters, but since there was not much to tell for this week, I let the newspapers speak for themselves. Hopefully, Silas Deane is satisfied with my work.

EDWARD BANCROFT: A PATRIOT NO MORE

11 August 1776

I supported my country, no doubt, but war was something I would not support. If the world was in order, and acceptable as it was, why risk making it better? Silas Deane and Benjamin Franklin were old acquaintances, but deep down I didn't agree with them.

Knock. Knock. Knock. A firm thump echoed through my house, interrupting my thoughts. I wasn't expecting company, but a familiar face awaited at my door. "Paul, I haven't seen you for years." I exclaimed as I gave him a sturdy handshake.

"Oh, yes. The good old days of 1764. Thank you for your help in Surinam. My plantation has improved greatly because of you," Paul Wentworth replied, nodding back with a crooked smile.

"Like you haven't thanked me enough. Besides, I enjoyed your company very much. Our debates were delightful, and it is hard to find a man who agrees with your worldview. So, thank you for that." Paul remained silent. "Well, come in, have a cup of tea. Y'know it's hard to get these days," I suggested, letting Wentworth inside.

Paul sat down in an oak armchair, thanked me, and leaned forward. "I understand you recently had a meeting with Silas Deane in Paris?"

I nodded my head, confused. How did he know this?

"I also understand you don't agree with the direction our new nation has taken."

I nodded again, though I was not surprised he knew this.

"Yes," I replied, "Now how—"

"That doesn't matter," Paul interrupted. "The point I'm trying to make is that I know how to help you."

"H-h-help me?" I wondered aloud.

"Yes, Edward, you are in a very convenient position. You are trusted, correct? Not only that but you have strong connections to the dealings in Paris. And, you have information. Yes, you hear it, you speak it, and you give it. The only wrong factor in that equation is that you don't want American independence. Nobody notices, but you disagree with everything about a Franco-American alliance, right? So, the information you hear, speak, and give, give it to me! Give it somewhere that will stop a French war!"

"What are you implying?" Confused, I awaited his response. Paul Wentworth took a breath.

"I'm saying, join Britain!"

"Britain? Explain!" I queried.

"All you have to do is say yes, and you are into the British Secret Society," Paul explained.

"The British Secret Society?" my voice faltered.

Paul suddenly laughed. "Edward, my friend, stop questioning everything I say!"

"I'm just shocked," I responded with a shrug.

"Yes, I apologize. I did spring it on you, didn't I?" I realized it was the chance I was looking for.

"So, you are telling me that Britain wants me to be a double agent? And that you are a spy for them as well?" I was tired of asking questions.

"That is exactly what I am saying," Paul replied.

My curiosity peaked. "What happens if I say no?"

Paul frowned. "That would not go well, especially since I just shared secret information with you."

"Let me think." I implored. Time was moving too fast. I had the chance to move from the Americas to the British side in a matter of minutes. I would betray my country. I would betray my friends. I would betray my honor.

"Yes," I said without batting an eye.

"Yes? You agree?" Paul confirmed.

"I agree but with conditions," I concluded.

"Conditions? I should've known you'd say that." Deep in thought, Paul wrung his hands. I watched silently waiting for a response. Finally, he checked his watch and looked up at me.

"I understand, Edward, though that will make it difficult. What do you have in mind?"

"Well, I have just one condition. I need to be paid exceptionally for this."

Paul chuckled.

"Don't worry about that. I wish we could talk more, but unfortunately, I must go," Paul said, abruptly standing up.

"Wait, but how will I know what to do? Or who to contact? Or—"

"I shall finalize your registered documents for you. You will know in time what to do but for now we need to know all the information you have. Just wait for now."

With that, Paul Wentworth left me alone.

13 August 1776

Paul Wentworth was true to his word. Two days after our meeting, Paul brought three men to my house, heads of the British Secret Society. One man seemed to be of higher command than the rest. His dark eyes scanned my soul as his bottom lip curved into a light smirk.

If I was meeting the heads of the British operation, Paul must have a great deal of trust in me, which created pressure. The dark-eyed man asked me pointed questions, though he already knew plenty about me, which was a frightening revelation. After the men were satisfied, the dark-eyed man motioned to Paul.

Paul set a written document on the table. "This is a, well, an oath I may call it." He told me, looking at the dark-eyed man, before staring at me sternly. "Sign this, and the British Secret Society will give you their trust and support."

"I already agreed, didn't I?" I queried.

"Yes, and that's all you had to do, but due to your *custom* request and the fact that we are yet to discover what Wentworth sees in you, you must sign this for the affirmation that you are giving your service to Britain. So that we all, not just Paul, know your pledge is in your life," another man stated.

Sweat beaded on my forehead as I reached for the feather pen. *Am I prepared? Is this a mistake?* Hands shaking nervously in anticipation, I signed the paper as a double agent for Britain.

The men finally introduced themselves. The dark-eyed man introduced himself as William Eden, head of the British spies. I recognized the family name as one of influence. The other two were named Suffolk and Weymouth. I knew Suffolk was a lord in Britain. Weymouth was an unusual but familiar man.

No matter, these men trusted me now, and I needed to trust them. And I needed to trust Britain. I wasn't doing this for money, though one of my requests was being well paid. No, I was doing this to save people, and to preserve our nation. This war destroyed my plantation and dye business, and all I wanted was peace. Now I realized the way to peace was through Britain, and if people saw me as a traitor, so be it.

History could twist my ambitions, but overall, I wasn't doing this for my reputation, I was doing this to make our nation better. If I fell, then so be it. If peace were in control, I would be satisfied.

12 March 1777

Dear Mr. Bancroft,
You have hereby been appointed Secretary to the American Commission in Paris, France, according to the recommendation of Benjamin Franklin. Please hasten your travel here immediately. Once you arrive, you will be assigned multiple tasks including negotiation meetings, interpretation, and secretarial matters.
Kindest and most important regards,
American Commissioners

I, Edward Bancroft, have been appointed Secretary in Paris! This cannot be true!

The timing was too perfect. Why? Not long before this felicitous letter arrived, I received immensely specific instructions from one of my British informers.

Retrieve information from Benjamin Franklin, but how? I wondered. Perhaps I could contact Silas Deane? Change my mind about attending the treaty signings? No, that could attract unwanted attention. This letter though, instead, gave me an unsuspecting pathway right to Benjamin Franklin.

Not only would I be in close contact with him, but I would also have the chance to discover and eavesdrop on other influential figures who trusted me, and the ones who didn't.

Perfect...but dangerous. How would I accomplish lying straight to the faces of my dearest friends? They thought of me to be an ally, a dear friend, an advisor, and a confidant. Instead, I was an opponent, an enemy, an infiltrator, and a turncoat.

I was another Judas, a wolf in sheep's clothing. No, I had to stop telling myself that. I was doing this for the good of America. They didn't know it, but I was *helping* them. Independence from Britain would end in chaos, so I was assisting my country the only way I could, by turning against what had been my lifelong mindset. So, I was going to Paris.

Hotel d'York, Rue Jacob, Paris, France
30 July 1777

I arrived in Paris and immediately was called to the Hotel d'York, where the American Commission was negotiating with France. Silas Deane and Benjamin Franklin received me warmly, while John Adams and John Jay nodded in my direction. Arthur Lee ignored me. He made me uncomfortable the way he looked down on me, always disapproving of everything.

"Edward, the meeting is this way," Silas Deane said as he caught my attention and gestured to an open room.

"Pardon me, I'm coming," I murmured. Deane nodded and disappeared through the door. *Prepare yourself for another day of arduous work,* I thought as I moved unwillingly towards the door. It was time for another day of spying.

I took in a deep breath of fresh air as I stepped outside. Laboring in a small, stuffy room along with others was not too much for my liking. In my head, I went over the information I learned. The French were skeptical of an alliance with America. They were waiting for proof that America was worthy.

As I sat down in the grass, a Black-Billed Magpie flew in the trees. It glided over the ground and landed but a few yards away from me, squawking in my direction. "Caw!" the bird croaked.

"Why, are you talking to me?" I laughed.

"Chak!"

"Well, I didn't mean to offend!" I said in jest. Landing closer to me, the bird let out another screech. "Hello there!" I welcomed it. Suddenly, a rustle in the bush behind the bird caught my attention. The magpie cocked its head.

Promptly, a beautiful black dog bounded out, a Newfoundland. I expected the magpie to fly away frightened, but to my amazement, it fluttered up on top of the great dog's head. "By Jove! What is going—." I was interrupted as the dog trotted forward and dropped a rolled-up parchment at my feet. It almost smiled while the magpie let out a squeak.

"You want me to, uh, read that?" I asked. *What? Now I was talking to a dog?* She nodded. I gaped at the creature, then closed my mouth. "I should've expected an answer to a question, huh?" I thought aloud.

Cautiously, I grasped the parchment and unrolled it.

Dear Mr. Edwards,

I gasped. Mr. Edwards was my name for contacting the British, and what they used to contact me. Was this a coincidence?

I'm guessing you are completely surprised right now that a dog has just given you a letter. I will explain. My name is Shadow, and the bird with me is named Nimbus. Shadow and I work with the British Secret Society, you might say. But the truth is, Nimbus and I are King George III's top spies.

I almost laughed. "Is this a joke?" I might've left the two animals sitting there, but this letter grabbed my curiosity. I read on.

I'm also guessing you just asked if this letter was a joke or not. I assure you; it is not. If you need proof, notice two things. One, the collar I wear on my neck right now. Second, the hopefully familiar signature at the bottom of this letter. I am here to help you so either speak now or forever hold your peace.

Sincerely,
Shadow

I LOOKED at Shadow's collar and noticed the British flag along with the sign of the crown.

Mmm, I thought. *The hopefully familiar signature at the bottom of this letter.* My eyes widened as I glanced at the bottom of the letter. "THAT'S KING GEORGE III'S SIGNATURE!" I yelped. "You aren't lying, are you?" I looked at the dog. "I could use help... I believe you."

London, England, 5 November 1777

The smoke-filled, gray roads of England provided quite a contrast to France's
bright-colored cities.
Here I was, back in London, soon to be arrested. Let me explain. The Parisians suspected me of my espionage in Paris. Trust in me was diminishing, replaced with doubt.

Arthur Lee insisted I was a double agent and convinced others to stand with him. Silas Deane thought it best that I return to London for the time being. That was where my plan came in. While in London, why not stage a fake arrest?

This would throw Lee off my trail and convince the French that I was spying for the colonies. Shadow and Nimbus sent the recommendation to King George III while I packed up for London. He had agreed it was a clever idea. So, here I was, in the middle of London, ready to be thrown in jail.

I checked the time— 8:58 am. "Bancroft! You are hereby under arrest for charges of treachery to the Crown!" a constable yelled, his voice bouncing off the cobblestoned streets. I made more of a scene by trying to run away. Surrounded by British constables, they took me.

THE EPIC STORY OF AMERICA 1777-1779

Hotel d'York, Rue Jacob, Paris, France
15 January 1778

"Edward, welcome back to Paris" Silas Deane greeted me as I walked into the Hotel d'York after such a long time.

"'Tis good to be back, Mr. Deane," I replied. "I was not too much for the smoky British air or filthy prison cells." I was released from prison a few days after my fake arrest, but the stench of the cells would forever be embedded in my mind.

I do not ever want to attempt a fake arrest again unless there is better lodging!

Tuileries Garden, 1st Arrondissement, Paris, France
9 December 1777

"Shadow, quick!" I called to the Newfoundland. "It's close to 9:30 pm!"

I raced through the changing leaves of the Tuileries Garden, trying not to gain attention. Shadow trotted alongside next to me, tongue hanging out. When I met her by the Hotel d'York, her wagging tail and person-like confidence affirmed our friendship and were the very assurances I needed that would bring success to our delicate venture. We established a mutual friendship and became close-working companions.

Every Tuesday, she would accompany me here where I would drop a small bottle of critical information for my British authorities. Today, the message was especially important. A few days ago, the news of the American win over the British at Saratoga reached Benjamin Franklin. Great news for the colonies, but not for Britain.

The victory at Saratoga was the push that gave France a reason to ally with America. The win gave America a chance to truly beat Britain in this war. King George III needed to know about the turn of events. Finally, I reached my destination. Looking over my shoulder, I carefully slipped the bottle into a hole in the tree.

Shadow jumped up and pushed a piece of paper into the hole as well.

"Shadow? Do you have a message to send too?" I asked. She winked at me and sauntered away. *Hmmn, what an unusual dog.*

Hotel d'York, Rue Jacob, Paris, France
6 February 1778

I burst out of the hotel, followed by Benjamin Franklin. France and the United States had become allied with a signed treaty. "HUZ-ZAH!" Franklin yelled triumphantly.

"Huzzah!" I smiled, though it was more of a wince.

"Let's have a drink! On me!" Franklin insisted giddily.

"I'm sorry, I have more business to attend," I lied.

Franklin frowned for a split second. "Well, yes, Edward, but I think we should be celebrating!" With that he left me, rejoicing quite well down the steps of the hotel.

Once I was alone, I called Shadow who wandered towards me. "France just allied with the former Colonies. Have Nimbus fly a message to King George immediately!" I thundered. Shadow scampered off to find Nimbus. *Uh, oh. King George is not going to be pleased.*

Passy, Paris, France
1 February 1779

"In conclusion, Edward Bancroft has supported the United States through and through. So, you must retract these accusations!" John Paul Jones declared, glaring at Arthur Lee and Musco Livingston, who both planned to challenge me in court.

They both knew in their hearts that I was a spy, and the fact nobody believed them drove them mad. So, Lee finally decided it was time to take things seriously. With Musco at his side, it seemed Lee would stop at nothing to finally put me in jail.

John Paul Jones, though, my dear friend and successful sea captain, believed in me and wore them down. After hours of arguing, Arthur and Musco were getting tired while John Paul still pressed on. "That's it! I'm finished! We renounce our claims!" Arthur Lee rose and strode out with Musco following. Relieved, I thanked John Paul.

"Of course. You don't deserve any of that for what you did," John Paul assured me.

I nodded warily. *For what I did.* I was a double agent, a traitor to my country. However, nobody knew. For now, I was safe.

SIR HENRY CLINTON: RESIGNATION DENIED

BY MADELEINE ROSE WENZEL

London, England
1 March 1777

I stepped off the dock onto firm ground for the first time in several weeks with Elias, my Carolina parakeet, perched on my shoulder. King George III granted me permission to return to England after my successful capture of Newport, Rhode Island, last December. *While I am here, I must request to resign or at least move from General Howe's command,* I mused sourly. *As well as publish my full account of the Battle of Sullivan's Island, to hopefully clear my name, which was tainted after our humiliating defeat there.* "You're going to be the most well-traveled parrot in the country by the time this war is over, little one," I muttered to my small companion as I gently tugged my wig out of his beak.

As I walked, I recalled my time in the colony of South Carolina.

Charleston Harbor, Sullivan's Island, South Carolina
15 June 1776

I had little hope of capturing Charleston and wished to go to the Chesapeake instead. However, Commodore Sir Peter Parker had different ideas and ignored my suggestions. The Rebels' unfinished fort was the only thing standing between us and capturing Sullivan's Island, and Parker decided to attack immediately.

We arrived in the beginning of June, but the weather turned against us, and we couldn't pass the Charleston Bar for three days.

Long Island (Isle of Palms), South Carolina
20 June 1776

By the 16th, we stationed our troops on Long Island, since it lacked an enemy fort, and the surf was calmer there than on Sullivan's Island. Our scouts told me that in the channel between the two islands, the water was only eighteen inches deep at low tide.

We soon discovered that it was much deeper than eighteen inches.

In fact, the water turned out to be seven feet deep, and we were stuck. We didn't have enough boats to carry us across, so the Rebels brought their artillery to the northern end of Sullivan's Island.

I stood on the beach, exasperated with both Sir Parker and myself. The more things went wrong, the more I regretted not pushing harder against taking this action. As I walked, I carefully watched my step to avoid trampling the jellyfish the tide washed up on the beach. *They look like cannonballs.* I gently prodded one with my boot. Sea birds flew overhead, and numerous other species fluttered in and out of the thin brush, singing cheerful songs. I gazed out over the channel, wondering what to do. We could shoot at them under the cover of night with the small field guns we brought with us while two battalions went over to take the post and hold it until we got reinforcements. However, I soon abandoned this plan.

I leaned against a palmetto. *The Rebels must have built their fort with this strange tree,* I thought sullenly. *There isn't much else out here other than sand.* As I stood there, a light weight landed on my boot, and I looked down at a bird. It was a parrot. They were prevalent here in the southern colonies, but I was surprised to see one so close. The creature's wing was bent at an odd angle, and I scooped the little one up to examine it. "Poor little thing," I murmured as I walked back towards our camp. "I'll see if the soldiers might know how to help you."

Long Island (Isle of Palms), South Carolina
28 June 1776

This wasn't right. Parker and his fleet attacked Fort Sullivan. The parrot, whom I named Elias, sat on my shoulder. He became quite tame after a few days of care, and a soldier splinted his wing, though he warned me that Elias would likely not be able to fly again. Our cannonballs were almost bouncing off the walls of the rebel Fort Sullivan instead of shattering them, while theirs gave our ships a beating! The closest we had come to destroying their fort thus far was knocking down their flag, which a soldier, who was either incredibly brave or terribly foolish, quickly scooped up. He held it high as the cannonade continued around him, keeping it steady until the others could rebuild a flagpole.

We continued to make no progress, and throughout the day it became painfully clear that we lost, reassuring me in my conviction that this was a foolhardy idea, but no one ever listens to me.

The battle continued until nightfall, and I later learned that the tide prevented them from drawing back, so they had to fight on.

New York Harbor, New York
5 June 1777

I hummed quietly to the tune of the British Grenadiers as I stepped onto colonial soil once more. During my time in England, I met a young Frenchman by the name of Lafayette, who visited King George III. I was not pleased to return here, and even less so to serve under General Howe. Instead of granting my request to resign, the King and Lord Germain gave me the Order of the Bath, knighting me.

Though this honored me, I remained hurt that they would not allow me to publish the full account of my time at Sullivan's Island and clear my name. I also hoped to receive the command of my friend, General Burgoyne, but he convinced the king to give it to him instead. Elias sensed my foul mood, as he remained quiet and well-behaved for the journey back.

Pennsylvania Countryside
11 September 1777

This evening I sent off small raiding parties to Elizabeth Town, Schuyler's Ferry, Fort Lee, and Tappan, and they arrived at their destinations at nearly the same time. The group at Elizabeth Town would act first, with the others ready to help should the need arise. We were going to make a quick sweep of the countryside to collect cattle for food, as well as disarm the colonists.

Had I known that Howe was attacking the Rebels at Brandywine on this day, I would have pushed my raids further to distract them. But alas, I had no such thought, since the weather was beginning to look menacing, my army had neither tents nor blankets, and the nights were growing cooler. Ergo, I ordered my troops to retreat with what little we collected, about four hundred cows of which twenty were for milk, the same number of sheep, and some horses. I do hope that these raids helped the commander, though he still refuses to listen to reason. The victory there cleared the way for Howe to take Philadelphia, which was formerly the Rebel's capital and home of the Congress.

New York
Mid-October 1777

In early October, I landed my troops at the west shore of Stony Point in the hopes of taking Fort Montgomery and Fort Clinton. I wished to take them with little struggle since the trails were too bad to bring our artillery, and the forts were out of range of our ships. The fog was thick as we came ashore, covering us as we marched inland. Burgoyne and I corresponded often since he started his campaign, and I was determined to help, over which fact, Howe and I argued.

When we arrived at the fortifications, I split my army into two and sent each to take a fort. Even though we had no heavy artillery by the next week, the Highlands were in British control.

Unfortunately, taking the forts was all I could do to help since I didn't have the men and arms to reach Albany without defeat.

I paced in my tent as I spoke to my spy, Lieutenant Daniel Taylor. Most of the correspondence I had with Burgoyne was encrypted in code, often with a masked letter, but this message was of utmost importance, and I felt it needed to be delivered by hand; so I tucked the message away in a silver bullet, and instructed Taylor to bring it to Burgoyne.

"If you're captured, do not hesitate to swallow the bullet," I ordered, rescuing it from the grasp of my ever-curious parrot. "Not you, Elias. Now, where was I?"

"You were telling me what I must do should I be captured," Lieutenant Taylor replied.

"Ah, yes. Once you ingest the bullet, you will have to watch carefully for it to re-emerge," I explained, gazing sternly at my spy, pulling Elias away from the edge of the table as I warned him. "Swallowing the message is your absolute last resort, understood?"

"I understand, sir."

I studied his face for a moment before pressing the silver ball containing my message into his hand, closing his fingers over it.

"You are to give this to General Burgoyne and no other."

"Yes, sir!" Lieutenant Taylor answered with a salute and left the tent.

I sighed and turned back to my work, only stopping to catch Elias before he tumbled off the table. Little did I know that my message would never reach Burgoyne; Taylor would be captured, forced to vomit up the bullet, and hanged as a spy.

Sandy Hook, New York
Late April 1778

I am now the Commander-in-Chief of the entire army here in the Colonies? I shouldn't be so surprised. I am—was—Howe's second-in-command! I turned to Elias with a smile. "Little one, we no longer serve under Howe!"

Elias gave a little squawk in reply, flapping his way up onto my head. I had sent an aide-de-camp to England to convince the king to let me take my leave and return. Now I'm glad that my request was denied.

British Headquarters, Philadelphia, Pennsylvania
30 May 1778

I arrived in Philadelphia from Sandy Hook on the 8th of May, and Howe left for England on the 25th, leaving me to my charge. My orders were to evacuate Philadelphia. I was not pleased with this, but if my first act as Commander in Chief was to retreat from Philadelphia, then so be it.

I sighed as I dipped my pen into the inkwell. His Majesty ordered me to write a letter to Mr. Washington and the Continental Congress to inform them that Parliament decided in their favor. My quill scratched on the parchment as I wrote, trying to keep Elias out of trouble. The little bird was attempting to grab the tool in his beak, bouncing around my desk playfully. "Elias, no, you mustn't be a rascal, or I'll have to put you in your cage," I chided him, moving him to the other side of the desk. He gave me a betrayed look, and I momentarily regret scolding him. But alas, I needed to get this done.

Headquarters, 30 May 1778

Dear Sir,

I was instructed by the King to send word to both you and the Congress of a few acts of Parliament in favor of the American Colonies. I will send my Adjutant General, Colonel Patterson, to deliver this to you, should you give me the time and place.

I have the honor to be, sir, your most humble and obedient servant.

H. Clinton

I had three bills of Parliament's decisions to send via Col. Patterson and hoped that I would soon get a reply from Washington. For now, though, I set them aside on my desk, one repealing the 1774 Massachusetts Government Act, and the other two being British peace proposals.

The next day, I learned that Washington refused to receive my letter because he wanted the bills enclosed in the letter, and not to meet with Col. Patterson in person.

Coopers Ferry, New Jersey
17 June 1778

Boats ferried my troops across the Delaware River following our evacuation of Philadelphia a few days earlier, moving as slowly as we could. I would likely lose a good part of my army when we arrived at New York City and wanted to make a move on Washington and his army while I still had the men to defeat him. This rebellion in the American Colonies was not the only war we had going on, and my latest orders from London required that I send some of my men to the West Indies, West Florida, and St. Augustine.

My plan was established, and I was ready to set off. I would lead my troops in a slow retreat across New Jersey to New York, which would hopefully lure Washington to attack us. I hoped the commander of the enemy army would not be too suspicious, but knowing how deliberately slow we were moving, I had my doubts.

Before leaving, I sent away the ill and wounded on ships, along with many heavy guns, taking with me 15,000 of our best troops on the march.

Mount Holly, New Jersey
20 June 1778

Our baggage train spread almost ten miles long as we marched across the New Jersey countryside. The Rebels harassed us since we crossed the Delaware into the colony, destroying bridges and wells, cutting down trees, and sending snipers to shoot into our columns. They did little to slow our march since we were already moving so purposefully slowly, but besides being quite annoying, their habit of filling in wells made it hard for us to find drinking water. As temperatures rose, my men suffered greatly from heatstroke.

Monmouth, New Jersey
28 June 1778

The heat and humidity were positively awful, and the mosquitoes were just as bad. I could feel my clothes clinging to my sweaty skin, and even Elias seemed subdued from his usual bouncy self as he sat between my horse's ears.

The haze of gun smoke made it hard to see and the deafening sound of musket and cannon fire left our ears ringing. The sulfurous scent of powder hung in the air like a heavy cloak, and my soldiers were dying from heat stroke in equal numbers as from battle wounds. The sweltering sun beat down upon us as it had all week from a heat wave that gripped the colony, bringing with it temperatures close to a hundred degrees.

As the sun slowly sank below the horizon at the end of the day, I sighed. Mr. Washington and his troops were in a more strategic position, and it would be foolhardy to attack them. My troops would move on to Sandy Hook, New York. The battle and heat exhausted both my troops and those of the enemy. The battle was a draw, although Washington claimed victory since my troops retreated. To my surprise, this army was not the untrained band of men it had been the last time I had encountered them. Something must have happened over the winter to train these men into the army I saw today.

British Headquarters, New York
2 December 1779

After Burgoyne surrendered at Saratoga in 1777, the French decided to ally with the Rebels, and they landed on North American shores in July 1778. On the 8th of August, they arrived in Newport Harbor, Rhode Island, and I sent off five battalions of soldiers to reinforce General Sir Robert Pigot, who defended Newport.

The city was under siege for most of the war, and our English troops occupied it since 1776. On the 29th of August, General John Sullivan decided to call off his siege and formed a defense across the island. Our forces could not break their defense, and though we kept the town, the battle ended in a draw.

During this time, I tried once again to get the King to allow me to resign or send me more soldiers. The government took ten thousand men from my army to reinforce other posts around the world, and still expected me to function at the same levels as before! So, in late 1778, I sent Major Duncan Drummond to plead my case to the King and his ministers. Yet again I was declined. King George told Drummond that even taking leave so that I may plead my own case was impossible and that I was the only man who may still be able to save America.

New York Harbor, New York
26 December 1779

I stepped onto the ship, wrapping my cloak around myself as the winter chill threatened to seep into my bones, Elias once again perched on my shoulder. We were returning to the colony where he was born, this time with the hope of capturing Charleston.

GENERAL CHARLES CORNWALLIS: A WAR WITHIN HEART AND MIND

BY PAYTON GRACE

THE EPIC STORY OF AMERICA 1777-1779

September 1777

*I*t broke my heart, all of it. The fighting, the bloodshed, the unfairness of it all. Never would I have believed my children would grow up in a time of such discord. *Jemima... Mary... little Charles...* A bittersweet smile spread across my face as I pondered my family back in Great Britain. How I missed them so.

Staring into the fire, I could almost see the loving faces of my wife and children, the memories of them warming me within, while the flames warmed me from the outside. But one could only stay warm for so long when submerged in the harsh coldness of war. All around me, soldiers, from boys barely reaching adulthood to weathered men both my age and older, milled about, enjoying this brief period of rest before we continued our march to Philadelphia. There, we would meet General Washington, that old fox, and his army that awaited us. Then we would rush into battle once more. Unfortunately, not all would return. I sighed, rubbing my temples as I read over the stack of reports and newspapers in the dim light.

Every day, I received news of battles, deaths, but I did not like it one bit. This would not have happened without taxing the Americans. Perhaps if I, or the four others in the House of Lords who shared my views in voting against the Stamp Act and the Declaratory Act, voiced our opinions louder, if we had shined more light on the situation, maybe none of this would have happened. Those fallen men, sons, fathers, and brothers would still be alive.

But there was no time to dwell on the past. What happened, happened as an indelible mark in the book of history. Now, we were at war. And no matter the outcome, sacrifices would be made. As much as I disagreed with the conflict between Great Britain and America, I made a commitment to my country and its army back in 1757, at the age of nineteen. My dedication got me promoted to Major General less than two years ago in 1775. I could not—no, I *would* not—let eighteen years go to waste. I could not ignore my duty.

My tired gaze rose from the papers in my hand to the sky above, which seemed to stretch endlessly, a sparkling blanket of stars. There was no telling how long this war would last, no telling how long I would have to stay apart from my family, or if I would even see them again. *Please, protect them.* I sent my wishes up to the stars. *Protect them, especially when I no longer can.*

Brandywine Creek, Pennsylvania
11 September 1777

"General Cornwallis, are you ready?" Howe's voice cut through the early morning silence.

It was barely dawn, the world around us was just beginning to awaken. The sky was still dark enough to see the stars, the silvery moon hanging to the west. A few birds had already begun their morning songs, their melodies ringing through the fog. And if I was being honest, I, as well as a few of my men, were not quite awake as well. But when duty calls, it does not wait until one is ready.

Washington, as usual, had been well prepared for our arrival. He had set up his men along Brandywine Creek to prevent us from reaching Philadelphia, the difficult terrain working to his advantage. As much as I hated to admit it, he was smart. Yet we had numbers on our side, and the man whose command I had been placed under, General William Howe, was even smarter.

With Howe's decisive planning, we had devised a strategy to work around Washington's set-up and hopefully break through it, using the weaker areas of the rebel defenses to our advantage. Seldom had General Howe's strategies failed us. And I had little doubt that they would fail us now.

I smirked as I imagined Washington's surprise when we managed to foil his plan. He had managed to best me months ago, when he tricked me and landed an attack on Princeton. But now, it was *my* turn.

"Yah!" I snapped the reins on my horse, riding forward towards the planned area of attack.

It was time to show him the true strength of Great Britain.

THE EPIC STORY OF AMERICA 1777-1779

Great Britain, Winter 1777

"Are we there yet?" I called the coachman for what seemed like the millionth time. I didn't mean to sound so childlike, yet I felt as if I could not wait another second for the trip to be over. I had ridden in a carriage multiple times in my life, yet somehow, this ride seemed much longer than any I had ever taken before.

"Not just yet, sir, only a little way left to go," the coachman replied amicably. "Excited to be home again?"

A smile bloomed across my face at the mere thought of it. "Absolutely."

Just a few months ago, soon after the battle at Brandywine Creek, I had taken part in yet another battle against the American Rebels, which had come to be known as the Battle of Germantown. Howe's strategy at Brandywine had led us to victory, yet the fight for Philadelphia had not ended there. Although I had succeeded in capturing Philadelphia on September 26th, the Rebels, as stubborn as they were, continued to fight.

I was impressed by their perseverance, I must say. Although they are but a new, young country, and had every reason to fear the well put together British Army, their passion and willpower made up for what they lacked. Fighting for freedom. I found it to be quite an interesting concept.

In fact, they nearly managed to apprehend General Howe in Germantown, aided by the cover of fog and the elements of confusion and surprise. I chuckled aloud at the memory. If it had not been for my arrival with reinforcements, the American general, General Greene, would have taken Howe and his men captive, if they were lucky, that is.

Wait. I snapped out of it with a start, shaking my head as if to clear my mind. *Stop thinking about such things,* I chided myself. *You are about to be* home *again.*

Even now, I could hear the joyous laughter of Mary and Charles Jr., the gentle voice of my lovely Jemima. I could feel the warmth that their mere presence brought me, see their bright smiles, and smell the delicious meals that we always enjoyed together.

We had been separated for far too long. I could not wait to see them once again.

"We've arrived, sir," the coachman announced, bringing the carriage to a stop.

At those words, my attention snapped back to the present, my excitement spiking even higher. I scrambled from the carriage, shouting a hasty farewell. Once I stepped foot on the familiar pathway, my pulse quickened. An inexplicable feeling of anticipation rose inside me.

Each step I took seemed too small, every second too long. Memories flooded my mind as I got closer to the house. I felt the urge to sprint, to rush up to the doors and throw them open. But at the same time, I wanted to savor each moment, no matter how small.

"*DADDYYY!*" The door flew open, and little feet flew down the steps and straight at me. Before I could blink, a small figure flung itself into my arms and clung on, enveloping me in a small but fierce embrace.

I smiled. I *knew* that voice. "Charles Jr.? Is that you, my dear boy?"

The little boy lifted his face from my chest, bright eyes sparkling, his tiny mouth spread in a wide grin. Each time I returned; my son had grown by leaps and bounds. At this point, I was afraid I would miss his entire childhood. But all those worries faded away as I embraced him. None of that mattered, nothing did, only that I was here, holding him in my arms.

"Daddy!" he said again, giggling.

"Daddy!" Mary, my little girl squealed, rushing over to be swept into a tight hug. My children... Oh how I missed them all.

A gasp came from the doorway. "Charles?"

My son and I both looked up at the name.

But that voice... No matter how long it had been, no matter where I went, no matter what, I would never forget that voice. Nor would I ever forget the woman who stood there, her eyes locked with mine, as time seemed to stand still. At that moment, it was as if we were the only two people in the world.

Jemima, my wife.

Every time I saw her, I fell in love all over again.

"Jemima." I set Mary and Charles Jr. down, opening my arms to embrace her.

"Charles!" In a flurry of laughter and tears, we held each other close, savoring being together once again.

Home. Home. Home, my heartbeat seemed to whisper.

I wrapped my family in a tight embrace, pulling them all close.

Home.

Yes. With a definite finality, yes, I was finally home.

***

"Goodnight, Mary," I whispered, brushing the hair from my sleeping girl's face and kissing her forehead. After making sure that she was snug beneath her blanket, I crossed the room to wish Charles Jr. a good night as well.

For a moment, I just stared down at their peaceful forms.

The war had not and would never cause me to lose sight of what I valued and loved most, my family. I fought, not only out of duty, but for them as well. I was helping to end this war so that my children may be exempt from further violence. The mere thought kept me going, especially when it got hard.

I could not bear to imagine Mary becoming a widow because her husband died in war, or Charles Jr. exposed to the gore of a battlefield. It pained me to think of them losing their innocence and positive outlook on life. It would happen someday, but not by war, not if I could help it. Not like that.

Once again, I looked out at the stars beyond the window.

For my children. I made the silent promise. *For Mary and for Charles.*

Monmouth, New Jersey, 28 June 1778

GENERAL CHARLES CORNWALLIS: A WAR WITHIN HEART AND MIND

Eyes closed, I tried to bring the images of my family to my mind's eye. The moments I spent with them... they had been so fleeting. And now, I was back in America, back to the war. Those wonderful five months now seemed like a dream, one that ended much too soon.

Now, I rode along with my men in the heat of summer. We received orders from the king to move from Philadelphia to New Jersey, another colony conquered by the British. Though of course, the colonists lacked the patience to allow us to travel in peace and picked yet another fight. Rebels, always making my life difficult. Although I agreed that their oppression had been quite unfair, if they had not openly declared war on my country, I would be at home, in the loving arms of my wife, watching my children grow up.

I sighed. If only serenity would last. When I opened my eyes again, the blazing hot summer sun greeted me, my vision nearly blinded by its overpowering light.

What a wonderful choice regarding battle conditions. I sighed, shielding my eyes. Since it was summer, the weather was already unbearably humid, and the thunderstorms from the previous night didn't help a bit. The heat was already getting to me. Beads of sweat dripped from my forehead and down my back. *If only I did not have to wear this thick woolen coat.*

I surveyed the area ahead. In the distance, a large group approached, the men uniformed in blue. If my intelligence was correct, George Washington's little sidekick, General Charles Lee was the general on horseback who led them. Even as he led his men onto the battlefield, he hesitated with every step. Perhaps that would work in my favor.

Would you look at that, we share a name, I sneered, narrowing my eyes. *Let that be the only thing we have in common.*

Adjusting my bayonet, I wiped the sweat from my brow, soaking my sleeve in an instant. Heatwaves rose around me. If the men did not perish in the battle today, they would melt to death in this sweltering heat.

It flabbergasted me that Rebel General Charles Lee marched into battle, yet was now... retreating. *Retreating! It's not even over!*

What a colossal coward. General Lee had his chance, but his uncertainty lost it.

Lee led his men in a hasty retreat. The poor soldiers panicked as they fled, a chaotic mess of people. At that moment, I felt a pang of sympathy. It was not their fault that everything went wrong. Their cowardly general was responsible.

Who in their right mind would put him *in charge?* I clicked my tongue, shaking my head. *If all their generals are like this, then the Rebels may as well surrender this very second.*

A cheer arose from my own men. I could not help but smile as I prepared to lead them in pursuit of the opposition. At least Lee's cowardice was good for something.

Not all the men had retreated when I spotted yet another American general on the battlefield. Contrary to General Lee, this general rode through the ranks, rallying the troops with his confidence, which spread throughout the field. Along with him, other officers also took a stand in leading the men back towards the battlefield.

Washington. I recognized him almost immediately. *I wondered when he would show up.*

But I had no time to observe him. I was a general myself after all. My job was to lead the men under my command. I raised my weapon in the air. "For Britain!" I shouted, riding into battle.

And just like that, the war was upon us again.

America, November 1778

My hands trembled as I read the letter over for the tenth time. It... could not possibly be true. It was not... Could it? All the while, my eyes were wide, and searching, as I blinked again and again. Maybe I was reading it wrong. Perhaps my vision was failing, or my mind was playing tricks on me. But no matter how many times I re-read the words on the paper, the contents remained the same.

Dear General Cornwallis,

GENERAL CHARLES CORNWALLIS: A WAR WITHIN HEART AND MIND

I regret to inform you that your wife, Jemima, is terribly ill.

IT FELT as if I'd been stabbed. Jemima was *sick*? I could not...I did not...She...The papers in my hand fluttered to the ground. If I had not grabbed the desk for support, I would have fallen to the floor with them.

A million emotions flooded my mind at once, but one thing was certain.

I was going back home to be with my wife, and no war would stop me.

CAPTAIN PATRICK FERGUSON: FERGUSON'S JOURNEY

BY ZOE MILLER

CAPTAIN PATRICK FERGUSON: FERGUSON'S JOURNEY

New Jersey, 1777

I, Captain Patrick Ferguson, am speaking to you of my time in the former Colonies. I was ready for a new adventure, and this place has proven to be new and exciting. Some places look quite different from where I have been before, but I did enjoy being in a new place and seeing new people. Some people here are exceedingly kind, but some are terribly angry that I served the king. However, I am loyal to the king, and I was there to fight against the idea that the Colonies are free to break away from the king. I was taught loyalty and dedication.

I was born in Edinburgh, Scotland, to parents who pushed me to work hard. My father was an attorney and later a senator. He was a good father, and he pushed me to be the best in everything I did. I worked hard at my responsibilities and earned the notice of my uncle, who encouraged me to join the military. Later, I became a Scottish officer in the British Army and began my military career. For years, I served with the Royal Scots Grays during the Seven Years' War before returning home due to a leg injury in 1772. I have answered King George's call to again serve with the British Army fighting the rebellious American Colonies.

I am here to fight for my country against those who want to tear it apart. I tell you just thinking of the disrespect to the king's authority makes me furious. I do not understand why they refuse to follow the rules of our good King George. The American Colonies are under British rule, and they are not free to make their own rules.

My men and I were in the colony of New Jersey during the summer. We spent much of our time trying to find where the Patriots were heading. However, we ended up spending most of our time chasing ghost Patriots, for we received false reports about where they were located. It was just a waste of our time and energy, especially sweating in this summer heat. "Ghost soldiers!" I laugh in annoyance when I think of it. My men and I focused our attention on finding Patriots. Our wish was to stop this fighting against the king.

Our wish started to come true in August, when we got the order to sail to the Chesapeake and help General Howe fighting to capture Philadelphia. During the voyage, I became tired of being on a ship. I remember speaking with the captain, Peter Smith on the deck.

"Peter, thank you for taking my men and me to Pennsylvania, but after being on a ship again for another extended period, I am ready to get back on dry land. How much longer will we be traveling?" I said in a calm, but exhausted voice.

"I would have thought you had your sea legs after all the time you spent on the ship here from England." Peter laughed and patted me on the shoulder. "It should not be much longer until we arrive."

When we got off the water and back on sweet ground, I went to my knees and thought how much I missed the sweet-smelling grass and did not miss the fish-smelling sea. The worst part of being on the ship was the blasted seagulls that would dive-bomb me every time I was outside on the deck. I was so thankful to be back on land. That night we set up camp somewhere in Pennsylvania, and I got a letter from General Cornwallis.

CAPTAIN,

I have some news for you, I have figured out where the Patriots have been hiding.

They are near a place called Chadds Ford in Delaware County, Pennsylvania.

I want you to take your men and head in that direction. We last heard that they were along a creek named Brandywine.

General Cornwallis

AFTER READING THAT LETTER, we needed to leave. I would give the order first thing in the morning after my men and I got a night of rest. As I was about to go to bed, I suddenly heard a rustling noise outside of my tent. I stepped outside of my tent with my musket wondering if the Patriots found us. It was dark, and there were no sounds except the rustling from some tall bushes. It was a mockingbird pulling at branches.

I laughed and shook my head "A mockingbird! Too funny!" I started to walk back into my tent when it flew at me and dove at my head. The bird brushed my hair as it passed.

"Get away from my head!" I shouted, waving my arms.

Finally, the bird flew in front of me and landed in the doorway of my tent. It turned its head to one side, and in the dim light its dark eye looked at me. Then I heard the bird say, "Hey." I shook my head. This journey had been a hard one. I was exhausted and hearing things. I shook my head again. It is just a bird, and they do not speak.

"Go away, bird," I demanded as I shooed it with my hands.

The bird answered, "Hmmn...let me think about it... No!"

"Go away, annoying bird!" I insisted in a stronger voice.

He boldly protested, "I have a name, and it is Archie."

I walked past the bird as I went back into my tent, thinking the heat and lack of sleep were messing with my mind.

I woke up, and the first thing I saw was the bird standing on my chest. Archie turned his head and looked at me with one dark eye.

"Did you get a good night's rest? Because I did. It's time to find those Patriots!"

The bird flew over and landed on a chair in my tent. For a minute I was confused. The bird was talking. I shook my head. The talking bird was not a dream, but I did not have time to think about anything other than General Cornwallis' letter. I quickly packed, and soon we were ready to leave.

The bird hopped about and said, "Come on, we've got to go to this area near Chadds Ford along the Brandywine Creek."

Then I gave him an annoyed grunt as I walked past him. The bird jumped off the ground and flew behind me. I mounted my horse, and Archie settled himself on my shoulder for the journey. As I began to ride through camp, I saw General Howe who motioned me over. He introduced me to the man standing beside him, Major Banastre Tarleton. This man was a legend among the British as he was fearless in battle, but it was not an honor to meet him. I heard of Major

Tarleton and his treatment of the Patriots. This was not a man I respected, and I did not agree with how he treated people.

I kept my greeting short and polite. "Hello, Major Tarleton, my name is Captain Ferguson." However, I could not keep the annoyance off my face.

"Hello, Captain," Tarleton answered flatly, seeing the look on my face.

General Howe noticed the look between us and waved to me onward. So, my men and I rode on toward Brandywine. After several hours of riding, I grew tired of the sounds of the moving army and thought I would talk to Archie, still sitting on my shoulder.

"I hope to return to England soon," I finally said to the bird.

I was expecting a response from Archie, but he was just snoring on my shoulder. A moment later this strange bird flew out of sight. I watched him fly away and felt a little loneliness as he disappeared. I shook my head and focused on the upcoming battle.

About an hour later, Archie was back. He flew to my shoulder and dropped a worm on my lap.

"Hi, I am back. I know you missed me. I even got you a snack," Archie said with a cheerful voice as he puffed out his feathers and settled in on my shoulder.

I flipped the worm off and said, "No, thank you." I smiled a little bit. Just seeing this strange little bird lightened my spirit.

With a snarky tone, Archie huffed, "Fine. Don't eat it!" as he flew to the ground. He scooped the worm into his mouth. After he ate it, he flew back to my shoulder and settled back to sleep. As we rode, I realized this little bird was not as bad as I first thought. I liked him.

Soon we arrived at Brandywine Creek, and suddenly an unexpected and loud gunshot echoed in the distance. One man went down. It happened so fast! I jumped off my horse to see who shot that man, and it was the Patriots! The battle had just begun! I could hear gunfire and men yelling as they ran and fought. I reached toward my horse to get my musket.

Archie was on the ground, gasping, "My life is flashing before my eyes! I am too young to die!"

I had no time for his drama. "Get up and hide yourself!"

I got my gun and began to join the battle. *BAM-BAM-BAM!* I was running and ducking. I looked to find Archie, but he was nowhere in sight. Right now, I could not focus o Archie, I had to focus on the Patriots. I felt pressure, and Archie was hugging my leg.

He looked at me with a terrified look. "What is happening?!"

"Archie, hide!" I shouted as I took cover behind a tree.

Out of nowhere a cannon fired. *BOOM!* Then smoke filled the air. My ears were ringing, and the smoke made it hard to breathe. I had to find General Howe. I started to run through the battle, ducking and shooting, and finally found him.

I warned my commander, "We are going to lose this battle if we are not careful!" I fired off a shot at a Patriot.

General Howe answered, "Do not worry, my boy, I have a plan, and it is going to confuse that no-good General Washington!"

At that time, General Howe tricked General Washington into thinking we were going to attack him in the front. Little did he know that we split our forces, and we were getting ready to hit him from the side.

Archie piped up and complained, "I am hungry. Do we have anything to eat?"

I frowned while looking through my spy glass. "This is not the best time!" It was at this time, as I was looking across the field of battle, I saw what appeared to be a Patriot officer, but this man was riding away from me, and I refused to shoot a man in the back out of honor. Then suddenly a horrible pain hit me in my right elbow joint. As I fell to my knees, I looked down and saw that I was shot. "I'm hit!" I yelled at Archie.

Archie flew to my aid and asked, "What do you want me to do?"

I answered with a grimace, "Go find me a doctor!" With great speed Archie zipped away into the sky and started his search for the British doctor.

After a few minutes I saw Archie zipping back through the sky and heading in my direction. "Get up, there is a doctor close by who is waiting to see you," Archie told me.

In seconds I arrived at the hospital tent where a great surgeon looked at my wound. While tending to me, the surgeon spoke up. "Did you hear that General Washington was on the field early today with another person dressed as a hussar?"

About that time, I remember the officer earlier today was with a person dressed like a hussar. "Rats, I could have taken a shot at General Washington, if only he was facing me. I do not regret it though, as I will not shoot a man in the back!"

The surgeon fixed my arm the best that he could. It was getting toward nightfall. As I came out of the hospital tent, my men shouted, "HUZZAH! HUZZAH! HUZZAH!" The Patriots were starting to retreat to the north and back to Chester. We were so exhausted that we decided to set up camp right on the battlefield.

As I laid down in my tent for the night, army drums got closer and closer to my tent. At first, I thought, "Wait, why am I hearing these drums? The Patriots are on the retreat."

Archie was banging on the drums, chanting, "We won! HUZZAH!"

"You're a crazy bird," I said with a laugh. "You scared me to death thinking that the Patriots were coming back for another fight. To be honest, I do not have the strength for another go around with them.

Archie said, "Oops!" Then he began to dance with his wings open, spinning like a tornado inside the tent.

Even months after the Battle of Brandywine, I suffered great pain from my elbow wound. More than once, the doctor wanted to amputate my arm, but I refused. Archie was always with me and just as annoying, asking questions at the wrong time.

During this time, I received sad news. My father passed away in Scotland months before Brandywine. I stepped away from military life to return to Scotland and recover from my wound and the loss of my father. Archie went with me for the next year. The little friend would sit on my father's grave and sing sweet songs. Someday I will be called to return to the Colonies and fight for our king once again, unless we stop them before I can return. If we continue this war, I will fight with all my might for the king, even if it means DEATH!

GENERAL WILLIAM HOWE

BY PIPER JORDAN

THE EPIC STORY OF AMERICA 1777-1779

Brandywine Creek, Pennsylvania
11 September 1777

The battlefield exploded with pops of gunfire and the pounding of galloping horses. Musket balls whizzed by, and dust made the air cloudy. General William Howe gazed over his soldiers, observing them as they pursued the enemy, forcing them to fight back. George Washington 'the Fox' was at it again, fighting back harder than expected.

The day is beautiful, thought Howe. There was a cool breeze, and the sky was partially cloudy, providing shade for the weary army. He smiled, letting the sun and the air lift his spirits high, filling his heart with joy.

A soft pounding came from the distance, heard over the rhythmic march of the soldiers. Quiet at first, barely audible, but still noticed by the general in front. As head of the army, he was its protector, and always alert to things out of the ordinary.

"Halt! Silence!" he ordered, pulling on the reins of his horse. The men stopped, listening. They heard it now, too: a horse in full gallop. "Be ready men. We do not know if he be friend or foe."

A man on horseback drew near. He was not dressed in the uniform of a soldier, but that of a courier. With a black hat that rippled in the breeze, and a long brown coat, he did not seem to be a threat to the army.

"Greetings, man. What be your business here?" inquired the general.

"I have a letter for General Howe."

"I am he."

Howe brought his horse closer to the other man's and reached for the letter he held. *A letter,* he wondered, *I hope it is not unwelcome news.* A letter in a war could mean so many things. Death, life, victory, defeat. It could be a request for surrender, or a message of peace. A light of hope, or a shadow of darkness. So many possibilities in one small, white envelope.

As the man on the horse rode off, Howe slowly opened the seal.

His heart skipped a beat, and he stopped. *Could it be my dear Frances?* She had said she would write to him soon, and he longed to hear her words. If it were she that wrote the letter, he could not read it now, not in front of the men.

On a beautiful day in 1765, he wedded a beautiful girl named Frances Connelly. She was radiant that day, and he had grinned like a puppy when he took her hand. But now a war separated them. He hated it for that very reason. He longed to see Frances and hold her in his arms again.

He coughed. "Alright, men. This is a fine clearing. Let us stop for now to rest." Obedient, as always, his soldiers gathered to make camp and talk with each other. Howe smiled to himself. With faces impassive in battle, it was easy to forget they were men. But they were, and they cared for each other—and their general—greatly.

He shook himself. Now was not the time for such soft-hearted thoughts. He had to focus on the letter—no telling what, or who, it would bear. Dismounting from his horse, he passed the reins over to a boy awaiting his orders, then he started again at opening the seal, a hundred possibilities filling his head. He lifted the flap and pulled out an official letter, signed by his fellow general, Burgoyne.

GENERAL WILLIAM HOWE:

My dear sir, now is the time we must seize. A plan has come to my mind to take New England, and finally end this war! General Barry St. Leger has agreed to join me, but I believe that only the three of us will make the victory sure. I am currently in Canada with my men, and we will drive south. General Leger will lead his troops down the Mohawk Valley in New York, and you will go north from New York City. In this way we will take New England. Sir, this war may finally be over!

Signed,
General John Burgoyne

. . .

HOWE CRUMPLED the letter into a ball and tossed it, glaring as the breeze blew it back at him. He had wanted to hear from Frances, for the time apart was a strain on his heart. But the letter was not from her. He snatched it up again. *New England.* Philadelphia was the colonists' capital, a much better location to seize. No, he would not go along with Burgoyne's plan. Besides, it would give Washington too much time to rebuild his army.

Shoving the letter in his pocket, he raised his hand. "Attention men! Onwards toward Philadelphia! It is there that we will conquer!"

"Huzzah!" they responded in a ferocious roar at the commanding words of their general. "On to Philadelphia!"

10 September 1777

It was late in the afternoon. Howe and his men had been marching for hours, and it was time for rest. "Alright, men! We will make camp here for the night and head out again early in the morning, so rest well!" They saluted, then broke up to make camp. *Tomorrow will be a big day, another battle,* Howe thought. They were going to storm the Continental Army and conquer Philadelphia. And they would win; there was no other option. *Besides, how could I tell Frances that I lost to those measly colonists again?*

11 September 1777

The bugle sounded to the rising sun at five in the morning. Groggily, Howe rose, pulled on his uniform, and made his way out of the tent. Many of his men were already up, taking down tents and preparing for the day's journey. It was going to be a tough battle. Although the British had believed at first that it would be a short war and a quick win for the crown, the colonists had proved themselves remarkably able to fight. Secretly, Howe admired that. They were beating the odds to fight for what they thought was right.

It was time to leave. Howe had received word from some local Loyalists that two forts located above the forks of Brandywine Creek were unguarded and would make the perfect place of attack. However, the forts were about seventeen miles away, and it would take at least seven hours to get there, not including rest periods. Therefore, they had to start the journey right away.

"Attention, men!" Howe called out. "We have a long trek ahead of us, and if we are to have any hope of getting there with daylight still left, we must leave immediately. Are you ready for what lies ahead?"

"Yes, sir!" they shouted in reply.

"Then to Philadelphia, men! Victory for the crown!"

"To Philadelphia! Huzzah!"

Howe smiled again at the joyful obedience of his men, but then sobered. Not all of them would see the sun shine tomorrow.

***

He was burning. Why, oh why, had he become a general? The sun was high in the sky and felt like fire. They had been traveling for hours and the sun was showing them no mercy. If he had not become a general, he could be home with Frances right now. If he had not become a general, they could have started a family. If he had not become a general, he would not be sunburned and sweating. He huffed. It was all true, but selfish. *My country needs me, and if that means sunburns, well, so be it.*

But then, just as Howe thought he may die from thirst, he heard a heavenly sound. Trickling water. It was flowing, it was gushing, rushing! Brandywine, they had arrived.

"Men! We are here!"

"Huzzah!" they cried, following their general to fill their canteens. Howe sighed as the water washed down his throat. To a parched man, cold water tasted better than something made by the King's cook herself. What a relief!

When the men had drunk their fill, Howe got to his feet. "We are close, men. The enemy lies just over that hill. Let us go and rest for a while before making our attack."

Gratefully, they complied and lay exhausted against the hill. Howe joined them, gazing up at the sky. *Oh Franny, where are you right now? What are you doing at this very moment? How I long for you! Are we looking up at this same sky, this very minute?* As his query drifted off into the universe, he remembered how she had looked in her wedding dress. And when he pictured her dress, he saw the clouds in the sky again, the same shade of white. It was that image that guided him to sleep.

"General, sir, they know we're here!"

Howe sat straight up. "Who?! What?!" Glancing quickly around he took in his surroundings and remembered. The journey, the plan. He dragged his hand over his face. He had fallen asleep on duty. How dreadfully embarrassing.

Howe got to his feet. "How do you know this, soldier? Did you see one of Washington's scouts?"

"Yes, sir," the soldier replied, "I saw him just on the other side of the hill. I know he saw us, but I do not think he knows that I saw him, sir."

Sighing, Howe rubbed his temples. "Well, there goes our element of surprise. Look alive, men! The enemy knows we are here."

Weary but rested, the army picked itself up. "Come on," one man said, "we may be tired—" someone huffed in agreement— "but we can win this battle. We have persevered through many battles before this one."

"He's right," another spoke up, "We can win this battle, and many more. Victory for the crown!"

"Victory for the crown! Huzzah!"

April 1778
Howe's Resignation Celebration

Fireworks exploded in the sky, bursting with color. The men had put on an excellent show. He was resigning from the army, and the soldiers wanted to hold him a celebration. Howe smiled.

They had won the Battle of Brandywine. The Fox and his men had put up a good fight, but Howe had won in the end. However, it was not the victory for which he had hoped. He lost five hundred men, and though Philadelphia was the colonists' capital, its capture was of no great value. Overall, it had been a pointless fight.

The letter. Howe recalled the message delivered by the man on horseback. He had been hoping it was from Frances. Instead, it had been regarding another battle, another plan to end the war. *What if Burgoyne was right? If I had followed his plan, would the war now be over?* It was possible.

But he had chosen his own path, and though he might regret it, he could not change it. He watched the sky, remembering that day by the hill when he had looked up wondering if Franny was looking up, too. He wondered the same thing now. *Franny, I have made mistakes. I wish I could change them, but I cannot. It is behind me, and the past will not change. But I can change the future. Oh, Franny, I cannot wait to be back home!*

KING GEORGE III: AMERICA'S LAST KING

BY BELLA WAUGH

KING GEORGE III: AMERICA'S LAST KING

St. James's Palace, London, England
23 February 1777

"We did WHAT?" King George III bellowed, slamming his fist on the desk, and jumping to his feet. His jeweled chair toppled over with a clatter, but he didn't notice.

Prime Minister Lord North wrung his hands. "Yes, Your Highness, we...er...lost the Battle of Trenton the day after Christmas."

The king slapped a hand to his forehead and paced around the room, ranting about the Rebels and their unexpected victory. His mind returned to December 1776, remembering when he toasted to the successive British victories.

"Oh, Lord North. What a victorious year this has been!" the king said with a proud smile. "Of the one-hundred battles and skirmishes fought this year, England won fifty-four, far more than the Rebels with only forty-six. With the majority of the battles in our favor, nothing can stop us now!"

A growl escaped the king's lips as he glared at Lord North, who shrank back. Lord North was far from responsible for the British defeat, but he was the only person present to bear the brunt of the king's fury.

"Blast those Rebels! How dare they oppose me so openly! They will pay, Lord North, they will pay. I shall not surrender those colonies, as long as I live!" The king engaged in another series of rants when a knock sounded on the door. "What is it?" he snapped.

"Your Majesty, you received a letter from General Howe," the messenger called through the door, his voice muffled.

For a moment, the king looked perturbed, but then his face softened, and his eyes lit up. "What, what? A letter from William Howe, my valiant general? Come in, come in!"

The messenger marched in and handed the letter to Lord North who scanned it. "As I was saying..." The king's voice rose again. "That blasted General Washington and his militia launched an attack on our men, and near Christmas no less!"

"Sir, while the news is quite disturbing, and I agree with you on all counts, General Howe has an urgent request," Lord North interjected.

"We shan't ever let such a loss happen again!" King George agreed as the prime minister nodded.

"Aye, never again. According to the general, this is not the end of battles to come," said Lord North as the snowy white curls on his wig bobbed up and down.

"I should say not! We cannot let them have the last word. The last gunshot on the plain. The last arrogant stance. Nay, we shall take those for ourselves!" The king puffed out his chest.

"However, in order to accomplish that, the general requires more ships and soldiers, Your Majesty."

The king frowned. "Of course, the kingdom will aid him, though what cost would that bring us, Lord North?" This war already had taken a great financial toll on England. His soul burned to win this war, yet his head reminded him that you can only fight a war when you have money and men to supply it.

Lord North paused and pointed to the letter. "He says here..."

"AT THE STATE *the Rebels are fighting back, I do believe we'll need more ships and men to fight this war for another year. Unless of course, the Rebels surrender early like cowards, in which case we could place the colonies back under the honorable rule of the Crown."*

KING GEORGE LAUGHED. "General Howe flatters me so, doesn't he?" North smiled a false grin, worried as well about the great cost of this war. "It's settled then." The king bobbed his head. "Write to General Howe immediately and inform him the supplies will come forthright. Loading of the ships will commence at daybreak!"

With a nod and a bow, Lord North left the room.

7 July 1777

"Look, Papa! A bird!" little Ernest cried out, pointing to the sky. Leaning onto his knees, King George spoke to his eighth child. "Is it now, Ernie? What color is it?" The king sat on the veranda with his family, enjoying the balmy weather. He glanced lovingly at his wife and smiled at their six-year-old son.

Ernie's face scrunched up as he shielded the bright sun from his eyes. "It's maybe...dark blue?"

"It's black, Ernest," George, their eldest son, snapped in a condescending tone.

"George!" Charlotte, the king's wife, reprimanded the fifteen-year-old without taking her eyes off her embroidery. The boy sulked as he whittled a stick with his pocketknife.

"Why, Father! It's our old friend, Nimbus!" their eleven-year-old daughter Charlotte, or Lotty as they called her, exclaimed with a hand on Ernie's shoulder.

"What, what? Lotty, is that so?" King George stood and walked to the balcony gazing at the sky as well. "My, isn't he a sight for sore eyes? Nimbus!" The king lifted his arm and whistled to the bird who circled and then swooped down, landing on the surprised young George's head.

"Chak!" The Black-Billed Magpie crowed and pecked him. The children laughed, and even the royal parents had to suppress their chuckles. Nimbus rose into the air to escape George's flailing arms, flapping over to land on the balcony railing by the children and the king. Eyeing them with a curious tilt of the head, Nimbus hopped closer. Noticing a band tied around Nimbus' right leg, the king unfastened it, revealing a folded paper.

"Oh, Father, what does it say?" Lotty asked, bouncing up and down.

"Let your father read in peace, Charlotte," the queen instructed.

Your Highness,

'Tis been a while since we spoke, and I have a new piece of intelligence for you. I have been watching one Edward Bancroft, the spy whom we commissioned to watch Benjamin Franklin back in March. While he has been doing *an excellent job, some suspect him. Bancroft is coming to London soon, and I suggest staging a fake arrest to ward off any suspicion.*

Your faithful companion,
Shadow

KING GEORGE WAS quiet for a moment, pondering this new information. When he first learned of his Newfoundland's uncanny ability to write, and act with utmost human intelligence, the monarch was flabbergasted, but he adjusted. Now Shadow was a faithful spy, and the king could rely on his information, for Shadow's advice proved to be quite helpful every time.

"Son, fetch Lord North right away," the king ordered George distractedly.

The boy shot the king an annoyed look and walked away, muttering under his breath.

The king sighed dejectedly, and his second eldest son, Frederick, called after his cheeky brother, "That's no way to treat Father, George!"

King George smiled wearily at Frederick, and George returned a few moments later with Lord North.

Bowing tightly, Lord North spoke. "Yes, Your Highness?"

"This way, North, I must speak with you." Turning to his family, the king waved. "I shall see you later."

"Now, North, I've just been inspired, though nature always does that to me. Do you remember Edward Bancroft? Well..."

The king's voice became quieter and quieter as he walked farther and farther away, dancing around the truth of his talented pets, but most of all relaying this important mission to North.

20 December 1777

"Your Majesty?" a voice called through a closed door.

King George stood and opened it. "Ah, Lord North, come in come in."

"A messenger has just arrived. We have news of two battles. May I---"

"Is it good news?" The king's heart pumped a bit faster than normal. This long war was taking its toll on the forty-year-old man, and daily he yearned to have a report that it was finally over, and that British rule prevailed.

"Aye sir, but there is bad news as well."

"Let's start off on a positive note then." The king walked further into the room as Lord North trailed behind.

Clearing his throat, Lord North read from the bulletin. "On September 11, our own General Howe and General Wilhelm von Kynphausen led a twofold attack against General Washington's men at Brandywine Creek. Thanks to heavy fog, Howe and his men were able to ford the creek and surround the Rebel men, leading to British victory!"

"Huzzah!" shouted the king, pumping his fist in the air. "That will show that Washington which George shall rule the colonies! Me! We shall win this war, North! We shall win!"

"Sir, we still have the other report."

The broad smile on the king's face faded. "Very well."

"The Battle of Saratoga was a face-off between our troops commanded by General Burgoyne, and the Patriot troops led by Horatio Gates. On September 19th, we attacked the Rebels, but Benedict Arnold anticipated this move and ordered his troops to surround our forces."

"Confound it! What an albatross that Arnold is. Though he does have a keen battle sense. If only he was on our side." The king's voice trailed off, and Lord North continued on.

"Then on 7 October, after waiting in vain for more troops, Burgoyne attacked again, but the Patriot forces again overwhelmed him, leading to his surrender."

"Surrender?" the king bellowed. "What kind of general is he? My army does not surrender!"

We should, Lord North thought, recalling the twenty-seven British losses this year. However, he didn't dare say it aloud.

THE EPIC STORY OF AMERICA 1777-1779

8 February 1778

Nimbus soared through the sky above London, his sights on the tall brick turrets of St. James Palace. He beat his exhausted wings, consoling himself. *Almost there, Nimbus ol' boy. In the name of the king, keep flying!* Encouraged by his pep talk, Nimbus flew toward King George's office where Nimbus hoped to find him this brisk winter morning. Once he got close enough, a glass opening in the brick wall (which humans called a 'window') showed King George indeed hunched over his desk. Eager to share the news, Nimbus flew straight towards the glass opening, increasing his speed until...

Thump!

The king looked up, seeing a black bird plastered on the window. Despite the feathers splayed out every which way, the king smiled when he saw it was his espionage messenger.

Nimbus recovered, trying to flap some sense back into his brain after his crash landing. At that moment, the glass opened, and the king poked his head out.

"Nimbus!" he thundered, beaming wide.

The shiny black bird shook his head once more and then flew to the windowsill. King George noticed a scroll of paper in the magpie's beak and held out his hand. Nimbus dropped the scroll and letting out a "chak," Nimbus stretched his cramping beak.

King George stared at the scroll for a moment before opening it. Something deep inside told him that this news wasn't good. Something deeper inside told him what was on this paper would change the course of the war. Something even deeper inside King George told him that England would lose. But curiosity overcame his doubts, and he tore open the wax seal and unfurled the parchment.

France has allied with the colonies. -Shadow.

What, what? No! Only six words, but they made the room spin. He took halting steps backward and sank into his desk chair. *No, no, no! Not this!* He grew frantic as all of his ominous feelings from a moment prior were realized. This news *wasn't* good. What was written right here *would* change the course of the war. They would indeed lose.

KING GEORGE III: AMERICA'S LAST KING

12 February 1778

King George knelt in the dirt beside a plant in the palace garden, observing its leaves, tendrils, and small buds. It had been only four days since he received the devastating news of the new French Alliance, and he was still shaken. Britain and France had their fair share of quarrels, disagreements, and even wars, like the war fought over European power in the mid 1700's, the Seven Year's War. That war had created a great deal of debt for England, which is why Prime Minister George Grenville urged the king to impose the Stamp Act in 1765. But not long after... *'Taxation without representation!'* the Patriots cried and revolted.

King George stood up and walked down the gravel path, rounding the bend. To his joy, a black dog bounded toward him with its tail wagging and tongue waving. "What what? Shadow, hello!" The king dropped to a knee, weaving his fingers in her soft black fur as Shadow barked.

"How's my little spy?" Another happy bark rang out. "Any more news for me, pup?"

Shadow didn't bark this time but walked to the garden next to the path and dug. Much to the king's amazement, within a few moments, a scroll of paper appeared in the soil, streaked with dirt but otherwise in perfect condition. Shadow nuzzled it with her muzzle, and the king knelt beside the hole, picking up the piece of paper cautiously. Shadow appeared to smile as she sat on her hindquarters, panting with her pink tongue. The king unfolded it and began to read.

YOUR MAJESTY,

Hello from your pet and spy, Shadow. I assume I brought you here, otherwise, you are the gardener or someone who should not read this. Do not continue unless you are His Majesty, King George III.

Since you have carried on, it's safe to assume you are indeed the king. (If not, off with you now!)

King George's forehead crinkled as his eyebrows drew up, staring

230

at Shadow with wide eyes. If he looked a few seconds longer, he would've witnessed Shadow's wink at him, but alas he already returned to the letter.

I hope you moved past your rage about the French Alliance, enough to consider your next move. However, I believe you are unsure what to do next, therefore this letter is for you.

Raising an eyebrow, the king gaped at the dog, amazed by the accuracy of Shadow's assumptions.

During the most recent battles, your goal has been to overtake the northern half of the Colonies, the site of so much political upheaval. However, we both know that strategy is not working. Therefore, I would like to make a suggestion. I recommend <u>shifting your Royal focus to the southern reaches of the Colonies.</u> I firmly believe this new tactic will bring the Colonies back into your grasp.

Your faithful companion,
Shadow

"Hmm..." the king murmured, rolling up the letter and squatting beside Shadow once more. "My dear pup, you may very well be onto something here."

11 October 1779

"Lastly I must thank Shadow, my dear dog," the king announced, gesturing to the sleeping canine. A few men and women threw each other sly dubious glances. Joyous about the great turn of the war's tide, the king threw this celebration, and for the past twenty minutes, he'd ranted about the war, the outrageous acts of the rebellious colonies, and of course the supremacy of the British Empire. However, he now had gone mad, thanking his dog of all things!

"Almost two years ago, as I walked through the garden with my precious dog, a wonderful idea came to me. We should focus on the Southern colonies, away from the north where achieving our rightful victory was proving elusive. Twenty months later, what is the result? Ninety-nine triumphs for the British Crown! Join me in a toast!"

The crowd sighed, relieved their king was not mad, at least not yet. Glasses clinked across the room as hearty cheers filled the air.

Lifting his glass, King George III beamed. "I've always known this war shall end with a British victory, and soon the world will know it, too! Huzzah for England!"

MAJOR BANASTRE TARLETON: TARLETON'S FIGHT AND NEWLY-FOUND FRIEND

BY CARMENE MILLER

MAJOR BANASTRE TARLETON: TARLETON'S FIGHT AND NEWLY-FOUND FRIEND

Brandywine, Pennsylvania, September 1777

Major Banastre Tarleton walked into his tent, went to his writing desk, pulled out a small brown book, and wrote.

My men are fighting bravely *and strongly. But we are exhausted. A few days ago, we got word from General Howe to march to Brandywine, Pennsylvania, so here we are. I am glad to be fighting for my country and my king. I do hope that I can return home one day. I miss my dear mother, my brothers and sister. But I will fight to the end, even if it means never seeing my family again.*

A soldier barged into his tent. "Sir, General Cornwallis wants you right away."

Tarleton put down his quill and marched over to General Cornwallis. "Sir, I understand you called for me."

"Yes, General Howe believes we can intersect the Rebels on Great Post Road and attack them in the late afternoon."

"Sir, I suggest we attack early in the morning, around five. If Howe's army is going to join us, we will have more soldiers and weapons and can catch them by surprise."

Cornwallis looked up with a smirk. "Well, Tarleton, you have the makings of a general. I will let General Howe know right away."

"Thank you, sir." Tarleton headed to his tent. As he got to the entrance, a red squirrel sat in a tree looking at him. Just for fun, he asked the squirrel, "Well, good day, how are you?"

To his surprise, the red squirrel nodded at him. Not thinking about it, he walked into his tent and picked up his diary. Then he thought, *Did that squirrel just nod his head to my question?* He got up and ran outside. The red squirrel was right next to his horse, Bess, looking at him with his pocket-watch in his mouth. Tarleton went up to the red squirrel and took it from him. With a confused look, he asked, "Now how did you get that?"

Dear Diary, the strangest thing happened. I asked a red squirrel a question, and I believe he answered. We don't have red squirrels in Britain that nod their head at us. He even got into my desk. Wait ... if the red squirrel can steal my watch without me knowing, then I wonder if he can spy on the Rebels without them knowing? Let's see.

He walked outside and asked the red squirrel, "Can you spy on the Rebels?"

The squirrel looked at him, nodded and ran off.

"Well, it looks like we have a new spy."

The squirrel returned at five in the morning, ran into his tent, and jumped on him.

"What are you doing here?" Tarleton asked.

The squirrel ran to his desk and wrote on a piece of paper. Tarleton walked over and asked, "What are you trying to tell me? Found.... them .... leave .... now? You found them, and you want us to leave now! I must go tell the general."

Tarleton ran out of his tent in his nightgown with his hands in the air."GENERAL, GENERAL, WE NEED TO LEAVE NOW!"

General Cornwallis came out of his tent. "What in the world are you doing, Tarleton?"

"THE SQUIRREL FOUND THEM. WE NEED TO LEAVE NOW!"

"Why should I believe in a squirrel?"

"Sir, trust me!"

"We will prepare for battle."

Tarleton ran back to his tent, yelling, "PREPARE FOR WAR. GET UP EVERYONE NOW!" He ran into his tent, changed into his uniform, and rushed back out to the men standing at attention. He mounted Bess and led her next to General Cornwallis.

MAJOR BANASTRE TARLETON: TARLETON'S FIGHT AND NEWLY-FOUND FRIEND

General Cornwallis said, "Tarleton, I sure hope you are correct about the Rebels." Tarleton felt the weight of the world on his shoulders.

As they got to the great road, the morning fog was upon them. It had provided them with perfect cover for a surprise attack on the Rebels. They went down the road as quiet as possible and then heard horses, people and the clanking of guns. But soon they heard a voice, "My men, be prepared for battle" and knew at once who that was.... GENERAL HOWE! General Cornwallis rode toward Howe's voice. Tarleton could hear the faint talking of the generals. After a few minutes, General Cornwallis, followed by General Howe, and his army broke through the fog. General Howe and another soldier joined General Cornwallis and Tarleton in front of the army. "So, who is this, General Cornwallis?" said GeneralHowe, looking at Tarleton. General Cornwallis lifted his head and said with a smirk, "This is Major Tarleton."

"Ah, I have heard a lot about you, Tarleton. You are doing a great deal for your country."

"Thank you, general. If I may ask, who is your companion?"

General Howe pointed to a young man. "This is Captain Ferguson. Shall we continue?"

"Lead the way."

They soon came up to Brandywine Creek. As they were about to cross, they heard gunfire. *BAM-BAM-BAM!* Before they could react, two men were already dead.

"REBELS!" the British yelled. The Battle of Brandywine began and would continue for eleven hours. *BAM-BAM-BAM-BOOM!* Men were fighting for their lives and country. The screams of soldiers and the smell of smoke filled the air. Sharpshooters climbed into the trees and shot down at their enemies.

One of Tarleton's friends ran to him. "My friend, I will fight for my country as you do. Now I plead, please take me to one of the nearby trees so I can climb it and destroy our enemy from above. If I die, tell my wife I died with honor." Tarleton gave him a sad look and nodded. Then the soldier jumped on Bess behind Ban, and they rode to the nearest tree.

Tarleton helped him up. "DON'T DIE!"

Then the soldier looked down at him. "I will try not to die, but in a battle like this it's hard."

Tarleton pulled out his gun and began to shoot the Rebels one by one. Men began to fall, and the British were losing more men than the Rebels. If they lost any more men, they would soon be outnumbered. Tarleton soon saw a man coming toward him fast. Then a cannon shot off, causing Bess to buck up and throw him to the ground. As Tarleton got up, the man rode right past him and into the battle. He was lucky that he got thrown to the ground, because that man could have killed him. But then Tarleton realized that it wasn't some soldier; it was none other than GEORGE WASHINGTON!

Tarleton yelled with more anger than he ever felt in his life. He whistles for Bess to come, and within two seconds she was there. He hopped on her and fought harder. Soon they lost more men. But they were pushing the Rebels back. A little spark of hope lit in every British soldier as they destroyed the Rebels. Soon, the Rebels retreated. After those long hours of fighting and death, the battle ended, won by the British.

"HUZZAH! HUZZAH! HUZZAH!" the British yelled. After that long fight and even though they lost men, they were incredibly happy. Tarleton snuck away from the crowd to his tent.

DEAR DIARY,

WE WON THE BATTLE! We fought for our lives and country, and it paid off. After the battle we sent men to go count how many died or were wounded. They counted 93 killed including my dear family friend John Campbell. 488 wounded including CPT Ferguson and 6 missing. I was told by a soldier that Ferguson was going to shoot a man in the back, but he didn't out of honor. The man was Washington. The war could have been over! If he was a true Loyalist like me, he would have SHOT HIM IN THE BACK! I must send a letter to John's wife.

. . .

MAJOR BANASTRE TARLETON: TARLETON'S FIGHT AND NEWLY-FOUND FRIEND

Dear Charlotte,

I hate to tell you that your husband, John, was killed in Brandywine, Pennsylvania. He told me to tell you that he died for his country. I am so sorry for your loss.

Banastre Tarleton

TARLETON WALKED over to his bed and fell straight to sleep. As he entered a world of his own, a terrifying dream interrupted him. The sound of gunfire filled the air, and he felt as if he is falling a long distance. The visions of violence, death and pain filled his mind. Then he saw his father and ran to embrace him. But it stopped when his father was lowered into the ground at his funeral. He screamed and then woke up. But when he did, the red squirrel's face appeared.

Both screamed, and the squirrel asked, "Why are you screaming?"

"What are you doing in here?"

"Well, talking to you."

"Why?"

"Because I am so bored."

"Okay, well, my name is Banastre Tarleton."

"That is a lot of letters .... B .... a.... n...a...s...t...r...e"

"Well, what's yours?"

"Are you ready to hear it?"

"YES!"

"Bobbly."

"What, wait, that's your name? Bobbly?"

"Nope. Ready for my real name?" the squirrel asked.

"Yes," Tarleton replied.

"Okay ... Eduardo Mateo Molinaro."

"WHAT?"

"Kidding. It's Billy Bob."

"What? You've got to be kidding me."

"But everyone calls me Billy the Great."

"I am glad I don't have to call you Billy Bob or Billy the Great. Just Billy."

Then out of nowhere, he started singing, "My name is Billy the Great. Tarleton gave me my name, and he loves me. That's why he sent me to spy on the Rebels. La la la la."

With a groan Tarleton said, "Please stop that wretched caterwauling."

"Can I please finish?"

"Fine."

"Alright. Ready ... BILLY BOBBB!"

"Are you done?"

"Yep, you should hear my friend Archie and me do it together."

"No, absolutely not."

Then Billy threw his hands in the air and ran out of the tent screaming, "ARCHIE, ARCHIE, LET'S SING!"

"No singing. I beg you please."

"Only if you sing with me."

"No."

"Please?"

"Fine."

"Ready on 3 ....1....2....3, BILLY THE GREAT!"

Tarleton wanted to throw the squirrel so badly, but he didn't. It reminded him of happiness and joy even in this dark time away from home.

Billy gave Tarleton a strange look. "You look too young to be in the war. How old are you, and what's your rank?"

Tarleton looked back. "I'm twenty-three, and I am a major. "

"Amazing ... you know what I am ... a squirrel."

With a sarcastic laugh, Tarleton said, "Ha ha, very funny." He gave a long yawn. "All right, Billy, I have got to get some rest."

Billy then ran out of the tent, screaming, "HE IS GOING TO SLEEP EVERYONE, SO BE QUIET!"

Tarleton walked over to his bed and laid down. But before he went to sleep, he kept thinking about the dream about his father's death, the sound of guns and men screaming. It sent a shiver down his spine. As he drifted off into a deep sleep, the dreams were not of pain, but

MAJOR BANASTRE TARLETON: TARLETON'S FIGHT AND NEWLY-FOUND FRIEND

seeing his family again and an unfamiliar woman named Susan Bertie who would later become his wife.

Tarleton woke up early in the morning to birds chirping and faint rustling. As he looked around, he saw his hat moving across his desk. Curious, he got up, walked to his desk, and picked up his hat. To his surprise, Billy was in it.

"Well good day, sir, my name is Major Tarleton," Billy said with a serious look.

Banastre looked at Billy and thought, *I can't believe I thought he could be a spy. The squirrel thinks that he is me. Strange creature.*

Billy then looked at him and said, "Here is a letter from your mother."

Tarleton grabbed the letter, tore it open, and read it aloud, because if he didn't, Billy would have run away with it.

My Dear Banastre,

How are you? I haven't heard from you in a very long time. Charlotte told me what happened. Your siblings miss you dearly. I pray that I can see you again after this war is over. Oh, and before I end this letter, please fight with honor.

Your mother,
Jane

Tarleton put down his letter with a smile. Then he said with a smirk, "Fighting with honor is how I would get myself killed."

Billy ran into the tent, hopped on the desk, and said in a dramatic tone, 'To fight with honor, or not to fight with honor. That is the question.' Do you know who said that?"

Tarleton gave an annoyed look. "William Shakespeare."

Billy walked over to the letter and started to read. "You have brothers and sisters?"

"Yes, I am one of seven."

"Wow, you're very lucky."

"What do you mean that I'm lucky?'"

Then Billy looked at him with a sad look. "Well... I had two sisters and two brothers. Before this war started, we were carefree, living in the trees. But when the war began, our family was torn apart. We all had to choose sides. It was brother against siblings against sister. I didn't get to choose what side I was on because I was so young. So, I got put with my mother... on the British side."

"Well, if you had to choose, which side would you be on?"

"None. I hate war. It's cruel. I would rather have everyone talk peacefully. Where no one would lose their families and homes. They came to us to talk. But of course, we said no. We need territory.

"Did you ever ask yourself if maybe the reason the Rebels are so mad is because the British slaughtered their families and destroyed their homes?" Billy asked.

Tarleton looked at the ground. *We are only fighting for our country.* Billy then got up off the desk and walked outside. Tarleton sat there for a moment and started to doubt the cost. *Is this really worth it?* He stopped worrying and wondering and started to once again go to sleep. But this dream was one he would never understand.

ABOUT THE AUTHORS

CHASE ADAM (Brigadier General Anthony Wayne)

Chase Adam is a homeschooled freshman, currently residing in the Midwest. When he's not tossing opponents in a fireman's on the wrestling mat, or tackling quarterbacks on the football field, you can find him reading anything he can get his hands on, or playing the Top Gun theme song on his trumpet. He hopes to one day become a lawyer.

DEDICATION: I would like to dedicate my chapter to my amazing family for all their support, and my favorite Coach Sibel because he's awesome. I'll always have peanut M&M's for you, Sibs.

And to all the Mad Anthony Waynes out there - while your hard work may not be recognized here on Earth, your Heavenly Father sees you, and your reward is in heaven. Never give up.

I am so grateful for this amazing opportunity to learn and research and write! I'm thankful that God provided a way for me to be part of this camp, the friends I've made (the Commonwealth Club) and the memories I'll have (pickles and chocolate - really?). Thank you, Miss Jenny and Miss Libby, for an unforgettable June!

AUTHOR'S NOTE: Anthony Wayne did not write a letter to Polly after Paoli. All the letters were either trimmed because of length, or cobbled together by quotes plus the retelling of the battle. When General Lee talks to General Washington during the Battle of Monmouth, no one knows what he said. In the actual quote that I included, he used the Lord's name in vain which I omitted. Other than that, it is word-for-word. In his second letter, Wayne calls Lee a "Caitiff." This was his favorite way to call someone a scoundrel.

BIBLIOGRAPHY: Mary Stockwell, *Unlikely General: Mad Anthony Wayne and the Fight for America*, 2018.

Bob Druey & Tom Clavin, *Valley Forge*, 2018.

www.ushistory.org/valleyforge/served/wayne.html

www.battlefields.org/learn/articles/battle-stony-point

www.battlefields.org/learn/revolutionary-war/battles/monmouth

www.thoughtco.com/major-general-anthony-wayne-2360619

MIKAYLA BADENHORST (Baron De Steuben)

My name is *Mikayla Badenhorst*, and I am 12-years-old. This is my second year participating in the Epic Patriot Camp, and I enjoyed it just as much this year last year. My favorite things to do, besides writing songs and stories, include playing volleyball, swimming and boogie boarding in the Gulf of Mexico, watching movies, and READING!! I also love hanging out with my family, friends, and three adorably crazy cats.

DEDICATION: I am dedicating my story to my mom who supported, guided, encouraged, and helped me, my uncle who promoted the stretching and training of my brain during summer break by sponsoring me for this camp, and my cat, Lewis, who offered tremendous emotional support.

AUTHOR'S NOTE: I loved learning and writing about Azor and Baron De Steuben, and I hope you enjoyed it too. Here are some fun facts about Azor. He *did* howl when the captain sang on the voyage across the Atlantic Ocean. Azor also helped drive the Baron into debt because of his giant appetite as well as leaping through the carriage door onto the Baron's lap. Something interesting about De Steuben includes the fact that Mr. Franklin and Mr. Deems fabricated his resume to make him look more tasteful to the American Congress. Astonishingly enough, the Baron was named after his godfather, King Fredrick I of Prussia. Baron De Steuben played a pivotal role in organizing and training the Continental Army, allowing these brave revolutionaries to gain traction against the largest military power in the world.

BIBLIOGRAPHY: Drury, Bob, Tom Clavin. *The Heart of Everything That is Valley Forge*. New York: Simon & Schuster, 2018.

Ellis, Joseph J. *American Creation: Triumphs and Tragedies at the Founding of the Republic*. New York: Alfred A. Knopf, 2007.

"General Baron De Steuben Arrives at Valley Forge." YouTube, uploaded by Valley Forge National Park, 1 October 2012. www.youtu.be/-u6K2MbuE5Q.

Lockhart, Paul. *The Drillmaster at Valley Forge: The Baron de Steuben and the Making of the American Army*. Narrated by Norman Diatz, Audible, 2008. Audiobook.

Raphael, Ray. *Founders: The People Who Brought You a Nation*. New York: MJF Books, 2009.

Rust, Randall. *Battle of Monmouth*. American History Central, 9 May 2022, www.americanhistorycentral.com/entries/battle-of-monmouth-1778.

"Presidents Day 2021: Who was Baron De Steuben?" YouTube, uploaded by Patriots Path, 15 February 2021. www.youtu.be/OC5Nz1QN_Lg.

JENNY L. COTE (Epic Patriot Camp Director)

Award-winning author and speaker Jenny L. Cote, who developed an early passion for God, history, and young people, beautifully blends these three passions in her two fantasy fiction series, The Amazing Tales of Max and Liz® and Epic Order of the Seven®. Likened to C. S. Lewis by readers and book reviewers alike, she speaks on creative writing to schools, universities, and conferences around the world. Jenny has a passion for making history fun for kids of all ages, instilling in them a desire to discover their part in HIStory. Her love for research has taken her to most Revolutionary sites in the U.S., to London (with unprecedented access to Handel House Museum to write in Handel's composing room), Oxford (to stay in the home of C.S. Lewis, 'the Kilns,' and interview Lewis' secretary, Walter Hooper at the Inklings' famed The Eagle and Child Pub), Paris, Normandy, Rome, Israel, and Egypt. She partnered with the National Park Service to create Epic Patriot Camp, a summer writing camp at

Revolutionary parks to excite kids about history, research, and writing. Jenny's books are available online and in stores around the world, as well as in audio and e-book formats. Jenny has been featured by FOXNEWS on Fox & Friends and local Fox Affiliates, as well as numerous Op-Ed pieces on FoxNews.com. She has also been interviewed by nationally syndicated radio and print media, as well as international publications. Jenny holds two marketing degrees from the University of Georgia and Georgia State University. A Virginia native, Jenny now lives with her family in Roswell, Georgia. Learn more about Jenny at www.epicorderoftheseven.com.

DEDICATION: IT'S FOR THE CHILDREN!

ACKNOWLEDGEMENTS: Thank you, God, for bringing each person and part of this project together. You get all the glory! I'm grateful to Banastre Tarleton, Mark Schneider, and John Slaughter for being the ones who got the ball of the Revolution rolling in my world to create the original Epic Patriot Camp. (See my opening comments in the front of the book for the full back story.) But Virtual Epic Patriot Camp would not have been possible without my dear friend, "spoon sister," and historical author extraordinaire, Libby Carty McNamee. While we suspect that we were separated at birth, I'm so happy to have connected with her to inspire the next generation of young patriots while having more fun than anyone should be allowed. Thank you, parents, for entrusting your incredible children to our care—your bravery is surpassed only by that of our Founding Fathers.

CHLOE FROST (Martha Washington)

Chloe Frost is a rising sixth grader at Westminster Schools of Augusta in Augusta, Georgia and the youngest of five children. She loves reading and writing and hopes to author a novel in the future, maybe more than one! She most enjoys writing fiction and hopes her flair for the imaginative shows beyond the facts about these amazing historical figures.

ACKNOWLEDGEMENTS: First, I would like to thank God for giving me the opportunity and gifts to be involved in this project and write my own chapter in a book. Next, I would like to thank my parents, Patty and Cecil Frost, for signing me up and supporting me. I would not have even known about this summer camp without my mom. Last, but not least, I would like to thank my oldest sister, Lani Frost, for helping me by making edits and making sure the format was correct. I am very grateful for everything. Thank you!

DEDICATION: I would like to dedicate this chapter to my sister, Lani. I love you very much. Thank you for helping me so much!

BIBLIOGRAPHY: "Martha Washington." *Omeka RSS*, marthawashington.us/exhibits/show/martha-washington--a-life/life-at-mt--vernon-before-the-/mistress-of-the-household.html. Accessed 27 June 2023.

"Elizabeth Willing Powel." *George Washington's Mount Vernon*, www.mountvernon.org/library/digitalhistory/digital-encyclopedia/article/elizabeth-willing-powel/. Accessed 27 June 2023.

"Martha Washington Timeline." *George Washington's Mount Vernon*, www.mountvernon.org/george-washington/martha-washington/timeline/. Accessed 27 June 2023.

"The Women Present at Valley Forge." *National Parks Service*, www.nps.gov/vafo/learn/historyculture/valleyforgewomen.htm. Accessed 27 June 2023.

"Washington's Vehicles Historical Marker." *Historical Marker*, 27 Jan. 2023, www.hmdb.org/m.asp?m=112850.

"Martha Washington." *Omeka RSS*, marthawashington.us/exhibits/show/martha-washington--a-life/early-life/childhood.html. Accessed 27 June 2023.

"Battle of Brandywine." *George Washington's Mount Vernon*, www.mountvernon.org/library/digitalhistory/digital-encyclopedia/article/battle-of-brandywine/. Accessed 27 June 2023.

"Conway Cabal." *George Washington's Mount Vernon*, www.mountvernon.org/library/digitalhistory/digital-encyclopedia/article/conway-cabal/. Accessed 27 June 2023.

PAYTON GRACE (General Charles Cornwallis)

I've written a biography before. I can do this again! A burst of confidence spread throughout my body, yet it only lasted for a second. *It can't be* that *hard to write another one.* Or so I thought. After mindlessly tapping the keyboard for a few seconds, I sighed. *Might as well stick to the script.* The information came to me almost immediately. 14-years-old, from Oahu, Hawaii, a voracious reader and writer. Yes, that was me. Somehow, I had written historical fiction twice now, a genre that I did not believe was my forte. In fact, every story I worked on up till then was nearly every single genre of fiction *except* historical. But I discovered there was something about taking facts from the history books and weaving it into your own words that was just... amazing. It is important to look back at the past and see how we grew and changed since then, both in the history of humanity as a whole, as well as one's own history. There would be no present or future without the past. As I pondered this, a quote came to mind. To get to where we are going, we sometimes have to remember where we've been.

ACKNOWLEDGEMENTS: As always, I am grateful for my wonderful family and friends, as well as my fellow campers and Jenny L. Cote and Libby McNamee for, once again, setting up and orchestrating EPC. It was yet another amazing experience. Each and every single one of you are a light, not only in my life, but in this world. Thank you for allowing me to see you shine. Continue to be your incredible, unique selves.

BIBLIOGRAPHY: "Battle of Brandywine – Brandywine Battlefield Park Associates." *Brandywine Battlefield*, www.brandywinebattlefield.org/battle/.

"Battle of Brandywine · George Washington's Mount Vernon." *Mount Vernon*, www.mountvernon.org/library/digitalhistory/digital-encyclopedia/article/battle-of-brandywine/.

"Brandywine." *American Battlefield Trust*, www.battlefields.org/learn/revolutionary-war/battles/brandywine.

The Battle of Brandywine Begins, 13 November 2009, www.history.com/this-day-in-history/the-battle-of-brandywine-begins.

"Battle of Monmouth · George Washington's Mount Vernon." *Mount Vernon*, www.mountvernon.org/library/digitalhistory/digital-encyclopedia/article/battle-of-monmouth/.

"Monmouth Battle Facts and Summary." *American Battlefield Trust*, www.battlefields.org/learn/revolutionary-war/battles/monmouth.

"The Battle Of Monmouth: The American Revolutionary War." *World Atlas*, www.worldatlas.com/us-history/the-battle-of-monmouth-the-american-revolutionary-war.html.

Wickersty, Jason R. "In the Heat of the Moment at Monmouth." *American Battlefield Trust*, 5 June 2019, www.battlefields.org/learn/articles/heat-moment-monmouth.

"Charles Cornwallis (U.S." *National Park Service*, 24 January 2020, www.nps.gov/people/charles-cornwallis.htm.

Copley, John Singleton, and Nathaniel Currier. "Charles Cornwallis, 1st Marquess Cornwallis." www.en.wikipedia.org/wiki/Charles_Cornwallis,_1st_Marquess_Cornwallis.

Dorney, Douglas R. "Lord Cornwallis: Defender of British and American Liberty?" *Journal of the American Revolution*, 1 June 2023, https://allthingsliberty.com/2023/06/lord-cornwallis-defender-of-british-and-american-liberty/.

Hickman, Kennedy. "Lord Charles Cornwallis, American Revolution Commander." *ThoughtCo*, 1 July 2019, www.thoughtco.com/american-revolution-lord-charles-cornwallis-2360680.

CAMERON GRAHAM (General Nathanael Greene)

Cameron Graham is a homeschooler from Arizona. He excels in STEAM activities and competes in challenges. His favorite subjects in school are military history and geography. Following his work in *The Epic Story of 1776*, he was excited to continue telling the story of Nathanael Greene in this second installment.

Cameron is active in his community and works with the homeless, children in crisis, and refugees in his city. He and his sister began their own ministry for refugees in 2021 to celebrate a child's first birthday in the USA.

Cameron is active in his local 4-H with a project on dogs as well as County STEM Ambassador. He also enjoys playing as a defenseman in the Youth Hockey House League. He plans to continue writing

Nathanael Greene's story as well as completing his series on military machines.

DEDICATION: First and foremost, I would like to thank Mrs. Jenny L. Cote and Mrs. Libby McNamee for the 2023 Patriot Writing Camp. Your passion for history is contagious, and I am grateful for all the guidance you gave me in becoming a better writer.

Thanks to my mom and dad for dedicating their time to help me in this endeavor and for the investment and belief in my success. Thanks to Madison for helpful tips from a fellow aspiring author.

AUTHOR'S NOTE: Hundley (high spirited squirrel) and George (turtle) are fictional characters who run through my story and assist the Patriots and Nathanael Greene. Hundley is just beginning to come into his full role as the trilogy continues into 1780.

I attempt to use Nathanael Greene's quotes and thoughts according to historical records to make the story as accurate as possible. At times I take liberty to place them inside a conversation that may not be historically accurate. For example, at times Greene speaks to Knox although he actually wrote those words to him.

BIBLIOGRAPHY: "The Conway Cabal." *Ushistory.Org*, 4 July 1995, www.ushistory.org/march/other/cabal.htm.

"George Washington Forges His Army | the Revolution (S1, E6) | Full Episode." *YouTube*, 10 Nov. 2022, www.youtube.com/watch?v=qWsi_LqPeP0&t=980s.

Greenwalt, Phillip S. "Nathanael Greene as Quartermaster General." *American Battlefield Trust*, 17 Oct. 2021, www.battlefields.org/learn/articles/nathanael-greene-quartermaster-general#:~:text=On%20-March%202%2C%201778%2C%20Rhode,the%20role%20of%20quartermaster%20general.

Hardy, Rob. "Cato." *George Washington's Mount Vernon*, www.mountvernon.org/library/digitalhistory/digital-encyclopedia/article/cato/. Accessed 27 June 2023.

Kelly, Jack. "Revolutionary Friendship." *Journal of the American Revolution*, 28 Aug. 2016, www.allthingsliberty.com/2014/07/revolutionary-friendship/.

NAOMI HAYES (Edward Bancroft)

Naomi Hayes lives in Nashville, Tennessee, along with her mom, dad, three younger brothers, and her energetic mini poodle-cavalier spaniel dog. She is 13-years-old and is going into the eighth grade. Ever since she was four years old, Naomi has dreamed of becoming a Christian author and influencing people with her work. Among writing, Naomi hopes to also become an illustrator, movie producer, or entrepreneur. She enjoys writing (of course!), soccer, basketball, art, and eating ice cream.

ACKNOWLEDGEMENTS: First of all, I wouldn't have been able to accomplish this without Mrs. Jenny and Mrs. Libby. Thank you for your patience, encouragement, and fun-ness!

I love you Mom, Dad, Gresham, Zeke, and Lachlan! Thank you for your help! Thank you to my teachers, Mr. Griffin, Mrs. Cruise, and Mrs. Gutierrez for being such incredible teachers and improving my writing! (Don't worry, I put some tropes in!) Also, thank you to all of the EPC campers, but specifically Bella, Christopher, and Gemma for your encouragement, friendliness, and awesome collaborating ideas!

DEDICATION: To my dear grandpa, Dwaine Cales. You helped me so much not just with this book, but with my entire life too. You have done so many incredible things, (including writing your own book!) influencing so many people, and you are an amazing grandfather. I love you!

AUTHOR'S NOTE: Many of the dates in Bancroft's life are unclear. For example, many sources explain that Bancroft left for Paris on 26 March 1777, but there are no hints when he arrived. For my chapter, I used the fact that in the 1700s, it took around six to eight weeks to travel between London and France. So, when I wrote that Bancroft arrived in Paris on 30 July 1777, that is just a mere estimate based on research. Another example is when Bancroft staged his arrest. I did not find exactly when it was, but based on his timeline, November seemed a likely time. At the end of my chapter, Bancroft is accused of treason by Arthur Lee but freed by his friend, John Paul Jones. Apparently this event happened "early in the year," so it could have happened anywhere between January and April. Also, when the

Franco-American Treaty is signed, historical resources say Bancroft was able to send a private messenger within 42 hours of the signing. Crazy, right? For my chapter, Nimbus the magpie was Bancroft's "private messenger." (Thanks, Bella and Christopher for that idea!)

BIBLIOGRAPHY: www.revwartalk.com/edward-bancroft
www.brewminate.com/edward-bancroft-double-agent-spying-for-both-sides-during-the-revolutionary-war/
www.en.wikipedia.org/niki/Edward-Bancroft
Schaeper, T. (2011). Edward Bancroft: Scientist, Author, Spy. Yale University.

PERI JORDAN (George Washington)

Peri Jordan is a teenage, Christian author from Columbus, Ohio. She spends her days reading, writing, and playing *far* too many board games for her sanity. Ever since she was little, she has loved writing about adventures to places she's never seen with people she's never met. Now, she is passionate about writing books to inspire and encourage young people to discover and deepen their relationships with their Lord and Savior, Jesus Christ.

ACKNOWLEDGEMENTS: So many people helped me to persevere and write this story. First, Mrs. Cote and Mrs. McNamee. Their input and critique on my chapter made all the difference, taking it from a rough draft to a polished story. I could not have done it without you! Second, I want to thank my mom, my dad, and my sister. Their encouragement was exactly what I needed to not throw my first, second, or final draft into the trash pretty much every time I looked at it. They prayed for me and worked with me through the entire process, and I am *so* grateful. Most of all, however, I would like to thank God for staying with me and being my number one fan even when my manuscript was, um... *not* the best. Thank you everyone! God bless.

BIBLIOGRAPHY: https://www.mountvernon.org/library/digital-history/digital-encyclopedia/article/george-washington-and-the-marquis-de-lafayette/#:
https://www.brandywinebattlefield.org/battle/

https://www.mentalfloss.com/article/612217/colonial-era-slang-terms

PIPER JORDAN (General William Howe)

Piper Jordan is a 16-year-old Christian homeschooler who likes to paint, draw, and write. She lives in Columbus, Ohio, with her mom, dad, sister Peri, and two cats---Fritz and Pixie. She is passionate about the love of her Savior, Jesus Christ, and hopes to one day express that through children's ministry.

ACKNOWLEDGEMENTS: First to God: Thank you for supporting me always. Though I had a couple tough moments with this story through research or writer's block, you got me through it.

To my parents: Thank you for encouraging me along the way and telling me I could do it. And thank you to my mom for reading Max & Liz to my sister and me—and doing all the accents.

To my sister: Thank you for supporting me in my writing and encouraging me. You were the one who first gave me the idea to write about the Battle of Brandywine. I do not know where my story would be without you.

To Mrs. McNamee: You were the first one to edit my story. I was very discouraged about it and scared that people would read it and think it was horrible, but when I read your edits, there was so much encouragement. You also had a lot of suggestions how to make it better. Thank you for helping me along my writing journey.

To Mrs. Cote: Thank you for having this class in the first place! I have written some here and there, but never a whole story and was never very committed. This class gave me the motivation and accountability to write an entire story. Thank you also for editing my story and showing me how I could do better. You and Mrs. McNamee are such a blessing.

BIBLIOGRAPHY: "Battle of Brandywine." *Wikipedia*, 19 June 2023, www.en.wikipedia.org/wiki/Battle_of_Brandywine.

"Revolutionary War: The Turning Point, 1776-1777 : The American Revolution, 1763 - 1783 : U.S. History Primary Source Timeline : Classroom Materials at the Library of Congress : Library of

Congress." *The Library of Congress,* www.loc.gov/classroom-materials/united-states-history-primary-source-timeline/american-revolution-1763-1783/revolutionary-war-turning-point-1776-1777/.

Robinson, Martha K. "British Occupation of Philadelphia." *Encyclopedia of Greater Philadelphia,* 26 Feb. 2022, philadelphiaencyclopedia.org/essays/british-occupation-of-philadelphia.

"William Howe." *American Battlefield Trust,* www.battlefields.org/learn/biographies/william-howe.

"William Howe." *Encyclopædia Britannica,* www.britannica.com/biography/William-Howe-5th-Viscount-Howe.

Yost, Russell. "The Most Complete Guide to General William Howe Facts." *The History Junkie,* 15 Sept. 2021, thehistoryjunkie.com/general-william-howe/.

ELLIOTT LAY (Benjamin Tallmadge)

BIBLIOGRAPHY: "Benjamin Tallmadge." *American Battlefield Trust,* www.battlefields.org/learn/biographies/benjamin-tallmadge. Accessed 27 June 2023.

"Benjamin Tallmadge." *Encyclopædia Britannica,* www.britannica.com/biography/Benjamin-Tallmadge. Accessed 25 June 2023.

"Culper Spy Ring." *George Washington's Mount Vernon,* www.mountvernon.org/library/digitalhistory/digital-encyclopedia/article/culper-spy-ring/. Accessed 27 June 2023.

Schellhammer, Michael. "Abraham Woodhull: The Spy Named Samuel Culper." *Journal of the American Revolution,* 28 Aug. 2016, https://allthingsliberty.com/2014/05/abraham-woodhull-the-spy-named-samuel-culper/.

"The Culper Spy Ring - Facts, Code & Importance." *History.Com,* www.history.com/topics/american-revolution/culper-spy-ring. Accessed 27 June 2023.

Yost, Russell. "Culper Spy Ring Facts and Accomplishments." *The History Junkie,* 29 Sept. 2021, www.thehistoryjunkie.com/culper-spy-ring-facts/.

LIBBY CARTY MCNAMEE (Epic Patriot Camp Director)

Libby Carty McNamee is a lawyer, speaker, and award-winning author of two upper-middle-grade historical novels, Susanna's Midnight Ride: The Girl Who Won the Revolutionary War and Dolley Madison and the War of 1812: America's First Lady, as well as their Study Guides. She loves making Author Visits to school groups in person and virtually. In addition, she would love to talk to your historical society and/or book club. Currently she is writing a third novel about a Civil War heroine, The Spy Who Won the Civil War: Elizabeth Van Lew. Sign up for her monthly Dispatch at LibbyMcNamee.com for fun historical tidbits. Find her on FB and Instagram @libbymcnameeauthor.

A native of Boston, Libby now lives in Richmond, Virginia. She is a graduate of Georgetown University and Catholic University School of Law. She also served as Major, U.S. Army JAG Corps, in South Korea, Bosnia, Germany, and Tacoma, Washington.

ACKNOWLEDGEMENTS: I would like to thank my fellow Epic Patriot Camp Director, dear friend, and "spoon sister Caroline," Jenny L. Cote, for inviting me again to embark upon this truly EPIC adventure! I am so thankful God brought us together through the American Friends of Lafayette just a few years ago. Huzzah!

In addition, I would like the amazingly-talented Mark Schneider for spending so much time with our starry-eyed campers as General Lafayette, Bruce Mowday for addressing our group author-to-author, and Richard Schumann for his fabulous voice-over as Patrick Henry for our Marketing Committee. Special thanks to my husband, Bernie, and son, Sam, for their support during the wonderfully hectic days of camp and editing "for the children."

DEDICATION: This is for YOU, the children—our twenty-five phenomenal campers who never cease to amaze, impress, and inspire us with their kindness, diligence, and dedication to becoming better writers. It has been such a joy and honor working with each and every one of you. HIP HIP HUZZAH!

EDAN MACNAUGHTON (Governor Patrick Henry)

Edan MacNaughton is a published author from California. He has a passion for both writing and sports.

DEDICATION: To my family, without your love and support this wouldn't have been possible. Love you all.

AUTHOR'S NOTE: The letter excerpts in my chapter are real. Patrick Henry did receive an anonymous letter inviting him to join the cabal against George Washington, and he forwarded it on.

William the servant is a fictitious character. Cato the cat and Charles the crow are also fictitious.

The journal entry Patrick Henry makes at the end is fictional, but I tried to capture his true-to-life thoughts as best as I could.

I only made a couple minor word changes in the letters. Some of the old English used was hard to understand. So, I found contemporary words with the same meaning and replaced them in an effort to make my chapter more enjoyable for you, the reader. If you would like to read the original untouched letters that Patrick Henry and George Washington exchanged, I recommend www.foundersarchive.org.

BIBLIOGRAPHY: "Colonial Williamsburg: The World's Largest Living History Museum." *Colonial Williamsburg Wax Seal*, www.colonialwilliamsburg.org/. Accessed 19 June 2023.

Cote, Jenny L. *The Declaration, the Sword & the Spy*. Living Ink Books, an Imprint of AMG Publishers, 2020.

Cote, Jenny L. *The Voice, the Revolution & The Key*. Living Ink Books, 2017.

Founders Online: Home." *National Archives and Records Administration*, www.founders.archives.gov. Accessed 18 June 2023.

Patrick Henry's Red Hill. *Patrick Henry's Red Hill*, 14 June 2023.

ROXANNE MESSIER (General Horatio Gates)

Hi! I'm *Roxy Messier*. I'm twelve-years-old and live in Raleigh, North Carolina. Next year, I will move to Greenville, South Carolina. My dad's new work will be in Traveler's Rest, the same name as Horatio Gates's plantation! I live with my mom, dad, and my four younger siblings! I LOVE to read, especially Jenny L. Cote's books! Her books were the reason I became interested in history and signed up for this EPIC camp! I've always loved to write, so getting feedback from my favorite author, AND getting published, is my dream come true! I also enjoyed reading Libby McNamee's book, *Susanna's Midnight Ride,* and I can't wait to read, *Dolley Madison and the War of 1812!* Soli Deo Gloria (Glory to God alone!)

DEDICATION: To Grammy and Pappy who sponsored me to this camp and always encouraged my writing abilities. Love you!

ACKNOWLEDGEMENTS: First, I want to acknowledge my parents, who supported me throughout this camp. Thanks, Mama, for helping me chop down my story (and kill several "darlings" in the process.) Thanks, Daddy, for helping me because Word is another language to me! You guys are the best! Love you!

To Henry, for always "supporting" my writing career (see those quotation marks, Henry? That's called *sarcasm*). Don't worry, I still love you though.

To Quincy: You are a cute little boy, even though I know saying that will annoy you. Love you! To Penny: Thank you for shamelessly snooping on m Epic Patriot Camp meeting, and for being my favorite sister (and only). Love you! To Teddy: You are so, so adorable, Teddy! From the way you pretend to shoot toy muskets, I can tell that someday you will be a little Patriot! Love you!

To Nena and Papa, who encourage my writing. And thank you for being interested in Jenny L. Cote's books and the book for research, Nena. Love you guys! Also, to my Aunt Blair, who helped cut down my chapter. Thanks!

And to Ms. Jenny and Ms. Libby: You both deserve rousing cheers from all the American Patriots! HUZZAH!

To the Epic Patriot Campers: For the laughs, the fake businesses, and encouragement of my story idea!

And finally, to God. Thank you for caring for me and giving me the chance to become a writer at this camp! Thank you for everything you've done in my life.

AUTHOR'S NOTE: Horatio Gates and John Burgoyne were in the same regiment from 1745-1747, but I don't know where they met. Bailey Tavern is a fictional tavern. Heinrich and Pleasant are fictional characters, but Heinrich's predicament of having no good chance in life was the problem of many peasants in the German countries. Hesse-Kassel was a real country, and Friedrich II was the ruler in 1777. I don't know if the ships carrying Hessian soldiers to America, recruited servants, but it is plausible.

The events of September 19th are all true, besides the dialogue. However, I don't know if Gates's generals lined up in his headquarters, but he would have received a report about what happened to Learned and his troops, although perhaps not in person.

The clock locket that Noemie uses is fake. As far as I know, there wasn't a French spy at the Battles of Saratoga. The plight of the French was real; they didn't want the British to know that they helped the Americans during the war for many reasons.

The word 'teleport' was not used until 1878. The mysterious figure and his bloodhound are fictional. James Wilkinson's report was loosely worded to a description in *Saratoga, Turning Point of America's Revolutionary War*. Horatio Gates' words were real.

I don't know where Horatio Gates was eating, but *Saratoga* stated at the mess. Mess halls were not used at this time, so Ms. Jenny told me to use "Officer's Mess." I do not know if Horatio Gates and John Burgoyne met the first time exactly thirty-two years before the surrender at Saratoga. Many friends became enemies because of the revolution, so maybe they were in that situation.

During the course of my research, I had the honor of seeing the papers of Horatio Gates in microfilm at the University of North Carolina, Chapel Hill (even though I'm an NC State fan)!

BIBLIOGRAPHY: Mintz, Max, The Generals of Saratoga, John Burgoyne and Horatio Gates

Ketchum, Richard, Saratoga, the Turning Point of America's Revolutionary War

www. en.wikipedia.org/wiki/Teleportation#

CARMENE MILLER (Major Banastre Tarleton)

My name is *Carmene Miller*. I am 14 and in 9th grade. I live in Concord, North Carolina, with my parents, two sisters (Zoe and Adie), two dogs (Eastway and Lexi), and two birds (Lafayette and Washington). I was so excited to return to camp this year and write about the famous Banastre Tarleton. I am a full-on history nerd like my dad and my grandfather, especially about the Revolutionary War. When I get older my dream job is to become a hospice social worker, because I want to help families, and also, I would like to be an author. God has blessed me to be here and the ability to grow my experience in writing.

DEDICATION: To my grandfather who is with God in heaven and to God for allowing this to happen and being by my side throughout my life. God bless you all.

AUTHOR'S NOTE: John Campbell and Billy are added characters to the chapter and not real. But don't tell Billy that he is a fictional character. He will go crazy. Hope you enjoyed the book.

BIBLIOGRAPHY: "Banastre Tarleton." *American Battlefield Trust*, www.battlefields.org/learn/biographies/banastre-tarleton. Accessed 28 June 2023.

"Banastre Tarleton." *Wikipedia*, 28 June 2023, en.wikipedia.org/wiki/Banastre_Tarleton.

"Banastre Tarleton BT GCB." *WikiTree*, 19 May 2023, www.wikitree.com/wiki/Tarleton-115.

"Battle of Brandywine." *Wikipedia*, 19 June 2023, en.wikipedia.org/wiki/Battle_of_Brandywine.

"Banastre Tarleton (U.S. National Park Service)." *National Parks Service*, www.nps.gov/people/banastre-tarleton.htm. Accessed 28 June 2023.

ZOE MILLER (Captain Patrick Ferguson)

My name is *Zoë Miller*, and I am 11-years-old and in the 6th grade. I was born in Concord, North Carolina, and I have been in martial arts for over a year. Also, I have two dogs (Eastway and Lexi), two birds (Lafayette and Washington), and two sisters (Carmene and Adie). My dream job is to be an ER doctor. Epic Patriot Camp was so fun, I hope to be part of it in the future. Ms. Libby and Ms. Jenny did a fantastic job, and I learned so much about the steps in creating a book.

DEDICATION: To my family

BIBLIOGRAPHY: "Brandywine Battlefield Historic Site: Patrick Ferguson." *Ushistory.Org*, www.ushistory.org/brandywine/special/art09.htm. Accessed 28 June 2023.

"Patrick Ferguson." *Wikipedia*, 2 Feb. 2023, en.wikipedia.org/wiki/Patrick_Ferguson.

"Patrick Ferguson." *American Battlefield Trust*, www.battlefields.org/learn/biographies/patrick-ferguson. Accessed 28 June 2023.

"Battle of Brandywine." *Wikipedia*, 19 June 2023, en.wikipedia.org/wiki/Battle_of_Brandywine.

KIT PACENTRILLI (General Henry Knox)

Kit Pacentrilli is twelve-years-old and lives in Virginia. She loves reading, writing, drawing, and playing goalie in soccer. She enjoys school, especially history, and hopes to one day become an author.

ACKNOWLEDGEMENTS: I would like to thank Jenny L. Cote and Libby McNamee for helping me write my chapter on Henry Knox. It has been a wonderful four weeks of writing, and they really helped. I would also like to thank my English teacher, Mrs. Purchas, because she taught me proper grammar and how to use commas. She also taught me numerous other skills that helped my writing. My French teacher, Madame Hyman, also assisted by teaching me French and French grammar. She even critiqued my French writing! I would also like to thank my history teacher, Mr. Borgerding. He taught me many things about the Revolutionary war – he spent four hours explaining an answer key for a Revolutionary War jigsaw puzzle, and everything helped. He let me look through his bookshelves dedicated to the creation of America to find information about Henry Knox. He knew which books had Knox in them! Finally, I would like to thank my parents for letting me do this camp, getting me to be able to participate even though I had school, and encouraging me to continue writing my chapters.

DEDICATION: For my endlessly hard-working teachers and my family. Thank you for all your hard work and encouragement.

BIBLIOGRAPHY: "Battle of Brandywine." *Wikipedia*, 19 June 2023, en.wikipedia.org/wiki/Battle_of_Brandywine.

"Battle of the Assunpink Creek." *Wikipedia*, 1 June 2023, en.wikipedia.org/wiki/Battle_of_the_Assunpink_Creek.

"Henry Knox." *Encyclopædia Britannica*, www.britannica.com/biography/Henry-Knox. Accessed 25 June 2023.

"Henry Knox." *Knox Museum*, www.knoxmuseum.org/henryknox. Accessed 25 June 2023.

"Henry Knox." *Wikipedia*, 28 May 2023, en.wikipedia.org/wiki/Henry_Knox.

ELLA QUILL (General Benedict Arnold)

Ella Quill is a rabbit author who loves spending her time (when she's not writing fascinating stories) eating and taking naps. She was "warren-schooled" and is a senior in rabbit school. She is currently frolicking around in the fields by Washington, DC, the US capital.

DEDICATION: For the Jason in my life. Thank you so much, brother! You have no idea how much you have inspired and encouraged this writer. God bless you.

I would like to give several very big thank yous! First of all, THANK YOU to my Lord and Savior. Without God, none of this would be possible. THANK YOU, Jenny and Libby! You all are such epic hosts, mentors, and friends! THANK YOU to Bella Waugh, my dear friend and budding author! You are one of my best friends, and I thank God for you! THANK YOU, Edan, Christopher, and Jacob, my epic camp friends! You three guys are amazing, and I've had so many fun memories with you all.

AUTHOR'S NOTE: Benedict Arnold, what a challenge! To create this chapter, I have added a lot of fiction and fantasy elements that I would like to point out. First of all, the character Ella Matthews is fictional. She and her family (Jason, Grace, and Andrew) are all fictional. So is their magical library. Benedict Arnold, however, is not fictional. He is a real man from the 18th century. All the events and places I have written in are accurate to history. I quote my friend

Lafayette (Mark Schneider) that Benedict Arnold is "neither black nor white but rather gray." I hope this chapter helps you see that.

BIBLIOGRAPHY: Sheinkin, Steve. *The Notorious Benedict Arnold; A True Story of Adventure, Heroism, and Treachery.* Flash Point, imprint of Roaring Book Press, 2010, Harrisonburg, Virginia.

Flexner, James Thomas. *The Traitor and the Spy.* Harcourt, Brace and Company, 1953, United States of America.

Philbrick, Nathaniel. *Valiant Ambition; George Washington, Benedict Arnold, and the Fate of the American Revolution.* Penguin Random House, 2016, New York, New York.

Hart, Benjamin. *Faith and Freedom; The Christian Roots of American Liberty.* Christian Defense Fund, 1997, United States of America.

ALEX ROBERSON (Alexander Hamilton)

Alex Roberson hails from Central Florida and is a native Floridian. She loves reading about the American Revolution and WWII. She is a competitive baton twirler and loves spending time outdoors. In addition, she loves spending time with her Holland Lop rabbits, Snickerdoodle and Ollie.

DEDICATION: Thank you to my parents for letting me have this incredible opportunity for a second time. Thank you to Jenny and Libby, for helping us grow as writers and the ability to write and publish a book.

AUTHOR'S NOTE: Hamilton was born 1755, but he subtracted two years (1757) to seem younger. During college he had a dispute with Samuel Seabury, writing *Farmers Refuted,* and going to taverns. His friends were fictitious. I created Snickers and Ollie to show the battles from a "bird's eye view."

BIBLIOGRAPHY: DeConde, Alexander. "Alexander Hamilton United States Statesman." www.britannica.com/biography/Alexander-Hamilton-United-States-statesman.

Groom, Winston. *The Patriots: Alexander Hamilton, Thomas Jefferson, John Adams, and the Making of America.* National Geographic, 2017.

History.com Editors. "Alexander Hamilton." *History.com,* 9 Nov.

2009, www.history.com/topics/american-revolution/alexander-hamilton.

Kanefield, Teri. *Alexander Hamilton: The Making of America #1*. vol. 1, Abrams Books for Young Readers, 2017.

Ryckman, Tatiana. *Alexander Hamilton: The First Secretary of the Treasury and an Author of the Federalist Papers (Great American Thinkers)*. Cavendish Square, 2016.

ANNA ROBERSON (Charles Gravier, *Comte de Vergennes*)

Anna Roberson, along with sister and fellow camper Alex Roberson, reside in Central Florida with their parents and rescued Labrador retrievers. When she is not busy studying, Anna enjoys drawing, playing the saxophone, and taking care of her hedgehog. Like her sister, Anna is involved with Children of the American Revolution as the descendant of a patriot.

AUTHOR'S NOTE: The conversation between Turgot, Charles, and King Louis XVI did not happen in real life. In this chapter, I wanted to add tension to this exchange. What better way to do so than to invite a former officer into a high-level meeting, and prove everything he said was wrong in an "I told you so" manner. Turgot did not want France to join America in war; he desired to keep his country peaceful. After he was released as comptroller general, the king agreed with Charles Gravier to forge an alliance with America.

BIBLIOGRAPHY: "Battle of Trenton." *Mountvernon.Org*, mountvernon.org/library/digitalhistory/digital-encyclopedia/article/battle-of-trenton/.

"Charles Gravier." *Battlefields.Org*, battlefields.org/learn/biographies/charles-gravier.

Chateau De Versailles. "Benjamin Franklin Has the Face of a Great Man." *Chateauversailles.Fr*, en.chateauversailles.fr/long-read/exhibition-visitors-to-versailles/benjamin-franklinv.

"Comte De Vergennes." *Americanrevolution.com*, americanrevolution.com/biographies/french/comte_de_vergennes

"Franklin's Favorite Foods." *Benfranklin300.org*, benfranklin300.org/etc_article_foods.htm.

History.com editors. "Battles of Trenton and Princeton." *History.com*, 9 Nov. 2009, history.com/topics/american-revolution/battles-of-trenton-and-princeton.

The Editors of Encyclopedia Britannica. "Charles Gravier, Count De Vergennes." *Britannica.com*, britannica.com/biography/Charles-Gravier-comte-de-Vergennes.

"Vergennes, Charles Gravier, Comte De." *Encyclopedia.com*, encyclopedia.com/history/encyclopedias-almanacs-transcripts-and-maps/vergennes-charles-gravier-comte-de.

HANNAH SCHNEIDER (Baron De Kalb)

Hannah Schneider is a creative thirteen-year-old who likes writing, drawing, and programming. She will read almost any book she can get her hands on, and has a lot of fabulous friends in her homeschool community. She lives in Manassas, Virginia, with her dad, mom, two brothers, and a butter-loving mutt, Jessie.

DEDICATION: For the children of the future. Never forget from where you came.

First, I'd like to thank Jenny and Libby for setting up this awesome camp, editing our stories, and teaching us everything they know about writing. You have worked so hard, and we're grateful you decided to spend a few weeks with a bunch of kids when you could have been working on your own books. Next, I'd like to thank my partner, Joy Elizabeth, for being a great and uplifting friend. You're an amazing girl. Finally, I'd like to thank my mom for discovering this camp, getting me research books, and doing super awesome stuff that only a mom can do, like being editor #4.

AUTHOR'S NOTE: It was difficult to find any detailed information about De Kalb. I found mostly general information about his military background, relationship to Lafayette, and a few locations he served in the Revolutionary War. The most detail I could find was the line in the military parade in May 1778. He did command the second on the left! None of my research specified if he got inoculated or if he talked to Baron De Steuben, but both may very well have happened. Also, we don't know if De Kalb had a real journal.

BIBLIOGRAPHY: Schenawolf, Harry. "Major General Baron Johann De Kalb 1721–1780. Foreign Soldier/American Patriot." *Revolutionary War Journal*, 28 Jan. 2023, www.revolutionarywarjournal.com/major-general-baron-dekalb/.

Heathcote, Charles. "Biography of General Baron Johann De Kalb." *Ushistory.Org*, July 1958, www.ushistory.org/valleyforge/served/dekalb.html.

Lewis, J.D. "Major General Baron De Kalb." *The Continental Army - Major General Baron Johann De Kalb*, 2009, www.carolana.com/NC/Revolution/continental_army_baron_dekalb.html.

THORSTEN SCHOEN (George Blakey)

I'm *Thorsten Schoen*, 13, enjoy playing soccer, biking, reading, swimming, fossil hunting, history, geography, languages, and traveling. I'm first generation American on my dad's side, but on my mother's side of the family, I'm deeply rooted in the building up of America from the mid-1600s.

My hometown is Dallas, Texas, but I've also lived in Germany, Austria, and France, one of many great advantages of being homeschooled. I have been to Europe 7 times, 8 different countries, and 12 states in the U.S. In addition to English, I'm fluent in Deutsch (German) and studying Nederland (Dutch).

ACKNOWLEDGEMENTS: I am deeply indebted to my mother, Beth, who inspired me to write about Blakey and supported me during the process. I'm extremely grateful to my Omi who helped me develop a love for reading, and my uncle, Thomas, for giving me feedback to polish my final draft.

This endeavor would not have been possible without the time and guidance of award-winning authors, Jenny Cote and Libby McNamee. What a blessing and opportunity they gifted me to write about my ancestor.

Jenny and Libby held me to the highest writing standards with grammar, etymology, dialogue, historical facts, deadlines, and more. I look at writing differently now but especially the road to becoming a published author. It is seriously an investment of time and hard work but worth the effort. Thanks to Jenny & Libby, I am a published author.

Also, a sweet thanks to my foster-fail-dog, Slate, who means the world to me. She helped me manage my stress, relieve any writing anxiety, and encourages me to always stay calm and carry on. Special thanks to my great-great-aunt, Florence Fogle Keahey. In 1953, she founded the George Blakey Chapter, DAR, in Bonham, Texas, and inspired us to complete his story.

Lastly, to my twin brothers, Franz & Matthias, I'm passing the writing-to-publish flame to you. Not the torch, but the flame! There is still more to George Blakey's story. Let's share it!

AUTHOR'S NOTE: George Blakey is my 5th-great-grandfather. It was exciting and truly an honor to write his story. I'm a history buff and to step into the shoes of my 5G-Grand-F, I lived history through him. It captivated and connected me to his story to tell with a different sense of belonging and identity. I have always imagined myself writing and publishing a fantasy story. Now I have written and published a story about my ancestor, George Blakey, and his role in the revolution.

BIBLIOGRAPHY: *Southern Campaigns American Revolution Pension Statements & Rosters*, revwarapps.org/w8367.pdf. Accessed May- June 2023.

"Princeton Battlefield State Park Overview." *NJDEP | Princeton Battlefield State Park | New Jersey State Park Service*, nj.gov/dep/parksandforests/parks/princetonbattlefieldstatepark.html. Accessed June 2023. And, "Princeton." *American Battlefield Trust*, www.battlefields.org/learn/revolutionary-war/battles/princeton. Accessed June 2023.

Full Text of "*a Genealogy of the Blakey Family and Descendants, with George, Whitsitt, Haden, Anthony, Stockton, Gibson and Many Other Related Antecedents. Compiled and Edited by Lue Adams Kress.*" archive.org/stream/genealogyofblake00kres/genealogyofblake00kres_djvu.txt. Accessed January-June 2023.

DAR Genealogical Research Databases, services.dar.org/Public/DAR_Research/search_adb/?action=full&p_id=A011051.

Accessed January-June 2023.

Kress, Lue Adams. *A Genealogy of the Blakey Family and Descendants: With George, Whitsitt, Haden, Anthony, Stockton, Gibson and Many Other Related Antecedents.* 1942.

Genealogies of Virginia Families: From the William and Mary College Quarterly Historical Magazine. Genealogical Pub. Co., 1982. AND Clearfield, 2006.

"Every Family Has a Story." *Ancestry | Family Tree, Genealogy & Family History Records,* www.ancestry.com/. March 2021-June 2023.

EMMA URRUTIA (General Charles Lee)

Emma Urrutia is a 15-year-old sophomore. She is an energetic creative writer who lives life passionately, loving God, family and friends. She enjoys reading fiction and cartoon-based novels. She totally enjoyed making more friends during her second year of Epic Patriot Camp 2023. Aspiring to be a musician, author and cartoonist, this imaginative teen hopes to change the world with these dreams, God willing.

AUTHOR'S NOTE: While yes, General Charles Lee *did* have a dog, he did *not* have a dog named Jupiter. The palmetto tress *did* indeed help the Continental Army at Charlestown. Lee *was* kidnapped by Tarleton in New Jersey for sixteen months. He *did* get scolded by Washington at Monmouth. He *was* shot at a duel during a court session. General Charles Lee *did* return in Virginia in 1779 for two years and then went to Philadelphia where he died in 1782.

BIBLIOGRAPHY: "Charles Lee | General - Wikipedia," 2023,www.en.wikipedia.org/wiki/Charles_Lee_(general)

"General Charles Lee - Revolutionary War," 2020, www.revolutionary-war.net/general-charles-lee/

"Charles Lee - George Washington's Mount Vernon," 2023 www.mountvernon.org/library/digitalhistory/digital-encyclopedia/article/charles-lee.

"General Charles Lee is captured at Basking Ridge - Revolutionary War and Beyond" www.revolutionary-war-and-beyond.com/general-charles-lee-is-captured-at-basking-ridge.html

JACOB WALTER (John André)

My name is *Jacob Walter*, and I am 15-years-old. I now live in Brasilia, Brazil, where it is always warm and almost always sunny. I have been homeschooled my whole life, but this winter (or fall for everyone living above the equator) I will attend Brasilia Christian International School for 10th grade.

DEDICATION: I would like to dedicate this to the real Ella. Thank you for inspiring me to get up off the ground after defeat, and write again. You are the only reason that I am writing today. You are also one of the reasons who I am today. Thank you as well for all the prayers, and encouragement you have given me. Thank you beyond words; you are a true friend.

ACKNOWLEDGEMENTS: I owe several thank yous. I will start with my family. Thank you to all my family, especially my sister, Eilana. Eliana thanks so much for being with me through the ups and downs, and always believing in me. I could never wish for a better sister. Thanks to Jenny and Libby. You guys are great and I have enjoyed this writing camp so much. You have made historical fiction writing such a fun experience and I am glad that this camp is always FOR THE CHILDREN! Thanks to all my friends outside of camp and your encouragement. I won't go into specific names but you know who you are so thanks for everything! I owe a special thanks to Ella Quill, Christopher, Edan, and Bella. You all are amazing writers, and I am glad to have you guide me through writing. I owe everything to my Lord and Savior, Jesus. He has blessed me with the ability to create and write, for that and everything else He has given me I am grateful.

AUTHOR'S NOTE: John André is a fascinating, yet little known character. Jason, Ella, and their parents are completely fictional. John André really did go to Head of Elk, New York, and the Battle of Brandywine. He also did have Protestant parents, one French and the other from Switzerland. He knew four languages and was partially driven to the military from a broken heart. The letter written to John André from Benedict Arnold, though, is pure fiction. John André swaying Benedict Arnold to hand over the fort and communicating through Peggy Shippen really did happen.

BIBLIOGRAPHY: "JOHN ANDRÉ: OFFICER, GENTLEMAN... AND SPYMASTER." www.intel.gov

"John André." American Battlefield Trust, 2023, www.battle-fields.org

"Spy System - Journal of John André." Historic Valley Forge, www.ushistory.org/valleyforge/index.html

"John André." Mount Vernon, 2023, www.mountvernon.org

Alan Alexlord. "The Real History of the American Revolution." *High Treason,* Sterling Publishing Co., Inc., 2007, pp. 289-295.

JOY ELIZABETH TARDY (French General Lafayette)

Bonjour! My name is *Joy Elizabeth Tardy,* I am a history-inspired homeschooled teen in my freshman year of high school. Epic Patriot Camp was such a blast with Miss Jenny and Libby! They put up with all our silliness like....at one point we young authors mused about spending the night at Patrick Henry's house *without* Docent Bob. It has been a pleasure to write another book with all these wonderful authors. As Miss Jenny says, "It's for the children!" Huzzah!

DEDICATION: To the girls in India and South America whom my family and I support. God has an amazing future in store for them. God also has an amazing future in store for you. As Jeremiah says in 29:11, "'For I know the plans I have for you,' declares the Lord, 'plans to prosper you and not to harm you, plans to give you hope and a future.'" Though you may not see what our Father in heaven has planned for you yet, just lean on Him. As He says in Matthew 11:28-29, "Come unto me, all ye that labour and are heavy laden, and I will give you rest. Take my yoke upon you and learn of me, for I am meek and lowly in heart, and ye shall find rest unto your souls." May you open your heart to trust Jesus as your Savior.

CHRISTOPHER J. WATT (Benjamin Franklin)

Christopher J. Watt was born in Johannesburg, South Africa, and loves history from the Dark Ages through the Colonial and Revolutionary Eras. Some of his favourite activities include drawing, designing, writing anything from newsletters to novels, horse riding, and discussing the characteristics of aristocratic crocodiles living in trees. Home educated since eighth grade, he now studies grammar and writing styles, graphic design, dog training, and carpentry. He co-authored *The Epic Story of 1776* and is now working on future projects. Christopher currently resides in Canberra, Australia, with his family and black Labrador Retriever, Shadow. Visit www.christopherjwatt.com for more insight into this writer's big world.

DEDICATION: My work this year is dedicated to the Author of All Things. I hope I have done well in writing my part of HIStory.

First, an enormous THANK YOU to my parents, John and Christl Watt, for allowing me to take part in Epic Patriot Camp 2023. This has been a life-changing experience, and I cannot thank you enough for letting me take part. Especially to my mom, Christl, for waking up at 4 AM with me every week in the middle of winter (time zones!) to support me as I joined each meeting. I'd like to thank *all* my fellow Epic Patriot Campers for the encouragement and joy you've brought me, especially Bella and Naomi for collaborating with me. This year has taught me the importance of reviewing my work and persevering. Thank you so much to my Grade 6 teacher, Mrs. Ellyn Clapham, who taught me to always persevere when it gets hard.

Of course, an *enormous* THANK YOU to Jenny L. Cote and Libby McNamee for all your hard work and encouragement in all things! You have both changed my life. Never before, Libby, have I ever found myself so immersed in studying my grammar! Thank you for reminding me that an author can always improve. Huzzah!

AUTHOR'S NOTE: Shadow is a British spy dog who first appeared in *The Epic Story of 1776*. Today she would be recognised as a Labrador Retriever, but Labs were only bred officially in the 1800s. Their ancestors were the Newfoundlands. Interestingly enough, Benjamin Franklin's son William had a black Newfoundland in the 1770s. Ben looked after the dog while he was in France, and the quote, "nothing shall tempt me to forget your Newfoundland dog" *is* historically accurate! Who voiced it and the situation around it is unknown, so I fictionalised it.

If you've read *The Epic Story of 1776*, you may remember that

Shadow was a St John's Water dog. Another term for this breed was the Lesser (or Short-Haired) Newfoundland. For historical accuracy, I changed it for this year's chapter.

Nimbus, Shadow's accomplice, has also evolved. He is now a Eurasian magpie, which is the European variant of the former black-billed magpie. I changed this to be more geographically accurate. (and so any colonial French ornithologists who may have noticed Nimbus on his mission wouldn't get suspicious!)

Some of the dates and times have been used fictitiously. I couldn't find a definitive source for the following dates and times:

It is not certain if Bancroft did a dead drop at 9:31 AM on 7 January 1777, but I assume he would have, as it was a Tuesday.

The exact date of his arrest in London is not clear, all we know was that it was in March 1777.

I have no idea when the commissioners learned about Spain's refusal, but I believe it was early January 1778, three weeks after the meeting with Vergennes. I added a few extra days for the response to reach France.

Lastly, you may have noticed my spelling is different from other authors. Words such as *honour* and *authorised* are not spelled incorrectly; I used British English.

BIBLIOGRAPHY: Franklin, Benjamin. "From Benjamin Franklin to the Committee of Secret Correspondence …." Founders Online, www.founders.archives.gov/documents/Franklin/01-23-02-0066.

"How Alexander Wedderburn Cost England America." American Philosophical Society, 9 January 2018, www.amphilsoc.org/blog/how-alexander-wedderburn-cost-england-america.

Isaacson, Walter. *Benjamin Franklin: An American Life*. Simon & Schuster, 2004.

Isaacson, Walter. "Benjamin Franklin Joins the Revolution | History." *Smithsonian Magazine*, 31 July 2003.

"Treaty of Alliance with France (1778.)" National Archives, 10 May 2022, www.archives.gov/milestone-documents/treaty-of-alliance-with-france-transcript.

BELLA WAUGH (King George III)

Bella Waugh is 16-year-old homeschooler who lives on a little farm south of Nashville, TN. She believes that learning our history is vital to her generation. There will be a great change in this nation if we place the value back in HIStory. Writing is a huge part of her life, and she feels the Lord has called her to be an author. More specifically, Bella writes in many genres from middle grade contemporary to historical fiction, and is currently writing a Biblical allegorical fantasy novel. As a veteran Epic Patriot Camper, she is so thankful for this camp and the amazing opportunity to become a published author—twice! You can find her at www.bellaraine.com.

DEDICATION: First off, I'd like to thank Jesus. He planted the seed of becoming an author in my heart, and He is the one who has fueled, encouraged, inspired, and continued it since! To my family- you guys were (and are!) so encouraging of me and my writing. Thank you so much for all of the edits and ideas you gave me! Jenny and Libby, you two are amazing! Your edits, advice and teaching were brilliant, and I'll carry them throughout my whole career. Thank you! Lastly, I'd like to thank my amazing Epic Patriot Camp friends, Gemma & Edan. It was a blast going to camp with you again. Thanks for all the help & support & friendship! Christopher and Naomi, I loved getting to collaborate with you two. To every other camper - Huzzah!

AUTHOR'S NOTE: As with all historical fiction, authors can't know every single detail about every single event and therefore must take some creative liberty. The major liberties in my chapter were specific dates which were fictionalized. The months and seasons, however, were as historically accurate as possible. Since there was no information on specific days, I improvised.

BIBLIOGRAPHY: "American Revolutionary War Battles." *Revolutionary War*, www.revolutionarywar.us/battles.

"The Battle of Brandywine." *George Washington's Mount Vernon*, www.mountvernon.org/george-washington/the-revolutionary-war/washingtons-revolutionary-war-battles/the-battle-of-brandywine.

"Descendants of George III." *Wikipedia*, 13 May 2023, www.en.wikipedia.org/wiki/Descendants_of_George_III.

"George III (1738-1820)." *The American Revolution*, www.ouramericanrevolution.org/index.cfm/people/view/pp0022.

"George III's Battle to Save an Empire." *Colonial Williamsburg Wax Seal*, www.colonialwilliamsburg.org/trend-tradition-magazine/autumn-2018/george-iiis-battle-to-save-an-empire/.

"Myths of the American Revolution." *Smithsonian.com*, 1 Jan. 2010, www.smithsonianmag.com/history/myths-of-the-american-revolution-10941835/.

MADELEINE ROSE WENZEL (General Henry Clinton)

Madeleine Rose Wenzel is 17-years-old and recently graduated from high school. Born in Norfolk, VA, Madeleine moved to Irmo, SC, at 18 months old, where she has lived with her parents, younger sister and brother, and numerous pets for the past 16 years. Madeleine loves animals, reading, and history, especially anything regarding the American Revolution. She would love to be a historian when she grows up, and possibly participate in re-enactments of Revolutionary War battles.

DEDICATION: To Dr. Anthony Scotti. Thank you for your encouragement and help in finding primary sources. My personal library continues to grow, thanks to you.

AUTHOR'S NOTE: I had the privilege of writing the scene for the Battle of Sullivan's Island on site at Fort Moultrie (formerly known as Fort Sullivan). The jellyfish that Clinton encounters whilst walking along the beach are called cannonball jellies. They commonly wash up along the coast here in SC. Sometimes they have spider crabs living in their bells!

The soldier who picked up the flag after it was shot down was Sergeant William Jasper. He was later wounded during the siege of Savannah in 1779 as he rescued his regiment's flags.

Elias is a fictional character. Henry Clinton did not have a pet Carolina parakeet. He certainly would have seen them since they were very common. Unfortunately, these birds are now extinct.

The letter in this story is based on: https://www.founders.archives.gov/?q=%20Author%3A%22Clinton%2C%20Henry%22&s=1111311111&r=1.

BIBLIOGRAPHY: Clinton, Sir Henry, and William B. Willcox. The American Rebellion: Sir Henry Clinton's Narrative of His Campaigns, 1775-1782. Yale University Press, 1954.

Edgar, Walter. Partisans & Redcoats: The Southern Conflict That Turned the Tide of the American Revolution. William Morrow, 2001.

Griffith, William R. A Handsome Flogging: The Battle of Monmouth, June 28 1778. Savas Beatie, 2020.

Lefkowitz, Arthur S. George Washington's Indispensable Men: The 32 Aides-de-Camp Who Helped Win American Independence. Stackpole Books, 2018.

Willcox, William B. Portrait of a General: Sir Henry Clinton in the War of Independence. Knopf; Distributed by Random House, 1964.

EPIC PUBLISHING TEAMS

EPIC TEAMWORK COORDINATOR
Christopher J. Watt

EPIC PRINTED MATERIALS ASSOCIATE
Cameron Graham

I. EPIC EDITING TEAM
Payton Grace
Peri Jordan
Piper Jordan
Elliott Lay
Roxanne Messier
Ella Quill
Emma Urrutia
Christopher J. Watt
Bella Waugh

II. EPIC MARKETING TEAM
Chase Adam
Cameron Graham

Naomi Hayes
Peri Jordan
Piper Jordan
Elliott Lay
Edan MacNaughton
Roxanne Messier
Kit Pacentrilli
Ella Quill
Alex Roberson
Hannah Schneider
Thorsten Schoen
Joy Elizabeth Tardy
Christopher Watt
Madeleine Wenzel

III. EPIC PROOFING TEAM
Mikayla Badenhorst
Chloe Frost
Cameron Graham
Naomi Hayes
Carmene Miller
Zoe Miller
Jacob Walter
Christopher J. Watt

Made in the USA
Middletown, DE
27 October 2023

41377969R00172